INGRID NOLL

Ingrid Noll was born in Shanghai in 1935, but later moved to Bonn and studied German and Art History there. *Head Count* is her second crime novel; her first, *Hell Hath No Fury*, received worldwide attention.

Hailed as 'Germany's Queen of Crime' (*Observer*), Ingrid Noll's novels have now sold up to 700,000 copies in Germany alone and have been translated into more than ten languages.

BY THE SAME AUTHOR

HELL HATH NO FURY

HEAD COUNT

Ingrid Noll

Translated from the German by
Ian Mitchell

HarperCollins*Publishers*

Collins Crime
An imprint of HarperCollins*Publishers*
77–85 Fulham Palace Road, London W6 8JB

Published by HarperCollins*Publishers* 1997

1 3 5 7 9 10 8 6 4 2

First published in German with the title
Die Häupter meiner Lieben
by Diogenes Verlag AG Zürich in 1993

Copyright © Ingrid Noll 1993

The Author asserts the moral right to
be identified as the author of this work

ISBN 0 00 232572 1
ISBN 0 00 232640 X (trade pbk)

Set in Meridien and Bodoni

Typeset by Rowland Phototypesetting Ltd
Bury St Edmunds, Suffolk
Printed and bound in Great Britain by
Caledonian International Book Manufacturing Ltd, Glasgow

CONTENTS

CHAPTER 1

Elephant Grey

Whenever I take up my microphone and describe Florence for the German-speaking tourists on my coach, they assume I am a student of Romance languages trying to supplement her pocket-money. They find me charming; one elderly couple told me straight to my face that they would have liked a girl like me for a daughter. They still haven't learned that the external and internal images of a person don't necessarily match.

Generally, my tourists are at the start of their Tuscany trips here, and they can't get to grips with all the noughts behind the lire fast enough. You might imagine that, because of this, they tip overgenerously, but unfortunately the opposite is the case. In order to make it more or less worth my while, I always warn my little flock at the end of the tour against thieves and purse-snatchers and illustrate this with the cautionary tale of a pensioner from Leipzig whose relatives all clubbed together to give her, as a seventieth birthday present, a trip to Italy, something that had long been her heart's desire. A few days ago, I tell them, she had all her cash stolen. Then I pass round a cigar-box, to take a collection for this pensioner. Most of them splash out pretty freely, since the person next to them is looking on to see what they contribute.

When the tour is over, I split the proceeds with Cesare, the coach-driver. In a way, this is really hush money, so that he won't blow the gaff to the travel agency about the old dear from Saxony.

Cesare accuses me of being unscrupulous. Naturally, the

root causes of such a condition lie all the way back in one's childhood; in my case, that was a dreary time, a time of misery and despair, which lies like a lump of lead among my emotional debris. It was only when I met Cornelia that things began to look up for me and I set about eliminating the unpalatable elements from it.

As a child, I never got what I needed. Not that I even had any clear idea of what I did need; today, it is clear to me that it was warmth and happiness. Like any other human being, I want to be loved, I want a bit of fun and adventure; I like friends with a sense of humour and a lively mind. Nor should they be without a modicum of education and culture. There was none of that at home. Bitterness was the order of the day there. Later, I simply took whatever I lacked; I suppose, in doing so, I did go over the score now and again.

My mother was a woman of few words, but whatever she did say was unerringly targeted nastiness. No doubt that was one of the reasons for my inexhaustible reservoir of suppressed rage, which just had to find violent release every now and again.

Even when I was still very small, whenever I ventured a naive or spontaneous comment at the lunch table, I could not help noticing my detested brother and my mother exchanging a split-second knowing glance. This glance told me that they had already talked frequently about me and my gaucheness, and that they would go on doing so regularly in the future. After that, I wouldn't utter a word for weeks on end. It was this repression of my fury that made me so devious.

When my brother Carlo was fourteen and I was ten, I stole his cigarettes, which he had bought secretly, and, on my way to school, I threw them into other people's refuse bins. Since he regarded me as cowardly and stupid and knew in any case that I didn't give a hoot whether he smoked or not, he never suspected me. He was convinced that our mother had got wise to him and was discreetly trying to prevent him ruining his health.

I took up stealing. I have never been accused of it, because the victim of my pilfering always assumed that any thief would want his ill-gotten gains for himself. What would a little girl want with cigarettes? What use to her is her aunt's perfume, when, after all, everyone would smell the expensive fragrance right away? In those days I stole door-keys, identity papers, teachers' spectacles, simply in order to throw them away – *l'art pour l'art*. It was only years later that I started to keep articles I had stolen.

Perhaps I would have turned out differently if my father hadn't deserted me so early. I say quite deliberately that he abandoned me, and not our family, for that's the way I saw it. I was seven years old when it happened, and up till then I had always been his 'princess'.

As in some Renaissance comedy, there were two loving couples in our family: one of high standing – the King and the Princess – and then the pair of servants – my mother and my brother. The king called me 'Princess Maya', and later, 'Infanta Maya'. Among his possessions, he kept a page from a calendar, with a picture of Spanish ladies-in-waiting in attendance on a young girl. Although my rather wispy light-brown hair contrasted with that princess's blonde tresses, my father nevertheless insisted that I looked just like her. I loved that picture.

Recently, I bought a reproduction of it and hung it next to my mirror. Right in the middle of the picture stands the delightful Infanta Margarita; her earnest child's face is framed by silky-soft hair. Like the older women, she, too, is wearing stiff crinolines, which explains why she is standing so erect, as if in traction. Clearly, Margarita is well aware that everything revolves around her. On the left of the picture, the painter has portrayed himself at work: a handsome, self-assured man. In contrast to him, on the right, stands a midget woman with a grimacing pug-face. Next to her, a child, or a dwarf-child, is trying to rouse a snoozing dog with a poke from its dainty little foot, but without success. The dog is the embodiment of tranquillity and dignity in this beautiful painting. There are other people to be seen, persons of historical significance, but they are of no interest to me. The colours of the background are grey, greenish and umber; in the foreground, a light ivory predominates, with a few exquisite splashes of carnation-red. All the light seems to be concentrated on the Infanta.

My father was a painter, just like that man in the background of this picture, who portrayed the Infanta all those years ago; when he went off and left me, all his own pictures disappeared as well. I found the page with the Spanish princess under a chest of drawers, all crumpled and tattered. I folded it up and hid it inside our Diercke's *Atlas of the World*, where my brother later discovered it and tore it to shreds.

No doubt, my brother suffered from the fact that he had never been a prince and his sister was set above him. He took his revenge whenever and however he could.

Usually, it was my job to lay the table. Once I stumbled over a worn bit of carpet, and three cups, saucers and plates were smashed.

'Like an elephant in a china shop,' commented my mother.

'The Infanta has turned into the Elefanta,' said Carlo.

She laughed approvingly. 'Nasty, but nicely put.'

So that's when I became the she-elephant. For years, my brother called me by that name. As for my mother, she addressed me as 'Maya' when she couldn't avoid it, but sometimes I would hear her saying to Carlo as I came in, 'Here comes the elephant.'

Cinderella marries her prince and becomes a queen, the Ugly Duckling turns into a swan. It was my dream that I would become famous and have the world at my elephant's feet. At fifteen, I decided to become a singer, a second Callas. From that time on, Mother and Carlo had to put up with the one aria from *Carmen*, over and over again. My voice was loud, my singing fiery. I was neither vocally gifted nor particularly musical, but it was a way for me to let off steam. 'She's singing *elefantabile* again,' my mother used to say.

One day, one of my classmates happened to hear what my brother called me. The next day, I was greeted in class with a deafening Tarzan-call. Even at school I had become a pachyderm.

Did I look like an elephant? In height and weight, I was around average for humans, my feet were dainty, my nose was nothing like a trunk, and my movements were neither uncoordinated nor lumbering. Only my ears didn't quite meet the norm; while they were average in size, they protruded a bit and stuck out through my straight rats' tails. Until I was too old for it, my mother used to comb my hair unmercifully after it had been washed, and as a result the teeth of the comb would snag on my ear and rake it downwards. Long after I was grown up, the same mishap sometimes befell a hairdresser. Whenever that happened, my entire body would be immediately swamped in goose-pimples as I recalled my mother, who could bring me to a state of physical discomfort in the course of other activities, too: her sharp-pointed fingers between my shoulder blades, the loud cracking of her fingers when she clasped her hands and the excruciating squeaking noises she produced while cleaning the windows.

My mother made sure that the elephantine in me was made manifest in my outward appearance as well. I needed a winter coat, and I asked for a fiery-red one. Allegedly we had no money for a new coat. Mother had a grey cape stitched up for me out of a handed-down llama-wool cloak, which left me looking decidedly shapeless. My shoes, too, were chosen in grey and one size too big, so that they would both match the cape and still fit me the following year.

A teacher heard my classmates' elephant-call and saw me stomping miserably through the November fog. 'Maya Westermann,' she said, 'that kind of name-calling wears off, given time. Besides, you shouldn't underestimate the strength of an elephant; sturdiness in a woman is something worth striving for!'

But I didn't want to be sturdy. I had fallen in love, and there was no place in my mind for anything other than romance. Of course, this wasn't my first time. That started as far back as my memory can reach, and the first object of my affection was my father. When he left me, I went into a state of mourning that lasted for a whole year.

Recently, my old geography teacher, accompanied by his wife, got into my tourist coach; it was the Easter vacation, which he was using for a short educational holiday in Italy.

We hadn't seen each other since I sat my final school examinations three years before, but we recognized each other at once, exchanged friendly greetings and, at the end, we wished each other all the very best. He had no idea that, for months on end, he had been the focus of my fantasies. Herr Becker and the dream of a career as an operatic diva were the only things that had prevented my slipping into depression, so grey and gloom-laden were both school and family life. Of these two ambitions for the future, one was as unrealistic as the other. All the same, I still have among my possessions a comb belonging to my teacher, which I purloined as a memento during my one and only visit to his house.

At that time, he was coming up for thirty years old, and I was already worried that I was suffering from an Oedipus complex. Overnight, I became a star pupil in geography.

Geography lessons involved studying the interrelationship of historical, economic and political factors. It always annoyed Herr Becker that most pupils read only the sports pages and the cinema adverts in the newspapers, skipping over politics and the financial section. Every morning, I had a row with Carlo, who would snatch the daily paper away from me without so much as a by-your-leave. When we came to talk, during the lesson, about the economic repercussions of the catastrophic drought in Chad, Niger and the Sudan, I would be the only one in class to put my hand up. Before Herr Becker could ask me a question, somebody yelled, 'No wonder she knows about it, since Africa's where she comes from anyway!'

'Were you born in Africa?' Herr Becker asked, interested but quite unsuspecting. Just like a real elephant, I charged out of the room to the accompaniment of my classmates' trumpetings, knocking over two chairs as I jumped to my feet. Outside the gymnasium, I subsided on to a low wall and used up my whole supply of paper handkerchiefs. What I was really hoping was that my teacher would come after me and find me. Perhaps I could get him to understand that I was a woman with an open mind. But nobody came. Later, one of the other girls said, 'Sorry about the Africa thing –

how were we to know you're one of the Indian kind?'

I've never stolen anything from my mother, even if some-times I could have wished her in hell. We had little money. From what my brother said – for my mother never talked about it – I knew that our father did in fact send something now and again, but very irregularly and we could never count on it. My mother worked as a nurse in an old people's home, and that was without a doubt the most unsuitable job possible for her. She had taken the course in geriatric nursing because the period of training was especially short. With her intelligence and speed of reaction, she could have learned any kind of office work with no trouble at all. Instead, she looked after old people with hard hands and a hard heart, as if they were lumps of wood.

It was not just because of our poverty that I didn't steal from Mother. The real reason was that I loved her with an unhappy, agonizing intensity. The older I got, the more clearly I saw that she was suffering a great hurt, and the wounds it caused her could never heal. We both, in our own way, grieved over the loss of the king, without being able to help each other. At that time, of course, I had no inkling of how cruelly I, too, would one day be betrayed by my father. But even my mother, who regarded my brother as a surro-gate for her love of my father, did show the odd sign of fondness for me. Despite all her nasty remarks and her refusal to take my wishes and needs into account, she resolutely opposed my intention to leave school.

'You'll be sorry one day,' was her main argument against my exasperation with school. The prettiest girl in our class wanted to leave and take up an apprenticeship in a chemist's shop. This was what started me thinking about how marvel-lous it must be to earn your own money and not have to doze away hour after hour in some stuffy classroom. However, I was not altogether sure whether an apprenticeship was the right thing for me either. School was a peaceful parking place. Without too great a show of rebelliousness, I allowed myself to be persuaded by my mother to continue my studies. Today, I believe that it was not merely ambition, but love, that made her take this stand. Things would have been easier for my mother if I had been bringing in money. That is one of the few things that I put down to her credit.

Incidentally, I was also grateful to her for my elephantine clothing in the end. Where I had done my damnedest to avoid wearing the llama cape (it was only that especially icy winter that induced me to pull on the warming wool), there then came a time when, even on mild spring days, I refused to emerge from my cocoon.

Herr Becker told me that, out of all the chic jackets and coats that performed a fashion parade in the playground during break, he liked my grey tea-cosy best of all.

'You're an individualist, Maya. I used to be exactly like you, I never wanted to go along with the crowd.'

Although he was wrong in assuming that I had opted for the elephant costume of my own free will, it was now dignified by his words. I was delighted that he thought that, deep down inside, we had something in common. I beamed him a big smile.

Anything I knew about love was purely theoretical and came from books – *Anna Karenina* and *Madame Bovary*. I had read about how women either dedicate themselves or throw themselves away. In my dreams, however, I was a world-famous singer, and Herr Becker could think himself fortunate that *he* might devote himself to me.

When I recently came across this conscientious, but strait-laced teacher and his good lady in my bus, I could only shake my head over my naïveté in those days gone by. Incidentally, I could, without the slightest risk, have slipped my hand into the good Frau Becker's handbag which, despite my usual sermon, still gaped open after she had handed over her donation. But Cesare was watching me in the rear-view mirror and giving me a reproving shake of his head.

When, at the age of sixteen, I got to know Cornelia, Herr Becker was already a back number, although the same could not be said of the grey cape. I had grown fond of it. At Christmas, Mother presented me with the red coat I had asked for a year before, which she was now able to buy cheaper in the sales. She had probably realized that I was already into my second year of going about looking like an elephant and that I now had a right to something a bit more elegant. Unfortunately, it was too late. To my mother's great chagrin, I never put on the red coat; I wanted to remain grey.

In my coach, I'm no longer a little grey mouse, but dressed up like some kind of stewardess, in a dark-green suit, white blouse and red silk scarf – the Italian national colours, in other words. My shoes, too, are red; I'm forever having to give the tourists the name of the shoe shop where I bought such smart footwear. In my handbag I also have the addresses of a German-speaking doctor and a priest, although the latter has been required on only one solitary occasion. They all dutifully note down the telephone code for Germany, my hints on national holidays, shop closing times, postage rates and even my tactful reference to the customary tipping procedures.

But by the end of a three-hour trip, with sightseeing and various photo-stops, my good advice has long since been forgotten, and once again they squint fearfully at the string of noughts on their banknotes. Then there are also the pedantic ones, who pull out their pocket calculators; I'm not exactly well disposed towards them, since their tipping is completely lacking in any spontaneity and they arouse in me neither malicious triumph nor moist-eyed gratitude.

When Cesare is in a good mood, he drives me home in his big bus, which is of course strictly forbidden. At first, he would never have gone in for such special favours, but through time I have managed to break down his inhibitions. He never gets out to come and drink an espresso in the pink villa, for he seems fearful that Sodom and Gomorrah could be lurking behind its doors.

I never bother to enlighten him as to whether I live alone or in company, whether I have any relatives or friends. My chequered past is none of his business; in any case, I'm sure it would far outstrip anything he could ever imagine or suspect.

CHAPTER 2

Celadon Green

Whenever Cesare spots a pair of lovers among our passengers, he is delighted and tries, with a wink or a smile, to draw my attention away from the sights outside to this internal one. He's a sentimental soul; families with lots of children, white-haired grannies and wrinkly newborn babes can distract his mind from the traffic and draw spontaneous expressions of tenderness from him.

I'm not like that at all, and I have my problems with loving couples. What's so beautiful about those vacuous adoring gazes anyway, that mindless harmony and tasteless fondling? On the other hand, everybody knows that this phase is short-lived, and I draw some comfort from that. But then again, maybe my touchiness comes down to the fact that I'm envious and not exactly proud of my own affairs (you could never call them romances). Recently, I saw a sixteen-year-old with her boyfriend of the same age, acting like some old married couple on an educational holiday. Sickening. Thank heaven I was never like that.

When I was sixteen, I still didn't have a lover, but I did at last have a friend. She was to become the most important person in my life.

Cornelia joined the class as an incomer. She was one of those people that get stared at by everybody. Not because she was strikingly beautiful (although she hadn't a blemish on her), but because she was so incredibly single-minded and had this total genuineness about her.

Cornelia sized up our class for a week and was, in turn,

observed just as closely. She fitted smoothly into the class-work, often talked nonsense but also had some brilliant ideas, and was never ashamed to admit it quite frankly whenever she hadn't a clue. Everybody was fascinated by her and began competing to get into her good books.

Cornelia, however, rejected all approaches and instead turned her attentions firmly and emphatically towards me. I couldn't believe my luck. Heaven had sent me a friend with sparkle, wit and imagination, with red hair and pretty forthright manners. Cornelia came from the very best of family backgrounds. Her father was a professor of Sinology and, as I was later to find out for myself, culture personified. After almost every sentence, he would put in a distinct, 'H'm, yes', and he talked like a book. At home, she was called 'Cora'. A Chinese student had even referred to her once as 'Miss Cola'.

Cora told me that she had been more or less slung out of her previous school for kissing the art teacher behind the stage set she had designed for a school play. Not that it was their first kiss. But on this fateful occasion, the headmaster, the school secretary and a trainee teacher had been involuntary witnesses. Cora found it highly amusing. The teacher, too, had had to get a transfer to another school.

Cora wanted to be an artist, and she showed me her enormous works, painted on brown wrapping paper. Her pictures were original and skilfully executed; all the same, they weren't always to my taste, because Cora revealed a slight tendency towards revolting subjects. In an attempt to impress her, I confessed my kleptomania. She was thrilled to hear it, although she considered it to be uneconomic, after all the effort expended on the actual stealing, to throw away the proceeds. In very short order, she got me to initiate her into the art of thieving. As part of the first lesson, I filched a scarlet lipstick before her very eyes in the Kaufhof store. But she wanted a gent's tie. I stole two ties from a revolving display rack, discreetly striped items, and from then on we wore them in school. I spun a yarn about 'Cora's brother's' to my mother, while Cora told a similar story at home. By these means, we gradually built up an increasingly distinctive wardrobe. Run-of-the-mill teenage clothes were not for us; everything had to have that touch of the out-of-the-ordinary about it. We owned braces and long johns, butcher's working clothes and mourning gear.

One day, there was an exhibition of Chinese porcelain in the museum. At the official opening, Cora's father delivered a speech in front of an invited audience. We were to play the charming little daughters, topping up the champagne glasses and handing round vol-au-vents and smoked-salmon sandwiches.

With half an ear, I heard the culture- and sherry-saturated father talking. 'Celadon green' was the only phrase that kept running around in my head. What was it? Cora patiently showed me a few dishes, round ones and square ones, in a milky-pale, exotic grey-greenish glaze, and I fell in love with them on the spot.

'Cora, I've just got to have that celadon-green dish!'

My friend nodded. No sign of hesitation, no scruples. 'Wait till the people start to leave. We'll help to clear up.'

Thus it came about, that, in my sparsely furnished room, there was to be seen a piece of ancient china with an engraved design of a dragon under the enamel, from the Sung Dynasty. My mother did not so much as notice this priceless unique specimen, for it was so noble, so fine and so restrained that the untrained eye simply overlooked it.

Stealing the dish had proved a very simple matter. The director of the museum was a friend of Cora's father. When, at the end, only the *crème de la crème* of the hand-picked guests remained behind, he opened the display cases and personally took out a few of the exquisite objects in order to draw the interested onlookers' attention to particular details.

There were about ten guests standing around the director and the professor as we began gathering up the empty champagne glasses. Cora covered me while I took the dish out of its case. We put four glasses on it, and Cora carried this miniature tray quite openly past all those present and into the side-room where there was a sink and the bottles were stored. Some time before, I had made a detachable bag that could be buttoned to the lining of my elephant cape, and could accommodate the results of my various trawling expeditions. We collected up all the remaining glasses, washed them in the side-room and then took our leave. Cora's father gave us an absent-minded wave. '*Jeunesse dorée,*' the museum director remarked. The professor had given us a fair bit of pocket-money for our services, thinking that the exhibition wouldn't be of the slightest interest to us.

Cora told me afterwards that the absence of the dish had been noticed by an assistant only two days later. It unleashed a colossal fuss. Police and insurance assessors pursued their investigation very discreetly, since, considering what distinguished guests had been there, nothing about the incident was to be allowed to appear in the press. Inquiries were centred on the guest list. Cora and I had, however, been completely forgotten. In the end, suspicion fell on the Chinese cultural attaché; it was claimed that, when he heard that all the Chinese treasures had come from museums in London and Berlin, his face had twitched quite distinctly. It must have been a professional who had helped himself, since, in the celadon-green dish, what was involved was a particularly old and exquisite piece which, nevertheless, to the layman would seem, if anything, quite unprepossessing.

'You've got good taste,' my friend told me. 'I would probably have gone for the oxblood vase. But that's all purely academic, since I can't very well display that kind of stuff on my windowsill the way you can.'

In the end, the insurers paid out a considerable sum in compensation to the Victoria and Albert Museum. The wife of the Chinese diplomat had flown to Peking two days after my deed, and that trip was regarded as proof of the Chinaman's guilt.

But the celadon-green dish would yet bring me misfortune.

It all began on Carlo's twentieth birthday, which fell on a Saturday. Mother was on duty in the old folks' home that weekend. Originally, she had wanted to swop with a colleague, so as to be free on her little darling's birthday. Carlo protested. He wasn't an infant any more, he said, for whom

Mummy had to bake a cakey. It would be enough if they could sit and enjoy a glass of wine together in the evening.

So Mother went off to work, and Carlo made plans to take advantage of her absence and have a little party. Because he had no option, or so I thought at the time, he let me in on his plan. He was intending to cook a meal for a few friends, and I was to invite Cora. Only much later did it dawn on me that he was putting the whole thing on for her sake.

In the morning, he sent me out shopping, giving me a list and some money. This new game, with him being nice to me, appealed to me, at least at first, and I obediently left the house, bought Spanish red wine, white bread and cheese, grapes and salmon substitute out of his money, and supplemented these, off my own bat, by stealing pâté de foie gras, caviare and champagne. There, however, I made a serious mistake, carried away as I was by enthusiasm and force of habit. The moment I reached our front door it was obvious to me that I couldn't unpack these delicacies in front of him. Later on, we could say that Cora had taken them from her parents' stock.

But as I opened the door, Carlo, looking very conspiratorial, beckoned me into the kitchen, without so much as a glance at my purchases. He gestured me to a chair. I sat down expectantly. Carlo drew an envelope from his pocket and handed it to me with great ceremony. Stupid ape, I thought, but naturally I was curious to know who the letter had come from.

'From Father,' said Carlo.

Now I got very flustered, tore the sheet of notepaper out of the envelope and read:

My dear son, if memory serves me right, today is your birthday. – Why had he never remembered my birthday? – *Please don't think I've forgotten you all. All the same, it fills me with shame to have to admit that my plans for building a proper life have come to nothing. For years I have hoped that, one day, my pictures would sell. Probably that will happen only after my death, and then you will be the lucky inheritors. Karin has left me,* – who in all the world was Karin? – *I now live alone and in seclusion, from one year to the next I am aware of more and more afflictions and*

*infirmities and suffer under unfortunate circumstances. Through
sheer necessity, I have had to take on the degrading job of a blood-
courier. How I would have loved to send you an expensive present,
but, believe me, there is many an evening when I go to bed without
having had a thing to eat. I am writing to you in the knowledge
that I do not have many years left. It is my great wish that Maya
and you can forgive me and can think back on your old father with
love in your hearts.*

'What about that then?' said Carlo.

'What's a blood-courier?' I asked.

He shrugged. We stared at each other, completely at a loss.

'Where does he live?' I asked, but then I saw for myself
that no sender's address had been given. We examined the
postmark and made out: Bremen. 'Our poor father,' I said
softly.

Carlo turned up his nose. 'What you should say is, our
poor mother! First he clears off with some other woman,
hardly ever pays maintenance, and now comes a begging
letter like this!'

'But there's nothing at all in there about wanting anything.
We don't even know where he's living.'

Carlo went across to Mother's desk and took out her bank
statements. 'In April last year, he sent a small amount, I just
happen to know that,' he said. 'I should be able to find the
transfer order, and probably it'll have his address on it as
well.'

Mother kept all her papers in order, and Carlo, as a trainee
in the bank, was used to sorting through things. He quickly
found what he was looking for. And, sure enough, there
was the address, stamped on the form. Father was living in
Lübeck, not in Bremen. For a second time, we looked at each
other, undecided. There was no way of talking to Mother
about our missing father, she refused to tell us anything at
all about him.

'We have to go and see him,' I said.

'Has he ever come to see us?' Carlo demanded. 'Has he
ever written to us before – when I did my final exams, at
Christmas – has he ever so much as asked whether we're
even still alive?'

21

I said nothing. Carlo hated him, but he was getting a reasonable wage, he was better able to help than I was. I had never stolen money, but perhaps the time for that had come. Or should I send Father CARE parcels made up of stolen foodstuffs? I lapsed into broody silence.

Carlo startled me out of it. 'For the time being, we'll tell Mother nothing about this letter and we'll talk about it again later. Now, my guests will be here in an hour; it's time to get on with the cooking.'

Without a word, I hid my stolen goodies under my bed covers, then sliced Emmental cheese into fingers, took the pips out of grapes and abstractedly carried out all Carlo's instructions.

When his friends arrived, my mind was miles away. I had actually been looking forward to meeting Carlo's new friend from the bank, since he had kept telling us how intelligent he was; but now I hardly even looked at this Detlef. I was thinking only of Father. Of course I had, for a long time now, been afraid that he was very poor, for if that hadn't been the case, he would maybe have sent presents for me. It often happens that an artist is not appreciated until after his death, he was right there. If he hadn't got in touch, then that was because he was ashamed. But why was it Carlo he wrote to now, Carlo and not me, since I had been his princess?

He isn't a painter any more, he's a blood-courier, I thought with a shudder. A terrible expression that reminded me of Dracula; I couldn't make head nor tail of it.

Then two more of Carlo's friends arrived with their girls, and we sat down to eat, Carlo next to Cora, and I next to Detlef. I would have liked to tell Cora about Father's letter, but I couldn't talk in front of such a bright set. We ate, and drank wine, there was lively conversation and laughter. At last I managed to steer Cora into my room. I lifted the bedcover; Cora caught sight of the champagne and said, practical as ever, 'Put that in to chill, right away!'

By the time I came back from the kitchen, she had already set out the caviare on my celadon-green dish. 'What's up with you?' she asked. Seeing the look of consternation on my face, she thought the police must be on their way.

Very briefly, I told her what had been in Father's letter.

'We'll go and pay him a visit,' she said. 'We'll work something out tomorrow.'

Cora seemed to find my arrogant brother not altogether disagreeable, and she laughed at his second-hand jokes, all of which I knew already. I was beginning to have some doubts about whether there was maybe more to it than her tried and tested trick of making a man fall in love and then leading him on a bit. Did she really like Carlo after all?

There was a conspiracy working against me. When I brought in the red caviare, which lay there looking very fine and almost like a goldfish on the greenish china, Detlef inquired whether that was a Chinese dish.

'Could be,' I replied.

Everybody suddenly fell silent and stared at the dish.

'Where did it come from anyway?' Carlo asked.

'From the flea market,' said Cora with great presence of mind, at which the general conversation started up again.

Detlef looked me hard in the eye. 'My uncle's a curator at the museum,' he said, meaningfully.

Unfortunately, I wasn't as cool as Cora; I flushed. 'So what?' I asked timidly.

'You know what, and I know what,' said Detlef. 'We'll have a chat another time about the Sung Dynasty.' Then he finished off practically all the caviare on his own. Cora took the plate away, washed it and put it in my wardrobe. With unerring instinct, she had caught the gist of our conversation while flirting routinely with Carlo. I was full of admiration for her. But for Cora, I would probably have run off to my room and wouldn't have had anything more to do with the rest of that awful party.

At last, Cora fetched the chilled champagne, got my brother to open it and gave me the first glass. I knocked it straight back, had to burp, at which everybody laughed, and so, in my embarrassment, I drank a second glass.

Ten minutes later, I had become quite talkative and was keen to sing a song, but Carlo put the damper on that. When they were all getting ready to leave, because my mother was

23

expected back soon, Carlo got up and took Cora home. I was hurt, because I had counted on Cora staying with me and the three of us clearing up. Now I was landed with all the work.

At the door, Detlef said, 'I'll be seeing you,' and there was something threatening in his tone. Then I was alone with my fears and the dirty dishes.

When my mother came home, she immediately threw all the windows wide open and suspected me of having been smoking, although she failed to notice that there was caviare on the carpet and the room stank of aftershave and stale wine. I pretended I had a headache and slunk out. Although I lay listening for him, I didn't hear when Carlo got back home.

On the Sunday, I set off, without breakfast, on the way to Cora's. My mother had already cycled to the old people's home, my brother was still asleep. In my fury, I poured two dessert spoonfuls of salt into the carton of chocolate drink that was usually the first thing he took out of the fridge on getting up.

Cora was still in her nightdress (an old heirloom in linen, trimmed with lace) and drinking black coffee in bed. She received me like some princess at her levée. Her parents, with the dog on its lead, had just been on their way out for a walk, and left me to shut the door behind them.

'Our daughter is still catching up on her beauty sleep,' announced the professor. 'Like a giant sloth, h'm, yes.'

Cora knew I wanted to talk about Father. 'We have to get some money,' she said, 'and then we'll go up there and sort everything out.'

To me, that seemed an impossibility. 'Firstly, I can't go off on a journey without telling my mother! And secondly, I don't know how to rob a bank.'

Cora grinned. 'Oh, Maya, that can all be fixed. Where do you usually go on holiday?'

Tears welled up in my eyes. We hadn't gone away anywhere in years, because there was no money. When we were small, Carlo and I would go down now and again to Mother's brother in Bonn. Uncle Paul had taken over our grandfather's little stationer's shop, had done it up and turned it into a successful computer store. Not only that, but without his regular cheques, we'd never have been able to live on Mother's salary. I didn't want to go back there any more, it was totally humiliating. My cousin was an absolute bore. Admittedly, my aunt always used to buy me some 'sensible' clothes, but I could do without that.

Cora listened to all this. 'Perfect,' she said. 'I've got to go and spend two weeks with my family in Tuscany, but that's not until the end of the holidays, and we've got any amount of time before then. I've got relatives in Hamburg, which fits in very nicely. Surely your mother will have no objections to my inviting you. Besides, both my uncle and my aunt are out at work all day and they couldn't care less whether we spend our days in a museum or in our beds.'

'Lübeck's not far, so I could go straight on.'

'No way,' said Cora. 'That would be unwise. You'll stay with me in Hamburg, and then we'll toddle along together to call in on your royal daddy.'

Cora was curious about my mysterious father. I would have preferred to meet him on my own, but I held my tongue for the time being.

'The second problem's the readies,' Cora said. 'And there, I have an idea. My parents will pay the fare, yours too, I'm sure. But we need a sub for the starving artist.' I wasn't too taken by her irony, but I said nothing and waited for suggestions. 'I read in the paper recently about how a con man studied the obituary notices in the newspaper every day,' Cornelia went on, 'and about two weeks after the death of some grandad, he'd ring the widow's doorbell and claim that the deceased had left a hefty bill unpaid. When the old lady then wanted to know what it was for, he'd pull out an order form and tell her, very quietly, very discreetly, that it was in connection with some items of pornography the dead man had ordered. All the old dears would go pale and cough up at once, so as not to be reminded of such a scandal.'

'That's mean,' I said with a laugh. 'But you can't be serious about drumming up money that way! And besides, we might be able to make ourselves up to look a bit older, but nobody's going to take us for porn hawkers.'

That set Cora off in a fit of laughter. 'That's not what I meant, Elephant Baby! But that story gave me a good idea. Now listen: my father is fantastically educated, but absent-minded, as you'd expect in his position. Recently, he forgot to go to a colleague's funeral, or at least to send a letter of condolence. Mother reminded him of the date only when it was too late and his dark suit was at the cleaners. Well, to cut a long story short, the family had requested donations instead of flowers. For a riding club of all things, as if it wasn't well enough off already! Father reached for his wallet, scribbled a few quick sincere words and sent me off to the bereaved family's house. Because there was money in the envelope, I was to hand it over personally.'

'You didn't keep the money, did you?'

'The very idea. Some old biddy opened the door and showed me into the study, even offered me tea. All the other relatives were at the cemetery. When the old dear went off to the kitchen, I was left alone with a desk covered in donations envelopes, which, of course, as a properly brought up girl, I did not open.'

I was fascinated. 'Can that be done, nicking money from a dead person?'

'It doesn't belong to the dead person, nor can it do him any good,' said Cora. 'We could go to the funerals of complete strangers, only rich ones, obviously. If there's something in the paper about donations for Amnesty or some children's home, then we don't lay a finger on it. But a golf club or a yacht club, that sort of thing – well, there, I wouldn't think twice. Don't you reckon your father needs it more?'

I nodded. But I wasn't all that keen on the idea. Stealing a lipstick had been a game. In the case of the china dish, it was only afterwards that it hit me what I had got into, and I was almost a little sorry. On the other hand, I loved that piece, whereas thousands of visitors to the museum would take as little notice of it as my mother had. When you came down to it, I had shown myself to be a connoisseur, and so had perhaps earned a moral right to the object. But stealing money was something I still considered criminal in those days, and even the thought of acting like some Robin Hood couldn't make it any easier for me.

All of a sudden, Cora leapt out of bed. 'It's been raining during the night. I've got to go on a snail-hunt.'

Mystified, I followed her into the garden. Barefoot and still in her nightdress, she stalked around in the damp flowerbeds and borders snipping fat slugs in two with a pair of secateurs. Spellbound, she watched as the oozing slime welled out on to the grass. I felt sick.

When I finally got home, Carlo mentioned with a leer that Detlef had been there and had been asking for me. He eyed me with interest.

'What was he after?' I asked brusquely, although I had a terrible suspicion – blackmail.

'He seems to have taken a fancy to you,' said Carlo. 'And, by the way, that Cora's terrific. If you back me up in getting going with her, then I can return the compliment and steer clever old Detlef into your clutches.'

'I don't want your Detlef,' I said, slamming the door behind me.

Soon, the holidays arrived. I longed for the chance of not seeing my gruesome family for a long time and of being out of Detlef's reach. Why did life have to be so complicated?

CHAPTER 3

Red as Blood

Recently, a father got into our coach with his little daughter.
It's actually a piece of nonsense taking children of that age
along on a sightseeing tour, and, as a rule, I don't approve
of it. Most children are a nuisance; they get bored, they
chatter loudly through my commentary, don't stay in their
seats, smear chocolate all over the upholstery and distract
even the most serious tourists from listening to me, and from
giving their tips. Fortunately, most parents are aware of this
and prefer to take smaller children to the seaside. But this
father was accompanied by a mature personality, who
appeared attentive, yet not at all precocious, no little sweetie-
pie, but a princess of royal blood. It stirred an ache in me.
Father and daughter made just as peerless a pair as I, as
Infanta of Spain, along with my regal papa, had done. Obviously I had gone too far in idealizing my father, who had
become no longer accessible at such an early stage. Perhaps,
though, this charming pair was also a distortion of reality,
and there was an embittered mother sitting at home waiting
for them.

Despite this analogy with my own past, I have not altogether
unhappy memories of our fund-raising operation on behalf
of my father, which of course took place before he showed
himself in his true colours.

Although Cora and I studied the death notices daily, no
opportunity presented itself for some time, because in most
announcements there was no reference to donations; in the
few cases where a bank account was specified, these con-

cerned some Protestant church choir or a pigeon-fanciers' club; to judge by the addresses and the wording, they involved surviving relatives who knew all the guests at the funeral personally. We would have drawn unnecessary attention to ourselves, and in any case the donations were likely to have been pretty small. Stealing from cancer funds and school support groups was something I refused to do. In the end, we came across the Freemasons; we weren't exactly sure what they were all about, but they were an exclusively male association, and Cora convinced me that this was no philanthropic organization, and we should go for it.

The villa stood on the banks of the Neckar, the finest of locations, and there was bound to be money about. Or would those attending the funeral prefer to work through bank transfers?

I signed a condolence card with 'Dr', followed by an illegible flourish. If asked, Cora was going to pass herself off as the daughter of a Frankfurt professor. Although not dressed in black, we wore muted, unobtrusive clothes, no make-up, altogether childishly neat and tidy in appearance. I plaited my hair into thin pigtails and put on Carlo's glasses. Cora had a dark wig which her mother had worn years before at a shrovetide carnival; she trimmed it into a sober fringe and, in corduroy slacks and a dark-blue velvet top, she looked like a twelve-year-old. 'Camouflage,' said Cora, 'that's the French for a kind of disguise, and it's very common in the animal world.'

At the house of mourning (a public service was being held at that very moment in the town centre), an elderly woman opened the door to us. Cornelia put on a schoolgirlish lisp and said her piece. The old Freemason biddy was hard of hearing, but she nodded and made to take the envelope from my hand. Not a word about asking us in. I was just about to give up, but Cora bawled into the old woman's ear (forgetting her lisp) that we had a long train journey behind us and were very thirsty. We were shown into the kitchen. No envelopes full of money lying about here, but plates of tasty-looking sandwiches. While I sat drinking lemonade, Cora shouted, 'Toilet!' and left the kitchen. The woman asked me about my parents. I pretended I was an orphan, and drank one glass after another. At last, my friend came back in, winked at me, drank a mouthful herself and, with great assurances of our gratitude, shook the woman by the hand. We left the house at a great rate of knots.

I asked, 'Did you . . . ?' and she nodded.

We went into a café in the pedestrian precinct, made a beeline for the toilet, bolted the door and tore open the envelopes. Cornelia had pocketed every last letter of condolence. Actually, I had assumed she would take only one or two, so that they wouldn't be missed later. In the first one, there was a cheque.

'Shit!' I said. But all in all, as it then turned out, we had made a good haul. In a first flush of enthusiasm, we ordered our favourite cakes, then, in a whisper, we agreed not to touch the rest, but to hand it over to my father. But he was sure to ask us where the money had come from.

'I'll think of something,' said Cora, and I believed her right away.

Twice I had succeeded in avoiding Detlef. He was short-sighted and so couldn't recognize me as quickly as I could spot him. On the first occasion, he was standing leaning against the wall outside our house as I came home in the late afternoon from my Spanish study group (which I was attending because it was taken by Herr Becker). Like a rabbit, I shot off to the side and hid, crouching in someone else's front garden. When at long last he pushed off, I crept out, stiff all over. The second time, he was sitting in our kitchen, pretending to my mother that he was waiting for Carlo. This time, quick as a flash, I thought up a white lie. 'Carlo says to tell you not to wait for him, he's gone to the cinema.' Detlef shot me a withering look, but didn't dare come out with an argument in front of my mother, and left. Shortly after, Carlo came home, and my mother was puzzled. But she was too tired to bring the subject up again, and, with a sigh, she put the kettle on and went for a lie-down to rest her swollen legs.

The next day, Carlo brought a letter from Detlef. 'Well,

well,' he said, 'so the elephant lady is trampling men's hearts underfoot!' He wasn't to know that, as the go-between, this was no love letter he was delivering, but a blackmail threat: *If you're not waiting at the back door of the bank at six tomorrow, I'm going to report you to the police. D.*

Cora advised me to go. 'First, we've got to hear what it is he wants and why he hasn't reported you up till now,' she said. She also offered to come with me, but I declined; I didn't want her to think me a coward.

Carlo usually came home around five, so I didn't have to worry about meeting him as well as I waited punctually for my blackmailer.

Detlef was friendly at first. He offered me a Cinzano in the café. In his own good time, he got to the point. Everything would be fine, the china dish could still be handed down to my grandchildren as a knick-knack if I did him a small favour. I acted dumb. He was going to have to call a spade a spade. And so we beat about the bush for a while. At last came his demand: I was to sleep with him. Just as I suspected. Nevertheless, I was speechless with indignation for a second or two. But I couldn't very well yell at him in front of everyone. I got to my feet. 'I'll think over what you've said,' I told him, desperate to talk to Cora. She would know what to do.

Ten minutes later, I was at her place. She expressed her approval. 'You did everything just great. All we really have to do now is get through the five days till we leave. Then we'll have shaken him off for the time being.'

'Five days is a long time, though! He'll ask me again tomorrow!'

'If the worst comes to the worst, you leave him to me, Maya. I can sort out a sandpit mafioso like him, and no trouble at all.'

'And then he'll end up wanting to sleep with *you*. Very likely in preference to me!'

Cora gave me a hug. 'Don't you worry about a thing, I'll cut him down to size,' and indicated, between forefinger and thumb, a tiny little mannikin. But I was so afraid that she promised never to leave me on my own throughout these five days.

31

My mother had no objections to my spending nights at Cora's; she felt flattered by my friendship with the daughter of a professor. I had spun her a tale about Cora's parents being away and my friend being frightened of staying alone in the house. Surprisingly, Mother suggested that Cora could sleep at our place for that matter, but then she recognized that the professor's house was bigger and more comfortable.

So we had managed to arrange it that we met our enemy, Detlef, only when we were together, and, with Cora there, I was able to come out with some fresh, teasing remarks that kept Detlef's hopes up.

On the very first day of the holidays, we took our seats in the train. Cora's relatives did not seem altogether delighted at the prospect of our visit; in any case, they had little time to devote to us. In actual fact, that suited us fine. She wasn't used to anything else, for her mother, too, was usually conspicuous by her absence. This striking woman, whom I had seen only seldom, was always on the go, as Cora put it. She attended lectures in psychology, frequented the openings of art exhibitions, did the rounds of the boutiques and would fly off for three days in New York. I admired her. Her sister in Hamburg was quite different, a serious workaholic. From morning till night, she repaired dentures in a joint dental practice.

After we had spent our first day in Hamburg catching up on our sleep, we went to Lübeck. I had never been so excited. Did my father still look exactly as in the photo I took everywhere with me? Mind you, that picture was nine years old. In those days, he had been a man with a lively imagination, by turns amusing and then broody and introverted. When he was painting, no one dared disturb him. He was slim and good-looking, with a little beard. Would I recognize him? I could no longer imagine the sound of his voice. How would Cora find him? That, too, was very important to me.

We had to stop and ask the way several times before we found the street. It was a basement flat. 'Roland Westermann', said a piece of blue insulating tape stuck beneath the other bell-pushes. We rang, tentatively at first, then harder. Just as we were about to give up, the door was flung open.

There, before us, stood a scowling man in a dressing-gown. He was a caricature of the king.

After a fit of helpless panic, I said, 'I'm Maya!'

My father tugged on the cord of the red-and-grey striped velour dressing-gown, which was much too small for him, lashing it tighter round his bulging pot-belly, and rubbed his eyes. He gaped at me, obviously even more surprised than I was. 'You mean, you're my daughter?'

I nodded and couldn't hold back the tears. The fat man drew me into the house, the baffled Cora following without waiting for an invitation. In a gloomy kitchen-cum-living-room, we sat down on some metal garden chairs with broken slatted seats. The place stank of beer, smoke, stale cabbage and unaired bedding, and through an open door a greyish-looking bed could be seen.

Father couldn't stop shaking his head. Then he glanced towards the clock which hung over the sink, next to a shaving-mirror. It was two in the afternoon.

'A bad time of day. I go to work very early and I was just about to have my afternoon nap.'

'We weren't to know . . .'

Cora looked at him. 'I'm Maya's friend.' She said it distinctly, as if she were talking to some mental defective. Father had a wad of cotton wool in his right ear, which he now dug out slowly.

'You were a beautiful child,' he said to me.

I didn't know how to respond to that. Wasn't I beautiful any more?

Cora opened the windows. Father got to his feet, pulled up the roller-shutters in the tiny bedroom and carried out a chamber pot. With moist eyes, I blinked at Cora once he was outside.

'Your father's a lush,' she said.

My own diagnosis hadn't progressed that far yet. When he came back in, I took a much closer look at him. White streaks in, and heavy bags under, his eyes, the beard gone, and in its place, unshaven stubble, thinning hair of an indefinable colour, straggly and sticking up. His paunch was bloated, a filthy vest showed under the dressing-gown and his legs were clad in pyjama trousers in olive-green and mousy-grey patterned flannel.

Father was embarrassed by my stare. 'I'll get dressed,' he said, closing the door of the little bedroom behind him.

Again, Cora and I exchanged glances. She drew the money from her pocket and handed it to me. 'The lottery, that's what we'll tell him,' she whispered.

When Father reappeared, he had tidied himself up. He was wearing a navy-blue sailor's jersey that was loose enough to conceal his paunch, had combed his hair and dabbed on a pungent eau de Cologne. He had put on black trousers, which were covered in cats' hairs.

'Well, kids, this is a surprise!' he said. 'Right, let's go to a pub, I'm afraid it's always a bit stuffy in here. Bad enough for a rheumaticky old man, but not at all suitable for young ladies.'

I gave him the money. 'We've had a win on the lottery!' I told him.

'I can't possibly accept this,' he exclaimed, counting the notes. 'I could never borrow off my own daughter.'

'It's a present,' I said.

Father pocketed it. I would have quite liked to be hugged, not by this rheumaticky old man, but by the king and artist.

In the pub, he ordered beer and schnapps for himself, I wanted coffee and Cornelia hot chocolate. I had to tell him all about Carlo and myself. After a few schnapps, Father became nicer, more relaxed, more amusing.

'What's a blood-courier?' I asked.

He explained that he set out very early in the mornings in a company van to call in at a whole lot of medical practices. At each, he would be handed a bag with various blood samples, which he then delivered to a central laboratory. 'I've got blood on my hands,' he joked. By noon, he would be back home, where he would have a nap, after which he would get up and paint. He had been hit by disaster the previous year, when he had had his driving licence taken away for six months and was out of work. Thank heavens, he had been given his job back after that. 'But I've got debts, girls. You can't live on social security.'

Naturally, I wanted to hear about his artistic work. He promised to show me his pictures back home. But when, three hours later, we left the pub, he packed us off to the station. He had work to do, he said, and we could come back and see him again in the next few days. Unfortunately, he wasn't on the phone, but late afternoon would be a good time to come.

For quite a while, I couldn't talk to Cora, but just sat beside her staring out of the train window. She had nothing to say either. At one point, I caught myself imagining I might bring some scandal into her respectable family home, so ashamed of myself was I.

The next few days we spent lazing about, sleeping late, going to the swimming pool or into town for an ice-cream; we hung about with other young people, coming home only when her aunt would be expecting us for the evening meal. Then we would let them force money on us for the cinema, and we'd fritter away the rest in amusement arcades and the like, even though we reckoned we were almost too old for that. Pretty soon, we got to know two young students on summer vacation. We invited the two of them to brunch in the aunt's flat. Cornelia soon grabbed the nicer one for herself and steered him into the kitchen, while I sat, bored to death, in the dining-room with his bashful pal. But I didn't begrudge Cora her bit of fun and was only too happy that no one in Hamburg addressed me as 'Elly Phant'. In my mind, I carried on endless conversations with my father. 'Don't you remember – I'm the Infanta Maya and you're the King of Spain? Why have you come down in the world so much? Who is Karin? What do your paintings look like?' All this and more I wanted to know in my fictitious dialogues. But I suspected that, the next time we met, I would ask only about the pictures.

Cora was no longer so keen on going back to Lübeck, but she didn't want to let me down. I assured her she could quite easily stay in Hamburg, but she thought that would be boring. We left her aunt a note, saying that we wouldn't be back by dinner time, and set off on our second visit.

It seemed almost as if Father had been expecting us. Both he and his surroundings were distinctly tidier. From his meagre supplies, he cooked a passable meal; it was only the grubby plates that put me off. I would have loved to give them a good wash in hot water, but I was afraid of offending him.

At my request, he showed us a few of his pictures. They were all small-format things, and very different from what I remembered. Cora, with her connoisseur's eye, noticed at once that he got by with only three colours.

'How right you are,' Father said, looking intently at Cora for the first time. 'I've made a virtue of necessity. You know how it goes in the fairy tale: white as snow, black as ebony, red as blood ... When I had no money to buy paints, I decided just to make do with the ones I had. Black as death, white as light, red as sin.' We sat listening, as if we were in school. He went on: 'The Nazis, with their black, white and red flags had probably touched the right nerve in their supporters with their swastika in its white circle against a sea of blood. With the same design in other colours, say, blue, yellow and green, they wouldn't have got anywhere. So it follows, if you dress yourselves up in a combination of black, white and red, you'll find any number of admirers.'

Cora said, 'I've no desire to draw crowds of fascists.'

I was thrown by this. Did this vivid red have anything to do with his job as a blood-courier? Much later, I mulled over why he chose those colours when he had denounced them as being associated with right-wing extremism. Could colours convey an ideology anyway, did they not exist in Nature, every bit as innocent in themselves as earth, sea and grass?

Father's paintings were all alike; there were always black insects – bugs, ants, moths – creeping around on red fruit. The backgrounds were white, mostly a tablecloth with folds and shadows painted in meticulous detail.

'Only in the face of limitations does the master really reveal himself,' he observed.

I thought back to his earlier pictures. 'You used to paint the sky and the sea, never pomegranates with bugs.'

'Is that so? Could be. Yes, as a matter of fact, you're right,' and he rummaged about behind his wardrobe, getting annoyed because he couldn't find what he was looking for, and digging out more and more black, white and red pictures. Amongst them lay one that surprised even him. A white, Christ-like corpse lay on black, charred beams, with blood streaming from its wounds. It bore Carlo's features. We stared at it.

'Must have done that when I was plastered,' said Father.

As on so many occasions, Cora expressed what I dared only to think. 'Herr Westermann, has Carlo been to see you lately?'

Father looked at her, disconcerted, and shook his head.

'How do you know what Carlo looks like nowadays?' I asked. 'He was only a child then.'

'That isn't Carlo.'

'Who is it then?' inquired Cora.

'Girls, girls, it's no one at all. A distorted product of my imagination. Does your mother know you've come to see me, Maya?'

'No.'

'What has she said about me?'

'Nothing.'

He believed me. We took our leave and promised to come again soon.

On the following day, Cora went to meet her student in town, while I took myself off on an expedition through the Hamburg shops. Actually, I didn't intend stealing anything; the pocket-money Mother had given me was, considering our circumstances, generous, and it more than covered tram tickets, ice-creams and other odds and ends. My personal requirements were modest, and it would never have crossed my mind to indulge myself in luxuries. Only a select few things could lead me into temptation. But for my poor father . . .

I stole neither money nor food, but paints. Their strange

descriptions fascinated me: caput mortuum, cerulean and madder.

Because it was summer and I couldn't go about in my elephant cape, I carried on my arm a large plastic carrier bag full of bread-rolls, into the depths of which I let slide a small collection of tubes of paint. The brush had to be of sable.

That evening, we went to a musical. Cora's uncle had got hold of some tickets. He fostered the hope that we would be going home soon.

Cora thought we should get the paints to Lübeck right away. Since seeing the picture of the corpse, she had formed a high opinion of Father's art, because this subject had appealed to her taste.

Father was touched by my present. 'But what on earth am I supposed to paint?' he exclaimed like a child.

'Us,' I said. 'A double portrait of Cora and me.'

'I haven't painted figures for ages.'

But Cora, too, badgered him, because she was taken by my idea. Father got quite fired up; the new colours stimulated him. He began by making several sketches, which turned out amazingly vivid. 'I'm going to paint you like two of Utamaro's courtesans.' Not a word about Spanish princesses.

After three sittings, he completed the picture in a tremendous creative frenzy. This work was totally out of character with his bug pictures, it was more colourful.

In it, Cora and I looked older and more worldly-wise, yet there was something childishly cruel in our expression, as if we had just pulled the wings off an insect.

Father was delighted, he embraced me for the first time, and then Cora too (not altogether decently, I felt) and expressed the opinion that this picture marked the start of a second career. That there had even been a first one was news to me.

Father wanted to give me the painting as a parting gift. But how was I to hide it from Mother? She would know right away who had painted it. I tried to explain this.

'Then tell her the truth,' he suggested.

'She doesn't talk about you. Carlo and I don't want to hurt

her; she's probably never got over you leaving us . . .'

As I said that, I became embarrassed, for I hadn't been as direct with him all the time we had been there.

He stared into space. 'A hard woman,' he said. 'Anyone would think I went to the nick of my own free will.'

Cora and I gave a start. What was that he said?

Cora asked politely, 'Why were you in jail, Herr Westermann?'

I would never have dared.

'Oh, hell . . .' Father went to fetch some schnapps and took a drink straight from the bottle. 'I'll tell you about it when you're older.'

When you're sixteen, that's the last thing you want to hear.

'Anyway, it was all a bad break. I've paid for it. If your mother had stood by me, I'd have been back with you years ago.' He let slip another obscure remark about other women being less hard-hearted.

Again, it was Cora who pushed him further. 'Did you marry a second time?' Never mind that she must have known that my parents weren't divorced.

'No, no,' he said. 'Karin's a nurse, a fine woman with no prejudices. At least, that's what I thought. Now she's gone, just when I'm getting old and need help.'

'Father,' I said, plucking up courage, 'do you remember how I'm the Infanta Maya?'

'What do you mean, Infanta?' he asked, poking around in his ear with a matchstick. 'We don't have that sort of thing here. And besides, Karin was no younger than your mother – in fact, a year older.'

I wasn't interested in his stupid Karin. 'Father, I mean the Velázquez,' I said, pleadingly.

'Velázquez? If I remember rightly, he painted pictures of the Spanish court, Infantas, too. What makes you think of that? I'm no latter-day Velázquez.'

That was clear enough proof that he had forgotten the child that had been his little daughter.

Cora packed away the picture. 'If Maya doesn't want it, I'll take it,' she said.

Father merely nodded. Obviously it didn't even occur to him to keep it himself, as a memento. We took our leave. We were intending to travel home the next day. There was a lot I had not managed to clear up or find out, new secrets had been added to the old. Disappointed and deeply hurt, I shook his hand.

'Well, cheerio then,' he said.

CHAPTER 4

Persian Pink

You can hate your parents, you can idolize them. Cora's parents were so much the opposite of mine that, leaving aside all petty squabbles and signs of everyday wear and tear, they seemed to me the epitome of a modern relationship between partners. My father was a drunk, my mother a depressive. Had she got that way because of him, or had Father taken to the bottle because of her? Whichever way it was, they had each done their very best to help the other along their disastrous way.

In spring, it can sometimes rain very heavily in Florence. When it does, hardly anything of the beauty of this city can be seen from inside the bus, with dirty rainwater running down the windows. The comparison with the tears in my grubby soul is probably not an original one, but it does keep coming into my mind.

On dreary days like this, my thoughts go back to our return journey from Hamburg to Heidelberg. As we sat there in the train, nodding goodbye to Cora's greatly relieved relatives, I had the feeling I was in for a dose of flu. As it turned out, I remained in good health, but my inner listlessness and tearfulness were very similar to the early symptoms of some illness. We talked about my father, or rather, Cora did. I hadn't the strength to work out my own theories about him.

'Are you going to put Carlo in the picture about our secret mission?' she asked. 'Without letting on about our win on the lottery, of course.'

I was horrified. 'That's absolutely none of his grimy little business.' At the same time, I was quite taken with the thought that I knew something he didn't, and that I could put him on the rack with a long-drawn-out report, with him having to drag every last little detail out of me. 'I'll have to think it over,' I said, snuggling up to Cora and falling asleep.

I woke after a feverish doze; a disturbing dream, which I couldn't put into words, was bothering me. It had something to do with Father's paintings. But soon Cora and I were going to be separated, and I would be totally at the mercy of my extortioner. Without my friend by me, I felt like a motherless child.

Cora had found a newspaper in the luggage rack. I had hardly opened my sleepy eyes when she started talking.

'There's something interesting here I must read out to you. Listen to this:

> During a teenage party in the county town of H., seventeen-year-old Markus S. was rushed to hospital with severe injuries sustained under tragic circumstances. After consuming large quantities of alcohol, he took a tear-gas pistol belonging to his father and, assuming it to be harmless, put it to his head and pulled the trigger. According to statements by his friends, he wanted to frighten a girl from his class in school, who had broken off a relationship with him. The boisterous party came to a terrible end. The shock wave from the detonation caused the young man a serious brain trauma. He was admitted in an unconscious condition to the University Neurological Clinic, where it took him three days to come out of a coma.'

Cora looked at me expectantly.

'OK,' I said, 'so there's something I'd never have known. I always thought these guns were only a deterrent, to frighten people but not to do them any injury.'

'Yes, sure, but this dope Markus held it right against his head, that's the difference.'

'Well, so what's it to me?' I said tetchily.

'Maya, my father keeps a gas pistol like that in the drawer in his bedside table.'

I gaped at her in amazement. What was she driving at?

'If this Detlef doesn't back off, it might be a possibility.'

42

'Are you wanting to do him in?'

'We could work it that he shoots himself, just like in this article. Nobody's to know about what we've just read.'

'Cora, that's going too far. We have to go about it another way. I think we've got to get something over him. Blackmail him back, if you like.'

Cora was picking bits of fluff off my lamb's-wool sweater. 'That might just work. My folks are away this weekend. On Tuesday we're going off on holiday, and we've got to have rescued you by then.'

'So what do you mean about the weekend and your parents being away . . . ?'

'Well, the party in the paper has given me an idea. Supposing we invite Detlef, Carlo too, and maybe a few others. Then we get the slimy jerk drunk and I give him the big come-on. I lure him into my parents' bedroom. He takes his clothes off and dumps his things in the bathroom, because that's the way I want it. The bathroom has two doors, so you sneak his clothes out and hide them, and when he's stark naked, I give him the slip.'

'Oh, Cora, what good is that? That won't bother him one bit. He'll just roll into your folks' bed, put on your father's pyjamas and sleep off his skinful. And anyway, he's not going to strip off unless you do it first!'

'I'll take off some of my things . . .'

Cora was way ahead of me, I was sure of that. But how far? I had never asked because I was convinced I wouldn't be able to match her on this subject. But I forced myself.

'Cora, just when did you first . . . with a man . . . I mean, really . . . ?'

'The day before yesterday.'

I didn't believe her and looked her straight in the eye. 'Not that student?'

She nodded. 'Honest.'

'And – what was it like?'

'You've missed nothing.'

I didn't yet know at that time that Cora regarded men as just some kind of mouse that you played with for a while, the way a kitten does, before satisfying your hunger.

43

There was a long silence as we sat looking out at the flat North German countryside. Then we came back to the subject of our blackmailer, and we decided to give the party idea a try. Without the pistol, but with the intention of somehow or other making him look stupid or giving him a real scare. It was no good running away from attempts at intimidation; attack was the best form of defence.

'And what if all that doesn't work?' I asked. 'Then you'll be far away, sunning yourself in Italy, enjoying your *gelati*, while I watch him skulking round our house.'

'Rubbish. You're a she-elephant and you'll trample him down.'

That gave me an idea.

Carlo seemed bucked by the invitation, obviously imagining that Cora was throwing the party for his sake. On the day before the event, I cycled to the old folks' home. I hadn't been there very often. I headed for the ward nurses' rest-room. One of my mother's colleagues, who didn't know me, eyed me with curiosity.

'So you're Frau Westermann's daughter! But you don't look at all like an elephant.'

I asked where I could find my mother, saying I had lost my front door-key. The nurse went off to look for her. The moment I was alone in the little room, I opened the medicine cabinet in search of sleeping drugs. Actually, I thought disapprovingly, they should keep this kind of cabinet locked; all over this place, keys had been left in locks, and yet they surely couldn't trust these doddering geriatrics. The biggest stocks they had here, apart from laxatives, were tranquillizers and sleeping tablets.

When my mother, somewhat puzzled at my visit, appeared in her white overalls, I spun her the lie about the house-key. As she gave me her own one, she scolded me. 'This sort of thing never happened to you when you were small.'

A doctor was standing in the doorway, grinning: 'Elephantile regression.'

*   *   *

Cora found a plentiful supply of drinks on hand in the parental cellar. We decided to cook a meal that would be heavy and hard to digest, something that would make the party guests soporific and tired. Using large white beans, fatty belly of pork, tomatoes, garlic, chilli, and red Spanish sausage, we concocted, in the middle of August, a meal for a winter's day. The only thing anyone would want after eating that would be a lengthy nap.

Carlo had passed the word to Detlef, who was now no doubt looking forward to an orgy. A classmate by the name of Greta was going to bring along her boyfriend, while Cora had invited a cousin who would also have a conquest in tow. Cora's brother, whom I hadn't met, was studying in the USA and wasn't due back until Christmas. So, we thought, with eight, you can have a party.

We had brought wine, beer and a lot of hard drinks from the professor's cellar-bar and laid them out at random all round the room. Detlef tried something of everything, and we kept busy topping up his glass. He beamed at me, while Cora gave him the come-on. Carlo was rather put out, since he reckoned she was fair game for him. Finally, we served up the heavy dinner. Cora and I made a great thing of having cooked it according to an authentic Peruvian recipe, and loaded our extortioner's plate with huge helpings. The first sleeping tablet was already nestling inside him, having been crushed into a spoonful of bean mush and steered into his mouth by Cora personally. She flirted with him on his left, while I did my bit on his right.

At one point, Carlo tugged at my sleeve and drew me into the kitchen.

'Listen here, pachyderm! I don't know what your game is,' he hissed, 'but you could at least give your pal a kick up the arse and get her to leave Detlef to you.'

'What for?'

'God Almighty, don't act so bloody dumb! It's no fun at all if the two of you make a play for the same joker and I'm left hanging around spare!'

'Then bugger off home! Cora and I, we go together like that, of one heart and one mind!'

He gave my arm a painful pinch and groaned at such gormlessness. 'You haven't a heart or a mind between the pair of you!'

After the second sleeping tablet, a lot of food and a lot of schnapps, Cora dragged Detlef away with her, to show him round the house. Carlo went home in a huff, while the other couples were busy with each other.

I slipped into the bathroom. I had dissolved more sleeping pills in some sparkling wine and poured it into a marked glass. Through the bathroom door, I could see Detlef sitting on the parental bed in his underpants. Cora took the glass from me and funnelled its contents into him. He was gawping glassily into space. I went in, and we both did a slow strip down to our bra and pants. Detlef grunted at the sight. 'My blood is like lava,' he burbled, then he keeled over and fell fast asleep.

We locked him in, went back to the other guests and announced that we had kicked Carlo and Detlef out because they were drunk. At this, Greta and her friend took fright and made off home, too. The cousin had settled down with his little precious in Cora's brother's vacant bedroom. But at last, as we were clearing up, we heard the front door slamming, and finally we were alone with Detlef. Like a flash, we shot into the parents' bedroom. There he lay, his mouth open and snoring reassuringly.

He was usually a very smart dresser; like Carlo, he had learnt at the bank that a career in business was not something you achieved by sloppy dressing. Purely from his outward appearance, we could hardly fault him. Mind you, he was, like his name, pretty wet, with his hair the colour of the bristles on a piglet and his boring, chubby baby face, but details like his blue signet ring and his poncy, flashy watch were a challenge to our creativity.

'We can do anything we like with him now,' whispered Cora.

'But what, though?' I asked, a good deal louder, because it was obvious that he was sleeping as if anaesthetized.

'Cut it off, for example,' said Cora, turning up the volume too.

That shook me rigid. 'And supposing he bleeds to death?'

'Don't be daft – his hair!'

We looked around, searching for ideas. I had seldom had a chance to have a good look at a parental bedroom. My mother slept on a three-seater sofa in the living-room. At my relatives' or Cora's, I had occasionally caught sight of a double bed, bedside tables and wardrobes, but none of them had the slightest erotic flair. Here, though, it was all different. Even Cora's parents' bathroom, with its oriental tiles, was reminiscent of the Blue Mosque. But what fascinated me much more was the bed linen; I had only ever seen white, checked or some other respectably patterned stuff. Here it was all pure silk in an exotic pink that, in the subdued light of the brass hanging lamps, seemed to me like sin itself.

'What a strange colour . . .'

Cora nodded. 'Persian pink, my mother's favourite shade.'

Detlef's piggy hair didn't go at all well with this colour scheme. His open, round mouth made the savings bank apprentice into a piggy bank, the kind where you shove your saved-up mark pieces into its porcelain snout. Cora picked up her mother's nail varnish – naturally, Persian pink. 'Help me turn him over on to his front,' she said, and then started daubing his back with the pink varnish.

In the meantime, I had frisked through his blazer and fished out his wallet. When I looked up, I read on Detlef's back, I AM. 'What next?' I asked.

'A SWINE,' Cora replied.

'Nothing original about that, I don't think.'

'OK, I AM A PERVERT,' and Cora dipped her brush.

'No,' I said, 'better than that: I AM IMPOTENT.'

'He'll not be able to get it off by himself, he'll have to ask somebody else to help. It would be an even bigger laugh if he didn't notice it and, all unsuspecting, went to the swimming baths.'

When the inscription had dried, we turned him over again.

'Cora, look at this. He's got love letters from two different women in his wallet!'

'Give them here, I'll bring them right back. Dad's got a photocopier, and a Polaroid camera as well.'

While Cora made the copies, I had five minutes to take my first good look at a naked man. By the time I heard Cora on the stairs, I had covered Detlef over again.

'Before we take pictures of him, he's going to get pink fingernails as well,' said Cora. Like a couple of mani- and pedicurists, we worked our way through ten finger- and ten toenails in Persian pink. It was a thoroughly satisfying piece of work. Finally, to match the rest, we painted over the face of his watch and his signet ring.

'Anything else?'

From the professor's desk, Cora brought a selection of rubber stamps. She read them out: 'Small Packet', 'Printed Papers', 'Recorded Delivery', 'Personal and Confidential' and so on. We decided in favour of PROCESSED, and with it Detlef's chest, on which only a few bristles sprouted, was duly branded.

'Makes a good picture,' said Cora. 'Just a pity that we can't get both the front and rear views on the same photo, with PROCESSED and IMPOTENT.'

'You know, while we're at it,' I said, 'we could give the savings-bank piggy a present of a free earring.' With a darning needle, Cora pierced his ear lobe while I held a piece of soap behind it and a paper handkerchief at the ready. Detlef let out some angry grunts, but didn't struggle. We drew some silver wire through the hole in his ear and attached to it a tiny plastic piccaninny that had come from a bubble-gum machine.

Then we took a whole lot of photos. Detlef from all angles, sometimes with Cora and me. Mind you, we didn't take off all our clothes for this, but simply poked our heads out from under the Persian-pink duvet cover.

Into his wallet, in addition to the original letters, we put one photocopy of each, so that he'd know that we had duplicated them, along with a few of the photos that had turned out particularly well.

While Cora read the love letters to me, I removed the golden anchor buttons from Detlef's navy-blue jacket and sewed them carefully back on a centimetre farther over. In the midst of my leisurely needlework, I was struck by misgivings. 'You don't think these are Nazi-style methods, do you?' I asked my giggling friend.

Cora put my mind at rest. 'Outwardly, there's nothing to be seen, apart from the pink fingernails and the black baby. He can say he did that for a bet. So don't go wetting yourself about that. Now we're going for a sleep.'

To be on the safe side, we left the bedroom lights on and set a plastic bucket by the bed for Detlef to use.

'Do you think we should get in beside him tomorrow morning before he wakes up?' I said. 'And then he'd think we'd been doing it with him all night and we were quits.'

'That wouldn't match up with the IMPOTENT on his back, and I can't be bothered taking that off again. Anyway, I don't know where the nail-varnish remover is.'

So we went off to bed, for my mother had given me permission to stay overnight in the respectable professorial home. We slept till two in the afternoon, when we were roused by the insistent ringing of the phone.

Cora groaned, 'That's bound to be my parents,' and went to answer it. But it was Carlo, who hadn't been able to contact Detlef at home and wanted to know of his whereabouts.

'How should I know?' said Cora. 'He was pissed out of his brains and said he was going on to a brothel, but don't ask me which one.' Shocked, Carlo accepted that.

We scurried into the pink bedroom. Our piggy had made full use of the bucket. Cora threw the windows open. Detlef looked ill, and I was almost sorry for him. We gave him a nudge or two, and he opened his eyes painfully.

'You'll have to go,' said Cornelia severely. 'Do you want my mother to find you in her bed?'

Detlef tried to look at his watch, saw the pink painted face and let out a moan.

'It's Monday morning,' I lied. 'If you get a move on, you'll manage to be at your counter at the bank by eight, but they'll be able to smell the drink on your breath even through the glass panel.'

We left the room and, after a few minutes, heard him cursing wildly, using the toilet and then rushing headlong from the house. Never again did he feel the urge to lean on us. He even broke off all contact with Carlo, and my poor brother never did find out why.

It was my secret dream that Cora's parents would invite me on the trip to Tuscany. For years, they had rented the same holiday villa near Colle di Val d'Elsa, and I knew there were four beds there. In previous years, Cora's brother had always been there with them. But I didn't like to ask (the professor had already paid my fare to Hamburg), because it seemed to me I was always cast in the role of the poor relation.

Although Cora had often told me about this holiday home (with its own pool, naturally), it didn't even occur to her to try to talk her parents into inviting me along.

Now she was gone and would be getting brown, improving her Italian by flirting with tanned Vespa jockeys, eating tomatoes with basil and drinking Chianti classico. And me?

'Tell me, are the two of you actually lesbian?' Carlo had demanded with biting anger after the famous party. I nearly tipped the contents of the overflowing ashtray all over his white banker's shirt. But what he had said gave me food for thought. We weren't lesbian, of course, but I had to admit that I had gone right off my geography teacher once my friendship with Cora had grown increasingly close. It surely couldn't be normal, I asked myself anxiously, that at the moment I wasn't in love with a single man? Cora was my be all and end all, with her I felt good and immune to all the nastiness of this world. Without her, I was only half a person. Was this great dependence a good thing?

In the two weeks while Cora was in Italy, I was profoundly miserable. I kept busy, changed my room around, cleaned the kitchen to take some of the load off my mother, and in the mornings, while she was at the old folks' home and Carlo at the bank, I rooted around among old papers. I hoped I might discover some kind of documents, letters or other mementos, to do with my father. Clearly, my mother had destroyed everything that had originally come from him. Only a few photos in the family album had survived, out of a sense of decency, or probably because a gap would really end up arousing curiosity and because she couldn't very well deny the fact that we did have a begetter.

What I did find, though, hidden in a little volume of Eichendorff's poems (which, curiously, wasn't kept in the bookcase, but among Mother's personal papers and letters), was several photos of a young man who bore a striking resemblance to my brother. Who could this be, and why was he kept secret from us? In one picture, he could be seen arm in arm with Mother, who might have been about twenty at the time. I could just decipher 'Elsbeth and Karl' on the back; the violet ink had faded. Could he be Carlo's father? I tried to puzzle it out. In looks, Carlo took after neither my mother nor my decamped daddy. He had black hair, very fair skin and blue eyes, was a mad keen sportsman (his racing bike meant a lot to him) and well muscled; quite a good-looking young bloke, actually, if you overlooked the pimples that attacked him like a rash every now and again. The man in the black-and-white photo seemed to be dark-haired, too, and I let my imagination run and put together a wild romance between him and Mother.

Who did I look like? In the past, I had always hoped that, like a genuine princess, I resembled the king. Now I was no longer convinced of that. My thin brownish hair could well be from him, and my slightly sticking-out ears too, but my melancholy features I had from Mother. I had no desire either to be or to look like her; most of all, I'd have liked to be a cuckoo's egg.

When I came back from shopping one afternoon – Mother often left me a list of errands on the table – Carlo was standing at the kitchen sink, quite uninhibitedly shaving his legs. 'Have you gone off your trolley? D'you want to turn into a transvestite?' I asked.

'All the pros do it. You don't think I train every day just for the hell of it, do you? I'm taking part in a cycle race tomorrow.'

'And I suppose you reckon you'll go faster if you're hairless?'

'A bit, maybe, but they do it because of injuries. It's bad if you get hairs in the wound; and in any case it makes things easier for the masseur.'

I was amazed. Had I underestimated Carlo? 'Since when have you had a masseur?'

'That'll come, when I turn pro. Now get your arse in gear, Elephant Woman. Either you bring me the big mirror from the hall, or you get the job of shaving the backs of my legs.' I hurried off to get the mirror, although I wouldn't have minded the chance to cut Carlo while shaving him.

'Just as well for you. By the way, I've been wanting to ask you for a while now, who painted the picture in Cora's room?'

'What were you doing in Cora's bedroom?'

'If you'd care to cast your mind back, not a bloody soul gave a toss about me during your kiddies' party. So I went off under my own steam and had a look round. So, who painted the two of you?'

I wasn't usually as slick at lying as Cora. 'It doesn't matter,' I said awkwardly. But it mattered to him, and he twisted my arm.

'An uncle of Cora's,' I said.

'Don't give me any of your lies. It was only later I twigged, myself, that it must have been painted by Father. His identification mark is at the bottom; it struck me as familiar right away, but it took a while before it dawned on me.' With his legs still wet, he trotted over to his desk, which he always kept locked, and dug out a small, scuffed landscape sketch. The symbol, an intertwined R. W., stood for Roland Westermann. I hung my head.

'Right, spit it out. The two of you must have been to see him. If you don't come out with the truth, and right now, I'll tell Mother.'

Why was it that I couldn't bear the thought of that? Because I had the feeling that, with revelations like that, I would break Mother's heart. The very topic of Father was strictly taboo, and to so much as touch upon it was enough to provoke a catastrophe. Carlo and I were still small when Father left us, and at first we would ask about his whereabouts. But the look of almost mortal dismay on our mother's pale, tearless face, and the trembling of her hands betrayed more than her tightly pressed lips and her helpless shake of the head.

'We were in Lübeck,' I admitted. Naturally, Carlo was bursting with curiosity, and I told him, bit by bit, about Father's job as a blood-courier, how terribly poor he was and how his surroundings were unfit for human habitation. About my own shock at his drink-sodden behaviour, his unkempt appearance and his self-centred attitude, I never let on, nor did I say a word about the money we had got together for him.

Carlo got so agitated, he forgot about scraping the black fuzz off his legs. His hatred for Father was fanned into flames by my report. He simply couldn't bring himself to understand how we could have gone there several times to sit for the portrait.

'And what does Cornelia think of this creature?' he asked, for her opinion meant a lot to him.

'She got on pretty well with Father,' I said.

Cora was the one and only person who had immediately recognized my disappointment, or to whom I could pour out my heart in complete confidence. With Carlo, who had never liked me, I just couldn't be sure that, despite his promise, he wouldn't tell Mother to hurt her, to make himself important, or to show her that I was a daughter who had gone to the bad and who had defied a taboo.

CHAPTER 5

Black Friday

Now and again, when I have an interested audience, I offer them the chance of a shopping tour. There are always some people who appreciate it if you can take them to the right shops. Naturally, I get commission whenever I bring well-off tourists into shoe shops, fashion designers' stores or antique dealers'. In the case of these last ones, I negotiate a favourable price for my own clientele, and the dealer puts on a show to make it seem we're doing some fierce haggling, a game that he enjoys just as much as I do. Altogether, I frequent three different antique shops in the narrow little streets around the Piazza Pitti, always giving each its fair turn. In each of them, I've stolen something just once, but I make sure I never do it a second time. I have among my possessions a Marie Antoinette fan in carved and painted ivory, a gold snuffbox in the shape of a seashell, with inlaid enamelwork, and a travelling sewing box in ebony and tortoiseshell, complete with not only dainty little scissors and needles, flacons and a drinking cup, but also a miniature weapon for the lady in distress, a tiny, but razor-sharp, stiletto. I had admired this sewing box on many occasions, but it just couldn't be squeezed into my handbag; so I asked a tourist from Zurich to tuck it into her very chic leather rucksack. I had previously slipped a plastic bag over it, and she presumably took my 'purchase' for a plain wooden box.

Cora, by the way, takes no great interest in my little treasures; she has bigger fish in mind, huge paintings from museums – a Tintoretto would be just up her street. But neither of us has the know-how for a job like that.

To my secret collector's gallery belong not only *objets d'art*, but also mementos with some personal or aesthetic interest, like, for example, a dented Italian signboard. I acquired it at the end of those holidays when we had visited my father and got the better of Detlef.

Cora came back from Italy with a blue picture-hat. She brought me presents, too. A purloined metal plate with the words ATTENTI AL CANE, which I was supposed to hang on my bedroom door. For herself, she had pinched DIVIETO DI CACCIA, a sign from the Tuscan forests prohibiting hunting. In addition, I got a diary in handmade paper and the skeleton of a bat, which she had discovered on the dried-up lawn. Cora's artist's eye saw this morbid object in a different light from my own one; the sight of these filigree ribs made me feel slightly nauseous.

We embarked on our final year at school without enthusiasm. Not that we had any problems with studying, but there were many things in life which we considered more vital than Macbeth and probability calculus. Herr Becker, whom I now regarded merely as an ordinary human being and no longer as an inspiring pedagogue, didn't teach our class any more. While I was still stuck with the name 'Elephant Girl', it was now used simply as a matter of course and no longer depressed me. I was considered to be arrogant, and there was some truth in that. Despite my pachyderm skin, I felt myself to be a princess among plebs.

'The honest man thinks lastly of himself,' our German teacher quoted from Schiller's *William Tell*. 'The honest woman thinks only of herself,' was the leitmotif I wrote in my new diary. Unfortunately, I have not always acted according to that principle.

Cora had a steady succession of different boyfriends, and even Carlo continued to court her favour. At times, she would behave charmingly towards him, and he would fancy his chances, and then she would swagger past him holding hands with somebody else. Where men were concerned, Cora didn't know the meaning of faithfulness, but towards me she was constantly dependable and caring, loving and sincere, but above all, honest.

She grew prettier and prettier. She wore her red hair shoulder length and tousled. Her figure had become more slender, and her dainty ankles were reminiscent of the bones in my bat. To some extent, Cora resembled the ladies in paintings of the Italian Renaissance, with her high forehead and plucked eyebrows and her determined profile. It was no wonder that she was such an object of desire.

And what about me? At seventeen, I didn't consider myself beautiful, although, with hindsight, I must say there was no real reason for that view. But sparkle and charm were what I lacked, and that's the way it has stayed to this day.

The day the disaster occurred, that black Friday in September, began like all the others. For all that, there was still a warm sunshine, and the day seemed golden to us; the prospect of a weekend at the swimming pool saw us coming out of school in high spirits. Cora's mother was, as so often, away on her travels. Her father had some organizational problems to sort out before the semester began at the university. I had already said to my mother the day before that I'd be going to Cora's after school and wouldn't be back till evening. We made ourselves a quick snack of cornflakes, milk and bananas, Cora lent me a bikini, and we took the bus out to the thronged outdoor pool on the edge of the woods. Cora had come out in so many freckles in Italy that, from a distance, she looked dark brown, while I, who actually took on a tan much better, seemed wishy-washy beside her.

Naturally, we were never alone, lying there on our towels; Cora was like a decoy who attracted drakes, peacocks and roosters in flocks.

At five, Carlo showed up. The hairs on his shaven legs had grown back again in a stubble. He put on an act on the diving board a number of times, and was no doubt thoroughly put out because Cora didn't even look his way. However, when he just happened by where we were camped, and with three ice-creams, she was suddenly as if transformed and laughed and chatted exclusively with him, so that two other contenders, who had been devotedly rubbing her back with sun-tan oil, immediately took off. I ate my ice and went off for a swim, although I took my time about it. After that, I chatted for quite a while with Greta, who was sitting reading at the far corner of the grassy area. Whenever Cora was putting on her big show, I never felt particularly comfortable in my role as an extra, least of all when the flirting was aimed at my brother.

When it was time for us to go, Cora and I packed our things together and took our rubbish to the wastepaper basket. Carlo was laying on some heavy hints about a surprise in the car park. I suspected at once that he had borrowed a car.

Cora pretended to be curious. And there, indeed, stood a not exactly brand-new sporty little job that belonged to the somewhat dodgy brother of a former schoolmate. Carlo opened the door for us. I knew very well that, if I had been there on my own, he would have slammed it in my face and left me to walk home. Well, at least this way we got home much faster than in the stuffy bus.

It goes without saying that Cora sat up front. Carlo's driving was awful. His experience with cars was limited to nothing more than the driving lessons he had taken when he was eighteen. But he swanked about, wearing an open red silk shirt and reflecting sunglasses, with a cigarette hanging casually from the corner of his mouth and his seat set far back. I would dearly have loved to give him a thump around the ear as he sat, like some playboy, next to Cora and gave her his inane spiel about how you could push this little bus to the limit. Without so much as an invitation, he came with us to Cora's and then insisted on having another look at our double portrait.

'O loveliness beyond compare! Were ever maidens half so fair?' he sang in a falsetto.

I found it hard to bear, standing together with him and Cora and surveying my father's picture, and so I went into the kitchen for a drink of mineral water. When I returned, ten minutes later, the two of them, sitting close together on

Cora's bed, fell silent; this was a reaction I had frequently experienced at home, whenever Mother and Carlo were together.

'I've got to get home,' I said frostily. 'You coming, Carlo?'

'Off you stomp on foot; there's a good grey giant of the jungle,' he said. 'I'm staying.'

Cora said nothing, didn't even look at me, and helped herself to one of Carlo's cigarettes.

I slammed the front door behind me and cleared off. I had almost reached our house, and my rage had still not subsided, but if anything, it really blazed up when I realized I had left my school things at Cora's and I urgently needed a biography of Goethe for a project.

Since that day, I have often asked myself whether it really was so urgent, since my assignment was practically finished anyway. Why hadn't I phoned and asked Carlo to bring my briefcase with him? Some intuition or other made me look for a reason to go back. I didn't want my brother and my best friend to be sitting on a bed under my father's painting, and the thought of such intimacy hurt.

Once I was standing outside the Schwabs' house again, I really did feel out of place. Cora would think I was jealous and was trying to spy on her. As for what my brother thought, I didn't give a hoot. The borrowed car was still parked in front of the neighbours' driveway.

Should I ring the bell? In two minds, I hung about at the door for a while. Then I slipped in by the garden gate, because I knew that the verandah door at the back was usually left open for the dog; if that were so, I could sneak through the conservatory into the hallway, where my briefcase lay. Did I really only want the bag? Or did I want to eavesdrop, to intrude, to annoy Carlo? Maybe it was a nasty sense of foreboding that drove me back there.

As I reached the verandah door, I heard alarming noises coming from the first floor. A stifled or strangulated cry, furniture scraping on the floor, and crashing sounds. I was wearing trainers, and reached the first floor in a few strides. Cora's bedroom door with the sign prohibiting hunting stood open. Carlo was crouching, snorting, on her stomach, holding one hand over her mouth and pinning her arms down with the other. For a second, he let go, trying to tear open her blouse, and Cora let out a piercing shriek. Why didn't I just grab him by the hair and come to the aid of my friend in this hand-to-hand struggle? My very appearance on the scene would probably have been enough to make Carlo let her go.

Instead, without stopping to think, I had rushed into the Persian-pink bedroom and seized the gas pistol from the drawer in the bedside table. Now, seconds later, I was standing by Cora's bed, pointing the gun and shouting, 'Hands up!'

My brother half turned his head towards me but made no move to obey. Instead, he yelled, 'Sod off!'

'Let him have it, Maya!' ordered Cora through Carlo's fingers, her voice breaking with terror.

I put the gas pistol to Carlo's temple and uttered the magic formula: 'I'm going to count to three!'

'Put that toy away,' hissed Carlo and, in a blind fury, let go of Cora's hands and tried to snatch the gun away from me. But because he turned so violently, it slipped from his head down to chest level and went off.

Did I pull the trigger? I suppose I must have, and yet I can't recall doing it. As we found out later, his cardiac muscles were torn by the force of the shock wave. On top of Cora lay a lifeless bundle, but we didn't notice that right away. Together, we pushed him off and stared at each other, quaking. We could neither cry nor talk. It was a few minutes before we heaved Carlo on to his back and realized, to our horror, that we were looking at a dead man.

Cora tried to feel his pulse. 'I think we're going to have to call an ambulance,' she said, unable to put the full reality of it into words.

'The picture in Lübeck!' That was exactly the way the black, white and red painting had looked. All right, my brother didn't have a bleeding wound, but the colours of the red silk shirt, the white bedsheet and the black hair were identical with those in that visionary picture of my father's. No other colour came into it.

In those gruesome minutes, Cora did precisely the right thing, she phoned her father. Fortunately, he could be reached at once, and I shall never forget all that he did for me in the time that followed.

While Cora's garbled message must surely have confused and shocked him terribly, he kept his head, telling us to wait for him in the living-room and he would be there right away. Simultaneously with the professor, a doctor friend and an ambulance with its siren howling arrived. Cora's father had, in addition, instructed his secretary to notify the family lawyer.

After the professor had promised the ambulance-men that he would inform the police, they left empty-handed. The lawyer was given a full description of the situation, and he was present at the subsequent discussion with the police, a psychologist and a plain-clothes policewoman.

To cut a long story short, the following weeks were sheer torture, but I wasn't committed to a young offenders' institution. The whole thing ended up being treated as an accident in self-defence, and the case was closed, although I alone knew that it could just as easily have been classed as premeditated manslaughter. I had been wanting to do away with my brother for many a long year.

Much worse for me than all the police investigations was having to face my mother. Here, too, Herr Schwab stood by me, the way, as it turned out, he took care of everything from then on. He got the police to drive the borrowed car back to its owner, he sent a telegram to his wife, and he dropped Cora off with his secretary before coming along with me to my mother. He had forbidden the detectives to break the news to her. My mother took one look at me and went white as a sheet. The mark of Cain was branded clearly on my forehead.

I was unable to speak. The professor, who did not even know my mother and was actually a man who did his best to avoid personal conflicts, handled things admirably. He drew her to the sofa, held her bony hand and broke the truth gently to her, at least in part. She never found out that her son had tried to rape my friend, and the professor avoided saying in as many words that I had used the gun.

But my mother, as she looked at him wide-eyed, suddenly pointed a finger at me. 'She did it!'

'No, Frau Westermann,' said the professor, 'a dreadful accident, h'm, yes, as in Greek tragedy. Three innocent young people, indulging in some horseplay, who couldn't have known that a gas pistol, fired from close range, can be dangerous. Even in the hands of experts, a case like this, with fatal results, is very much an exception. Frau Westermann, it is a misfortune for all of us, but most of all for you, inconceivable and tragic, but please, you mustn't put the blame on Maya.'

My mother just kept on staring at me. 'An accident,' she said, very slowly, 'that's what Roland claimed too. Maya's going to end up in jail, just like her father.'

It was some considerable time before the professor left us together; obviously he felt it was high time he concerned himself with his nearly raped daughter. I saw him to the door, where he got me to write down the telephone number of my uncle in Bonn, no doubt intending to pass any further responsibility on to him. My father wasn't on the phone.

Now I was alone with Mother, and I began to feel afraid. She still did not say a word to me, didn't cry, but just sat staring into space, a crazed expression on her face, which drained me of any courage to try and comfort her, with either words or physical contact. For that matter, I could very much have done with some consoling myself, more than at any other time in my life. All of a sudden, I had the urge to throw myself out of the window and put an end to my utter misery. Imagining a double funeral actually ended up offering me something bordering on consolation, because the mental picture of Father and Mother, united in sorrow, weeping at our graves, enabled me to shed tears of my own at last.

'Leave me alone,' murmured my mother at some point during the evening. I was relieved that she actually spoke to me at all, and went off to my room to have another good cry.

When the phone rang, Mother didn't pick it up. She was still sitting there exactly as before, quite motionless. It was her brother in Bonn, whom the professor had called and who now wanted to talk to Mother. 'Uncle Paul,' I said, holding out the phone to her. She wouldn't take it, so my uncle promised to come the next day.

There was another call – Cora. She sounded composed, but with my rigid, glassy-eyed mother there in the room, I didn't dare talk to her at any length. Normally, I always used to take the phone into my room, but on this occasion it wasn't a matter of schoolgirl secrets, but fratricide. Cora seemed to have understood what the situation was. 'I'll be over tomorrow morning,' she promised.

During that sleepless night, I must in fact have dropped off at some time, because when I woke with a start, somewhere around three, I noticed that the light in the living-room was out and Mother had gone to bed. Tearfully, I fell asleep again.

When Cora appeared the next morning, Mother was still asleep, and I didn't have the nerve to open the door to Carlo's room, for it seemed she had gone in there to lie down. It was Saturday, she had the day off and we didn't have school.

Towards noon, Uncle Paul arrived from Bonn. We went into Carlo's room together. She had obviously taken an overdose of sleeping pills. Now I almost felt I had committed matricide as well, because I hadn't been able to pluck up the courage to go to her bedside sooner. But it wasn't too late. Mother was still alive, but had to have her stomach pumped out. All the same, when she was discharged from hospital a few days later, she was not allowed home, but was transferred to a psychiatric clinic. She steadfastly refused any visits from me.

My uncle stayed for a few days and wanted to take me with him to Bonn. I turned that idea down flat. While he did get in to see Mother every second day, neither of them seemed to have any idea as to how things were to go on from there. Mother had lapsed into a severe depression, and the doctors had made it clear we had to be prepared for an extensive period of hospital treatment.

In the end, Uncle Paul agreed that I should stay at the professor's for the time being and work on towards my final school exams. Cora's mother had flown straight back from the States and suggested I stay 'until further notice'. Apparently this lady, who was always gallivanting in foreign parts, was now suffering pangs of conscience over not having spent enough time at home and having neglected her parental duties.

Once the first few terrible weeks had passed, Cora and I were obliged, on the professor's orders, to undergo psychotherapy; for his daughter, he had arranged for communication therapy, and for me, psychoanalysis. Cora's mother went to exhibitions with us and took us to concerts and plays and did her best to welcome us home every lunch time with an Italian meal.

It was some weeks after Carlo's death before the funeral could take place. For one thing, the pathologists apparently had not had the time to deal with the case at once, and for another, they had hoped that my mother's condition would have stabilized sufficiently for her to be able to attend. But that was not to be, for the doctors treating her considered it to be too risky, while she herself expressed no wish to be present at the burial of the urn with his ashes.

But my father came. I was ashamed to admit to the professor that the dilapidated figure in the borrowed dark suit was my father. However, he didn't disgrace me, because he didn't utter a word to anyone, but merely shook hands all round, with a vacant expression on his face. Uncle Paul and he ignored each other, although they must have been in touch by phone. That evening, I was alone with Father in our flat, from which I had in the meantime removed all my things to Cora's. Only the celadon-green plate couldn't possibly have a place in the Sinologist's house; by a stroke of good fortune, he hadn't gone into my room during his visit to our house.

Father was to sleep in Carlo's bed, and I, for the last time, in my own. We sat in the kitchen over scrambled eggs and bread; my father had got in beer and schnapps. I drank tea. Cora had left me after the funeral and had got into her parents' car in a flood of tears. Since I had already started my course of therapy, I knew that there were a number of points that had to be cleared up, so I took my courage in both hands.

'Why were you in jail, and how were you able to foresee Carlo's death?'

Father drew out a filthy handkerchief – he actually was crying. I would have loved to see those tears on my mother, who seemed to have turned to stone.

'You've a right to know the truth,' he began, like some third-rate actor, and then fell silent again.

I topped up his schnapps glass. 'I'm listening.'

Blowing his nose, he started again. 'Your mother had two brothers, Paul and Karl. You probably won't remember Karl.'

The photo! I thought. So Mother hadn't had a lover after all, sadly it was only her brother.

My blubbering father went on: 'Elsbeth loved Karl more than Paul, and more than me. Carlo was named after him, and I had a hard job getting her to accept the C and the O. Karl and I hated each other from the very start. He was studying chemistry and was regarded as the one in the family who would make something of himself. At that time, I had already given up my studies and was working as a postman and doing some painting. Elsbeth had faith in my art and gave me some encouragement. Karl considered my pictures feeble.'

'So is the dead man in the black, white and red picture not supposed to be Carlo at all, but Karl?'

'That's right. I killed Karl when I was drunk and I landed in prison. I must have painted that picture years later.'

'Why did you do it?'

'In the heat of the moment, out of jealousy and rage. I belted him over the head with a beer bottle and he died instantly.'

'Had he attacked you first?'

'Only verbally, but that can be awful, too. He wanted me

64

to give your mother a divorce. He reckoned she was wasted on a failure.'

I stirred my tea long and slowly, while Father used a fork to scrape the dirt out from under his fingernails.

'Your mother was never able to forgive me.'

'Nor me, either,' I said, bitterly. I looked at him and thought, My father is a murderer, I'm a murderess. A fine king, a fine princess. The real victim is my mother, for the people dearest to her have been killed by us. Beside our family drama, Greek tragedies were children's fairy tales.

Once Father had got pretty drunk, he admitted he had never loved his son, because he resembled Mother's brother so damned closely. At the same time, he was well aware of how wrong that was and had, perhaps for that reason, thought of Carlo more often than of me. He pleaded for me to tell him about my brother, and at that, I lost the self-control that I had maintained only with great effort. I cried, he cried, and we could neither comfort each other nor fall into each other's arms.

After an extended belch, Father fell asleep at the kitchen table, and I went to lie down in my cell, for my room seemed to me like a prison in which I had lived for years.

Father made no effort to assume responsibility for my life or to involve himself in future plans for me. I told him I wanted to live at my friend's and that Uncle Paul would take care of my upkeep. He just nodded; perhaps he was ashamed. He said he had had a hard job getting his train fare together. The purchase of two bottles of schnapps didn't seem to have caused him any problems.

'Well, cheerio then.' Once again, that was all my father could come up with as we parted. But I couldn't forget his sad eyes and, in the time that followed, I thought of him not only with contempt, but also with some sympathy.

Cora and I had sworn never to tell a soul about that newspaper article we had read in the train. Not even to our psychotherapists, who were professionally sworn to secrecy, did we come clean, least of all on this point. Everyone, from the police to our parents, from our teachers to our schoolmates, believed that I had used the weapon only as a threat and that I had been convinced it was harmless. Similarly, Carlo's ugly part in the affair was withheld from public knowledge, although in this respect the detectives, Cora's parents, the lawyer and the psychologists knew that an attempted rape had taken place. The version given out to the press, the school and my mother had it that, in the course of an innocuous tussle and some play-acting, I had inadvertently pulled the trigger of the gas pistol. Everybody, apart from my mother, was able to summon up some understanding and sympathy, no doubt every individual endowed with a spark of consideration sensed how gruesome it must be to have the death of your own brother on your conscience. Only with Cora could I talk about how I saw myself as a murderess, and she alone was capable of talking me out of my feelings of guilt.

'For it to be murder, there has to be evil intent, and you were trying to help me! Murder must be committed out of malice and viciousness – neither of these applies here! Then there's also the motive of "in the furtherance or the concealment of another criminal act" – that certainly wasn't the case either.'

I could see all that, and yet I knew that, in the remotest corner of my brain, a desire to kill had existed, the kind of thing probably many people drag through life with them, without it all ending in disaster.

But, in my case, there was one additional morally incriminating factor: I was happy to be able to live at Cora's, freed from my mother and brother. I had never in my life had it so good.

CHAPTER 6

Sienna

There are few people who travel abroad on their own. That in itself makes them more interesting than the herd. There is, for instance, the lone-wolf type, mostly male and a bit of an esoteric. He seldom goes around in the tourist coach, but rather is a loner with a thing about art, who collects a special kind of bell-tower or some other out-of-the-way trophies. Women who travel alone are usually not so head-in-the-clouds, but are making the best of their situation. Still, all of them, male or female, have something sad about them, as they spend their holiday in solitude and sit down to eat without friends or family around them. Then, Schubert's 'Winter Journey' comes unbidden to my mind.

Among all the various sorts of couples, there are also occasionally pairs of siblings. When I see brother and sister sitting together in obvious harmony, it gives me an uneasy feeling. Because of me, my brother Carlo will never again be able to travel abroad, go on cycle trips, sleep with girl-friends or own a car. And thanks to that fact, I have a new family.

After Carlo's death, I would have been overjoyed if Cora's parents had suggested we should be on first-name terms, that I could address them as 'Ulrich' and 'Evelyn'. But this thought never entered their heads, and 'Herr and Frau Schwab' remained the order of the day. It could have been worse, I might have had to say 'Professor' and 'Doctor', but Cora's father didn't allow even his students to use that form of address.

With no great enthusiasm, but out of a sense of duty, Uncle Paul paid for my keep. While I was well aware that this allowance would have been enough to cover my previous needs, it was quite inadequate for the lavish lifestyle in this household. The food was of better quality, the linen was changed more often, a domestic help kept the house clean; tickets for me to go to cultural events were paid for, I was bought clothes and underwear, books and cosmetics. I quickly grew accustomed to a higher standard of living, yet, at the same time, I couldn't shake off a feeling of uneasiness, because I had no real right to these privileges. Admittedly, everything was given in that spirit of kindness and natural-ness that was so characteristic of my new family, but still, what Cora, as their daughter, was entitled to, was by no means mine by right. Sometimes I dreamt that I had been thrown out, or that Cora had got fed up with me and had persuaded her parents that I was no fit company for her. These fears had no foundation in fact. Cora's parents treated me almost like a daughter and, as far as material things were concerned, made no difference whatsoever between us. But because of my subconscious insecurity, my fear of making myself conspicuous through some piece of inappropriate behaviour, I stopped stealing, was attentive in school and scored top marks all the time; maybe I did become rather boring for Cora, and she didn't find me as much fun as before. On the other hand, she did understand that my high spirits should have deserted me as a result of that Black Friday. She, too, had to work hard at getting that trauma out of her system.

At least once a month, the professor's family went out to a Cantonese restaurant. I always enjoyed it when Cora's father chatted away in Chinese with the waiters and the diners at neighbouring tables turned to look at us out of curiosity and in total admiration. Even Cora and I would say 'Ni hao!' to the lady receptionist in the silk dress with the slit up the side.

Frau Schwab had red hair, just like her daughter, but she looked very different. She favoured delicate, subdued colours, long strings of pearls and elegant Italian shoes. How I would have loved to be the daughter of such parents! Whenever strangers took me as such, then that in itself gave me a lift.

Cora's mother, who now did everything she possibly could to look after us, enjoyed advising us in questions of fashion, but, for all that, her ideas were by no means restricted to her own very ladylike style. Cora rejected everything that was to her mother's taste, so that the frustrated adviser took increasing pleasure in fitting out my wardrobe. Whenever the three of us went shopping together, Cora would come home with a pile of extravagant gear, cheap stuff that had soon had its day. I, on the other hand, would be togged out very tastefully and much more expensively, because I knew how to appreciate quality. Unfortunately, though, it often happened that Cora neglected to hang up her clothes and, as we were rushing off to school, she would grab something of mine, as if it stood to reason that what was mine was also hers. Her mother would give a satisfied smile whenever she saw Cora in my cream linen jacket, and sometimes the nasty thought crossed my mind that, ultimately, she was in fact merely kitting out her own daughter by a roundabout way, through myself.

How long would I be able to stay in this family?

I pictured my mother coming back again, stony-faced and empty-eyed, and the two of us having to live together once more in our miserable flat. Now and again, I went back there for a few hours, running the vacuum cleaner over the place, airing it and trying to crack open Carlo's locked desk. My therapist had advised me that, if I ever felt the urge to write to Mother, I should do just that. Three times, I did in fact have the inclination, but this soon gave way to a sense of bitterness, for she did not once react. From Uncle Paul I heard only sporadically that she was still in a bad way and that no one was willing to speculate about a date for her discharge. Naturally, I hoped that Mother would, at some time or another, become a normal person again (it was doubtful whether she had ever been happy), but as far as I was concerned, her depression could last until after I had taken my final *Abitur* exams.

Cora started putting her therapist to the test. 'How am I supposed to know whether the guy is any good?' she asked me, and told him about an imaginary dream. Afterwards, she told me that was the first amusing therapy session she had had.

The 'guy', who had his work cut out with her, was a gentle, tubby man, who would look searchingly into Cora's green eyes without ever noticing that she was lying. My therapist was much stricter; I was not allowed to wander from the subject in hand and, at first, I wouldn't have dared pull a fast one on him.

Cora said, 'I never knew you were such a coward.'

To please her, I made up my dream of the little bird of the forest. In it, I was a little bird which, like an owl, would fly at night towards brightly lit windows and watch the people inside. It was obvious to my therapist that what we had here was the Freudian childhood scenario and I had, in my early childhood, caught my parents at it in bed. Again and again, I had to relax and make free associations with suggestive ink-blots. Because it worked a treat, I finished up thoroughly enjoying this game. But I kept quiet about my real day-dreams, in which I worked out how I would marry Cora's brother and thus secure my surrogate parents for myself, legally.

For precisely this reason, I was in love with her brother long before I met him. He went by the rather old-fashioned name of Friedrich and was studying physics. Cora sometimes bragged about him, going on about how fantastically intelligent he was, a second Einstein.

One week before Christmas Eve, the whole Schwab family went to fetch the prodigal son from Frankfurt Airport, without me of course, because there wouldn't be enough room in the car with all the luggage he was expected to bring. (As it happened, Friedrich had one solitary holdall with him.) He wanted to be addressed as 'Fred' and, as we sat down to the very first meal together, he informed us that he was as good as engaged. His American fiancée was called Annie; in the photo he showed us, she was wearing a silver brace on her teeth and looked podgy. I found myself developing something of an ambition to make Fred forget all about his American dream. But he hardly seemed to notice I was there; in any case, he liked sitting together with Cora, swopping childhood memories. I felt distinctly *de trop*. Friedrich was a few years older than Cora, but not much more serious; as a lover, it seemed to me, this Einstein was by no means the answer to a maiden's prayer. Otherwise he would have twigged that it was not by chance that I regularly bumped into him in my underwear. When, three weeks later, Friedrich flew off again, all I had achieved was that he had managed to remember my name. He had arranged with his parents that he would come to Tuscany in the summer with Annie, so that we could all get to know his future wife. I began to fear for my holiday billet. It was a fact that there were four beds there, and, with Miss Tin-Teeth, that already made five people, not counting me.

Apart from that, my first Christmas without Mother and Carlo went off relatively carefree. There were only a few presents and the festival was celebrated in an unsentimental and not particularly Christian way. Now and again I would play cards with Cora and Friedrich until daybreak and we had lots of laughs. I considered cheating to be part and parcel of playing cards, and Cora was of the same mind. Friedrich couldn't figure out why he never won. Sometimes he would give us lectures on physics that were monumental in their tedium. If he had been my brother, I would have emptied the professor's sherry decanter over his scholarly skull.

With the gradual approach of summer, Cora's mother took her two 'daughters' on a shopping expedition. By this time I had found out that, while the professor was pulling down a good salary, his wife was by no means impoverished herself. She could look forward to an inheritance and, since her marriage, received a sort of dowry from her father, her 'shoe and stocking allowance'. Out of this money, she paid for all our clothes.

'We have to think of Italy,' she said, and from that I drew renewed hope of being invited along. Cora put together a pink, purple and orange ensemble that was bound to clash horribly with her red hair and the inevitable freckles. Her mother decided on a stylish mixture of cool sea-green and lavender.

'Maya, you ought to wear natural colours,' she advised me. So I got a sand-coloured cotton sweater, a short, off-white linen dress and shorts in umber. 'All you need now is something in terracotta or sienna,' she reckoned.

'What kind of colour's that?' I asked.

'Just wait,' said Cora, 'till we're sitting eating ice-cream on the Campo in Sienna in the summer, then you'll never be able to forget this colour. It's a warm, reddish-yellowish brown. The houses all round the Campo just radiate these shades so intensely in the evening sunlight that you'll want to sit there forever . . .'

I acquired three-quarter-length slacks in sienna, along with the certain prospect of being able to wear them in Tuscany in the summer.

Shortly before the long vacation, I received, for the very first time, a letter from my mother (there had never been a word from my father). In it, she wrote, in very matter-of-fact terms, that she was getting better, but she would never be coming back home again, since our flat was steeped in too many memories. It wasn't reasonable to expect Uncle Paul to go on paying the rent for it if there was no one living there. They had offered her a job in the convalescent home at the spa as a nursing auxiliary while she continued her psychotherapy treatment, and she had been doing that for six weeks now, on a trial basis. A one-room flat with kitchen attached was available for her. Uncle Paul would be coming over in the near future to take care of clearing out the old flat. Any furniture she could use would be sent on to her, while Uncle Paul was going to put the rest in store. I was to collect my own things. (All that amounted to was the celadon-green plate.) She closed with the words, *Your mother, on whom you have brought unhappiness.*

There was not a word in this whole letter about my future. Of course, the professor had accepted me into his family, but on the firm assumption that my mother would be fit and active again within three months. I was mortified.

When I stood at Herr Schwab's desk with this letter in my hand (I had decided he would be the first to hear about it), he looked up from his translation with a friendly smile.

'Soon be off on the summer holidays, h'm, yes,' he said. 'And then life looks rosy again for you and your confidante, chasing the boys and eating ice-creams, h'm, yes.'

I laid Mother's letter on his leather-covered desk-top. He had to admit he hadn't reckoned with putting me up as a permanent guest. 'But that will make it all the more of a pleasure for us all when we celebrate a double success in the *Abitur*,' he concluded with charming kindness, and reached for a bulky dictionary. With that, the matter was closed.

Cora hugged me. 'Without you, I'd just waste away. It was awful, vegetating almost like an only child, when Friedrich first went off to the USA.'

Cora's mother, too, welcomed the fact that I'd be staying in the house for another year. 'If you were to go to your uncle in Bonn, you'd have to break off your therapy, and that would be too bad.'

It would have been very good if I had kept on with my therapy for much longer, but unfortunately things turned out differently.

One evening, as Cora and I were sitting in our nightdresses looking at photos from earlier holidays in Tuscany, I asked tentatively, 'There are four beds, but, with your brother and Annie, there'll be six of us – will we have to sleep in the tent?'

'Nonsense,' said Cora, 'we don't have a tent. There are three holiday flats in the house. At Christmas, my mother wrote and rented the smaller flat for Fred and Annie. All taken care of.'

'And to think I was afraid you'd go without me!'

'Are you serious?' Cora asked in amazement. 'Why didn't you simply ask?'

That was exactly what I found so hard to do. I'd be looked after for another year yet; I didn't dare ask even Cora what would happen after that.

But she herself started talking about the future. 'Maybe I'll study in Florence, painting or architecture. Although I'd have to take the language examination first; I can speak a bit of Italian all right, but that's not enough. The best thing would be if I went to Italy straight after the exams and made a serious start on preparing for the language test. And what are you aiming to do? Are you coming with me to "the land where the lemon trees bloom"?'

Although I could expect to get a grant, I'd never have the means to move to Florence. 'I'm going to study, too,' I said. 'German language and literature, and drama, and then I'll go in for theatre management.'

'Well, in that case, I'll give architecture a miss and become a stage designer instead, and later on we'll join the State Theatre together. Is that a deal?'

I nodded, although I knew exactly how unrealistic these dreams were.

At the beginning of June, I really was in Italy. Colle di Val d'Elsa was a small town, and from there, the road went on to the village of Gracciano. A gravel track led up to the holiday villa.

The house itself stood on a hill, with five tall oak trees on either side. The plot where Cora had found the bat's skeleton was surrounded by golden cornfields. In the early mornings and in the evenings, pheasants could be heard, cackling almost like hens. To the west lay a gently sloping field of corn, its edge marked off on the horizon by a single line of well-spaced trees. The professor found that, in the light of the setting sun, this field looked just like the evening field in Gottfried Keller's story of the village Romeo and Juliet.

I adored that landscape and its houses from the first moment I saw it. Our old house had been built, in the traditional Tuscan style, out of different-sized blocks of natural stone, bound together with mortar to form a lovely jigsaw pattern. Cora and I spent most of the time in the pool. Three swallows played above the water, nose-diving steeply to its surface and snatching up a little beakful of the chlorinated

74

water. As soon as darkness fell, they metamorphosed into bats.

The room I shared with Cora was darkened during the day, to keep it cool. The ceilings were high, with oak beams forming a load-bearing network, on which heavy reddish bricks had been packed in. When we lay side by side in bed, we could spend ages looking at the mosaic of these stones till our eyes became heavy with sleep.

After three days there, my skin had taken on that golden bronzed shade that was the envy of everyone, while Cora and her mother had to make do with a sprinkling of freckles. The professor always sat in the shade, reading. The American soon-to-weds hadn't arrived yet.

Cora's mother had the regular job of driving us to the bus stop, and she yearned for the day when we'd have our own driving licences. In Sienna, Cora showed me some of the intriguing sights, like the head of St Catherine in San Domenico, but most of the time we would sit around on the Piazza del Campo, getting chatted up.

Our pocket-money didn't go so far as to allow us to indulge in one ice-cream after another, since here they cost three times as much as anywhere else. But we were quite happy to lounge about on some set of steps or another, stretching out our tanned legs in front of us, and munching rolls filled with Tuscan ham. We fed the pigeons, and that brought us into conversation with young men next to us, managing to get through in a mixture of three broken languages, and in no time at all we would be treated to more expensive ices. The men were either fashionable young Italians or tourists with bulky rucksacks, trainers, sweat-stained T-shirts and cut-off jeans.

That was the course Cora's holidays had always followed, ever since she had been allowed to go into Sienna on the bus by herself. All the same, we had to be back in Colle di Val d'Elsa at a set time, for Cora's parents would be waiting for us to go out with them for a meal.

It was right at the start of the holiday, even before Fred and Annie arrived, that we got to know two German medical students who were heading for Sicily in a clapped-out old Volkswagen bus. I fell for Jonas on the spot. Cora, for once, didn't fancy either of them. My plans for getting my hooks into her brother over the summer were forgotten in a flash.

Jonas had eyes that were almost black, and I found him handsome and manly. He just kept looking at me all the time; he was the first man who didn't go after Cora first off.

In my lucky, sienna-coloured corsair trousers and a skimpy top in yellow-ochre, and with my brown skin and gold-and-brown flecked hair, I felt excitingly attractive; and here was a young man gazing into my eyes, only mine – could there be any greater happiness? We hardly noticed Cora ambling off with the other student – he was called Karsten – and into the zebra-striped cathedral to do her tourist-guide thing.

Only two days later, I slept with Jonas in the VW bus. He had turned up at our holiday villa, without his companion, but with a bunch of flowers he had picked himself, and took me off for a drive. From then on, I had nothing else on my mind. Cora observed, 'You've got it bad, all right!'

Poor, disappointed Karsten hitchhiked his way to Sicily, while I was able, day in, day out, to enjoy an all-consuming love life in the camper. Cora's parents made no move to interfere.

When at last Fred and Annie Oakley arrived, Cora was immensely dissatisfied, more than anyone. 'He's really got himself an absolute dog. I'd have credited him with a bit more taste. And that piercing Mickey Mouse voice!'

Annie was charmed by us all, found Europe wonderful, giggled inanely and talked in a horrendous language that had next to nothing to do with our school English. Good-naturedly, she did everything to please Fred. As for me, I was swimming in such a sea of happiness that I paid Annie and Fred no heed whatsoever. But my very lack of interest, accompanied as it was by my almost bride-like blossoming, seemed to have set something going in Friedrich, for he kept cutting his Annie short and laughing far too loud and long at the simplest of witticisms that dropped from my lips.

Cora observed the scene closely. 'Could you not drop Jonas

for Friedrich, then we'd be shot of that empty-headed bitch. That would be sensible, after all.'

I stared at her in bafflement. Since when was love supposed to be sensible?

'Forget it,' said Cora. 'There's just no talking sense with you these days.'

We were sitting on the grey stone outside steps leading to the upstairs flat, painting our toenails pink. Cora's mother came and sat down with us. 'And what about our little fingers then?' she said, and disapprovingly raised her daughter's fine hand. 'Where can these black mourning edges have come from, when you're diving into the water every hour of the day?'

I, too, examined my hands in embarrassment. Basically, we painted our toenails so that the fresh pink would distract attention from the dust off the road, but we considered varnished finger-nails to be too ladylike. Cora's mother showed us the way Frenchwomen do it, a French manicure: naturally, the nails cut short, filed into an oval and highlighted from underneath with a white nail pencil. While she was filing at my finger-nails to give us a demonstration, she remarked, quite casually, 'Should I lend you some of my pills? I've brought two packets with me.'

I blushed from head to foot, and I was lost for words. Cora, on the one hand jealous of these maternal attentions, and on the other, constantly in opposition to them, hissed at her mother, 'You're forgetting Jonas is a medical student. He knows better what he's doing than you do. Isn't that right, Maya?'

I nodded. Jonas always took care, as he had assured me he would, but he didn't like talking about sex, he just did it. Of course I would have liked to 'borrow' the pill, but solidarity with Cora took priority for me.

I have often looked back and wondered why on earth I should have fallen in love with Jonas, of all people. Very likely, I had no choice, even if that's not the way it seems. In those days, I was as ripe as any windfall; I had rid myself of my debilitating family, I felt at ease within the surrogate family of my choice, I considered I looked beautiful in my good clothes and with my tanned skin, and I was happy to be able to enjoy, for the first time in my life, a holiday in Italy, something that, for my classmates, no longer counted as anything out of the ordinary. The young men who, on those first days, had sat down beside us, had all thrown themselves at Cora. Now at last, along came one who looked only into my eyes – probably I would have melted even if the object of my love had been a far more unsuitable one than Jonas.

What did I know about him? He looked good, radiating, just like myself, that holiday *joie de vivre* that young people have, he sported a tan and was growing a wild beard. I loved it when our warm, sun-smelling skins touched. Jonas was more serious, more taciturn than I was, he was a trusting type, and I took care not to tell him anything about earlier misdeeds. I had in fact hinted that my brother had died the previous year in a tragic accident, but Jonas simply took me compassionately in his arms and wiped my nose with a rustic-style checked handkerchief; he wasn't interested in details.

He asked no questions, and neither did I. We were so taken up with our physical pleasures that we accepted each other without restraint, marvelling at everything we had in common and finding any differences interesting and exciting.

It was only much later that I got to know Jonas.

CHAPTER 7

Saffron

I received a call from the agency recently, asking whether I thought I could take on 'the grand tour', as my colleague had been suddenly taken ill. The big tour takes twice as long as mine, six hours to be exact, with Fiesole on the programme as well, of course, as the Uffizi, allowing a generous amount of time for the contemplation of Botticelli's allegorical *Primavera*. So I memorized the fact that the large-scale wooden panel was painted in 1478; on the left, Mercury stands guard, on the right, Zephyr chases the women, while Cupid fires his arrows from above. And in the foreground can be seen the man who commissioned the painting, Lorenzo Medici, gazing at the wispily clad Graces. Cora doesn't like this painting, although at certain moments she bears a slight resemblance to Flora. She loathes loveliness, and she does everything she can to camouflage her own by the way she dresses.

I've managed to get through the full tour a few times now. My twenty-strong flock would tick off the sights on their list and then devote themselves to shopping: hand-hammered writing paper, raffia and basketware, Florentine lace and gold jewellery with coral and pearls.

In a fury, I watched a seventeen-year-old as her parents gave her every single thing she pointed at. The old folks were so charmed by their darling child's having done them the favour of travelling to Italy with them, that they shelled out for the most senseless souvenirs, and would have gone running to Gucci and Fendi if their daughter had so desired.

*   *   *

My first trip abroad had taken place in the company of someone else's parents. Even though I can only sing the praises of Cora's parents over and over again, the fact remains that they still weren't my own. Maybe that was the reason why, at that time, I clung so passionately to Jonas.

When the end of the holidays finally came, there was a heartbreaking leave-taking. Annie and Fred went off to Paris, because the American girl didn't want to go home without seeing the Eiffel Tower. Friedrich's enthusiasm for the States and for Annie of the Sweaty Palms had waned in proportion to his increasing attraction to me. Doubtlessly he was already hatching plans to shake off his betrothed by ditching her somewhere along the way.

It was the parting from Jonas that I could hardly bear. I wasn't in the least ashamed of bursting into tears in front of the assembled family, of hanging on to him like some spider-monkey, or, in the end, of slumping into the professor's family's car as if deprived of all willpower, like a Hindu widow shortly before suttee.

The professor had accompanied my passionate farewells with rather impatient urgings: 'Ready now, h'm, yes.' Cora and her mother exchanged a rare glance of fellow feeling.

Jonas was studying in Freiburg, and so it would take him only two hours at weekends to be at our door to take me off on a romantic outing. He kept this promise. He himself lived in a Catholic student hostel, where female visitors, while not generally forbidden, were certainly frowned upon. On several occasions I asked him why he didn't look for a room elsewhere. There were financial reasons. Through some clerical connections, Jonas got a hefty rebate on his rent; his elder brother had entered a holy order. His parents, who owned a farm up in the Black Forest, had brought up all their seven children strictly and devoutly. So it was, then, that I never visited Jonas, but he was our guest every weekend. Only our love life took place in his camper (especially once the weather turned colder). At countless Sunday meals, Jonas was present in the role of parasite. At the outset, the generous parents would watch this additional member of the family with interest, but that soon flagged. Jonas's main quality lay rather in his being a good listener than an entertaining conversationalist.

Five months before the *Abitur* exams, I had a dreadful suspicion that I was pregnant. The first person I talked to was Cora.

As always, she knew what to do. 'On no account must you mention it to my parents, otherwise there'll be an enormous hoo-ha,' she said. 'We'll get a pregnancy-test kit from the chemist's. If it turns out positive, you'll have to phone Jonas right away. He's studying medicine, so he'll know how to go about it.'

Jonas was in his second semester, but I had boundless confidence in him and his comfortingly warm voice. The test did come up positive, so I called him. 'I'm pregnant,' I announced.

Silence.

I tried to picture his face. After a lengthy pause, I said, 'I'm sure you'll know how we go about getting rid of it. As far as I know, I've got to go to an advice centre first.'

He still said nothing, and it was beginning to give me the creeps. Maybe he wasn't on his own? 'Maya,' he said, barely audibly, 'you must never say such a thing again.'

What was that supposed to mean? Surely we had to talk about it! I got very agitated. 'Well, say something, for heaven's sake!'

'I'll have to think it over,' said Jonas, so slowly that it was obvious he was playing for time. 'Abortion is murder. A sin.'

It finally dawned on me that his profound faith was going to prove an additional problem. But if faith was supposed to be able to move mountains, couldn't it prevent a belly from swelling? With shame and dismay, I pictured myself sitting in Cora's room with a screaming infant, with no money, no husband, no job, wholly and completely dependent on the charity of parents who weren't my own. It was one thing for Jonas to be sharing their table now and again, but the constant presence of a baby was quite another.

'Jonas,' I threatened him, 'if murder and sin is all you can come up with, just give a thought to your part in this whole sorry story . . .' I couldn't keep the tears back any more.

81

'It's a nuisance, but our priest is still away on holiday,' said Jonas. 'I'll not be able to speak to him until next week.'

At that, my anger boiled over. When I lose my temper, I can trample everything underfoot. 'Leave the God-botherer out of this!' I yelled. 'It's a gynaecologist I need most of all! But I'll find one by myself!' I hung up.

After this conversation, Cora came rushing into the room; no doubt she had heard me shouting. She took one look at my puffy, tear-stained face and took me in her arms. 'We don't need that dead loss, we'll manage everything without him. Just think of Detlef.'

I couldn't raise a laugh. The kids' stuff with Detlef was a far cry from having a child in your womb.

The next day, I was sitting in a gynaecologist's waiting-room. Cora held my hand until I was called. The doctor confirmed the fact that I was pregnant, and I dissolved in tears.

'You're only just eighteen,' she said sympathetically and gave me a searching look.

'I don't want a child now, maybe when I'm thirty . . .'

She understood that only too well. I told her how I had been taken in by a friend's parents and was living as their guest, my own mother suffering from depression, my father a drinker!

In the end, she offered to do everything she could to stand by me; she arranged an appointment for me at a family-planning advice centre and wrote down the address of a regional abortion clinic. Somewhat relieved, I returned home with Cora.

The VW minibus was standing at the front door. Jonas tumbled out, embraced me and was in an awful state. Even before we got in the door, he cried loudly, 'We'll get married!'

The theory is that it's one of the high points in a woman's life when she gets a declaration of love and a proposal of marriage. At that time, my feelings were in such a state of disarray that I felt no sense of joy. Because of his inability to react quickly, Jonas had aroused my anger; I had, of course, not taken into consideration that he was only three years older than I was, but no less hungry for love and every bit as inexperienced. I had scared the life out of him with my message.

Jonas was a man who needed time. I had known him for only a few days, when his way of eating was already getting on my nerves. He could spend a whole hour munching on one slice of bread, so that, in my impatience, I felt like spoon-feeding him myself. But was that such a bad thing? On the contrary, thoroughness and meticulousness were his strengths, and certainly not mine. I didn't respond to his proposal with a grateful embrace, as Jonas had expected. Instead, I remained obstinate and answered coldly, 'I don't need any favours.' Cora slipped away.

Once I was alone with Jonas, he started reproaching himself. My pregnancy was his fault, and his alone. As a good Christian, he would do everything in his power to assume responsibility for the new life.

'And how do you see that working out?' I demanded. 'Neither of us has any money or training for a job.'

'As soon as you've got your *Abitur*, we'll get married. You can live with the child at my parents', until I've completed my studies.'

I could just picture myself, in my peasant costume, making hay and schlepping pig-swill into the sty, all the time with a whimpering child on my hip. 'I'd sooner go to America,' I thought. To flee from prospects like these, maybe to Friedrich, that would be just the very thing.

But Jonas recognized that he couldn't simply offload me on to his parents. He drew a picture of a small, inexpensive but cosy flat and a loving couple, happy in their own modest way with their child. 'One happy little family,' he said.

At the word 'family', I forgot my anger and defiance. Wasn't that the panacea for all problems? To set up a new family that was different from both the sickening one I had been born into, and the other one, to which, as an outsider, I had no right; a family with a child of my own, a husband and a home in which everything belonged to me, where it would be up to me where the lamp should hang and when we would eat. Suddenly, this family of my own seemed to me like the paradise I had been searching for, ever since my father had deserted me.

By the time Jonas had to leave – he had a mid-term exam the next day – I had made up my mind to have the child, to become a good housewife and companion. Cora came in to me as soon as she heard the minibus roaring away.

'Don't even think about it!' she warned me.

If I had listened to her, my life would have taken a different course. But who has ever taken well-meant advice where matters of the heart are concerned?

I didn't go to the family-planning people. I sent word to my therapist that, for the time being, I wouldn't be able to spare the time for any consultations because my preparation for the *Abitur* was more important. Cora, too, broke off her communication therapy; the novelty had long since worn off for her.

As a matter of fact, I did study very hard at that time, presenting some excellent seminar papers and thus giving the lie to the theory whereby pregnant women are supposed to be so preoccupied with their womb that they have nothing left over for their brain.

It was my intention to inform the outside world only once the deadline for any possible termination had passed. That would then amaze them all, my parents and Cora's, my teachers and classmates.

Frau Schwab was not one of those mothers who get up early to put the hot chocolate on. Whenever Cora and I left the house, usually without breakfast, she would still be lying beside the snoring professor in their Persian-pink bed. But that didn't mean she was asleep or that she was deaf. On the contrary, she had pricked up her ears at the sound, coming through several walls, of my early-morning retching and, with razor-sharp logic, had drawn her own conclusions. No doubt she was, despite the shock, relieved that it wasn't coming from her own daughter.

At first, she had tried to sound out Cora. But my friend wasn't for coming straight out with the truth to her parents.

I'm sure this detachment, this cutting of the umbilical cord to her own begetters, was particularly difficult for her, because, unlike myself, she had so little reason to find fault with her parents.

'You'll have to ask her,' Cornelia told her mother, who, rather embarrassed, put the crucial question to me: 'Maya, are you expecting a baby?'

Both of us went red. How difficult it must have been for the professor and his wife to digest this situation. I had only just turned eighteen, they had assumed responsibility for me and were accountable to my parents. Naturally, they offered me the chance of a quick and confidential abortion – in fact, they tried to force it on me. If it had been their own daughter, they would have acted no differently. But my defiance was complete. Right now, I'm really fighting for my child, I thought, and I enjoyed the sense of power in being able to intimidate my ersatz parents with my problems. For sure, they hadn't deserved that; I was taking it out on the wrong ones, punishing them for the humiliation that they were not my proper parents. The memory of my own instinctive revolt against the unwanted child had been quickly suppressed.

The Schwab family was forced to concede defeat; Cora was the first to do so. She accepted my pig-headedness. At last, when I was in my third month, I wrote to my parents and Uncle Paul and talked to my teachers. I no longer had to take part in games lessons (instead, I had to attend the local antenatal exercise sessions), and kept on being asked by the girls in my class about how I felt and getting rather perplexed stares from the boys. Cora took driving lessons, while I knitted a little baby-jacket in saffron yellow, a colour that was suitable for both sexes and would go well with the anticipated dark eyes.

In the meantime, Jonas had been thinking things over, and had spoken to his father confessor, even though it did take him longer than was comprehensible to me. He had given up his medical studies 'for the time being' and started a short course with a pharmaceuticals firm. In as little as six months, he could begin work as a rep, calling on doctors.

Even during training, he got a salary, which would rise. Medical representatives were well paid. We were going to look for somewhere inexpensive to stay, in the Mannheim area and possibly in a rural community.

Jonas's parents had received his confession of the news without undue emotion. When you had seven children, all brought up strictly and devoutly, it seemed you were used to some sort of derailments along the way. I was invited to come and visit them, and the wedding was to be held there, too. Well, where else?

One springlike Saturday, Jonas drove out with me to the family farm. He was much more excited about it than I was.

If Jonas was a man of few words, then the rest of his family seemed almost to be made up of deaf-mutes. There was coffee and a wonderful sponge cake with crumble topping, and they kept putting another slice of it on my plate without saying a word. I could barely understand their local dialect. They accepted me without great enthusiasm, but also, without prejudice. My fears that these pious country folk might write me off as a fallen woman proved absurd. These parents took things just as they were. The mother asked if I was going to turn Catholic. I shook my head.

'I can understand that,' she said, 'but the child must be.'

I nodded. Fine by me.

In actual fact, I could find no objection to these people; they were all right, there was no false heartiness and no nosy interrogation. But it was just not my world. Saying grace at table was alien to me.

I was reminded of a meal around Christmas time at the professor's house. Fred from America was present. We were having braised heart, and as it was brought to the table, we sang, in four parts, '*Bonjour mon coeur!*' At that, my own heart had soared, for jokes like that had been unknown in my own family. I wanted to establish a new one, in which such a merry time was had by all.

As we were leaving, the grandmother, who was sitting at the coffee table knitting, asked me what colour I wanted the baby's things to be. She wanted to make a start on the work. 'Saffron yellow,' I said, and everybody gawped at me. But from that day on, the great-grandmother-to-be stuck strictly to my instructions. Jonas told me the people in the village had been quite keen to adopt this baby colour as a novelty.

To jump ahead a bit – when the child was born, it was already suffering from jaundice, and nothing could have looked worse on it than an all-saffron outfit.

Once Cora had passed her driving test, we sometimes drove to school in her mother's car. I was overcome by a cautiousness, even fearfulness, that I had never previously experienced, and I was constantly on at Cora to drive more slowly.

'You're making *me* nervous,' she said. 'A pregnant elephant's worse than any mother.'

Cora could take the liberty of saying things like that without my temper flaring. As a matter of fact, I was gradually changing into a shapeless creature that could only move at a very leisurely pace.

It was as we were getting out of the car one day that it happened. Infected by my jumpiness, Cora dropped her car keys, which disappeared down a drain. Lessons were just beginning, and there we stood, staring helplessly at the mouth of the culvert.

'If you squat down and put everything you can into heaving up the cover,' Cora said, 'you could bet on having a miscarriage by tomorrow.'

She gave me a hard look. I didn't go along with her suggestion. I could feel the child, alive and kicking, and I said nothing. In the end, Cora lost that trial of wills, one of the few times when I didn't do what she wanted. After a few minutes, we walked, without exchanging a word, into the school building; later, we got the janitor to prise up the drain cover and fish out the car keys.

Nevertheless, the conflicting feelings, on the one hand, of longing for a new life with a new family and, on the other, wanting to be rid of this foreign body inside me, were intensifying. How vital some therapy sessions would have been just at that time.

In addition, I was having some first doubts about the solicitous Jonas. The physical pleasure that we took in each other had been our most important bond. This attraction was now losing some of its power. Jonas and I couldn't really talk to each other, except about practical things like home, furniture and first names. He seldom laughed, he rarely read, he wasn't the least keen on music. His interests lay in the realms of science. But, in contrast to Cora's brother, who studied physics but could still indulge in childish fun, Jonas was devoid of all humour. Or was it my fault? Was I, in Cora's company, so set on acting downright silly that a serious man like Jonas was repelled by it? Sometimes I put all my fears down to my condition. Ahead of me lay the *Abitur*, the written exams first, then the orals, and two weeks after that, the wedding at a strange farmhouse, and not too long after that again, giving birth. It seemed a pretty busy schedule.

The written exam in mathematics that we had to do for our finals was the one tricky bit. Cora had a tried and tested system of cheating all ready. We copied out the questions, I went to the toilet and tossed the sheets of paper, which I was able to conceal without any trouble in my voluminous maternity dress, into a prearranged wastepaper basket. A boy in the fifth form, who worshipped Cora, smuggled our questions out of the school building, where two maths students were waiting. In a café, they feverishly worked out the answers, which had to be back in the same wastepaper basket by a certain time.

A heavily pregnant pupil is usually allowed by the invigilating teacher to make repeated visits to the lavatory. With the completed answers secreted about my bulging person, I returned to the exam room, where, pretending to feel slightly queasy, I asked Cornelia, under the beady eye of the teacher, for a sip from her bottle of lemonade. While she bent down to rummage for it, I let the paper with the answers meant for Cora drop to the floor and, as I did so, I attracted all eyes to my pregnant lump by letting out an ominous moan.

'I think that could have been a contraction,' I said, and no one paid Cora the slightest attention. Once I was 'feeling better', I copied out the students' work, and no teacher on earth would have dared to keep a close eye on what I was doing. In those exams, Cora and I turned in the best mathematics performance of our whole school careers. All the other exams we passed even without outside assistance.

I invited my father, my mother and my financial backer, Uncle Paul, to the wedding. Mother declined by letter, but she did give us to understand that she would come and see Jonas and me once our child was born. Uncle Paul couldn't come either, not altogether out of lack of inclination, but because he would be away on a photo safari in Africa at the time. Father hadn't sent any word at all, but, lo and behold, there he was at the wedding.

'I'm sorry I haven't brought any presents. I'm the surprise myself,' he said, standing there before us in the same black suit with the greenish sheen that he had borrowed for Carlo's funeral.

The professor's family represented my side with great dignity, while Jonas was supported by half the village as well as his six brothers and sisters, some of them already with large families of their own. Karsten and Cora acted as witnesses.

My in-laws had gone to a great deal of trouble. It was a glorious summer day and, just as in the picture books, we were all able to sit out in a large meadow under the apple trees to celebrate the occasion. A wedding feast straight out of Brueghel had been laid out, with roast pork and crackling, freshly baked bread, and beer. Before very long, Father was half-cut, not because he couldn't hold his drink, but because the unaccustomed suit brought him out in a sweat and he was rapidly knocking back one schnapps after another, always along with a beer as a chaser. He kept on wanting to have a chat with his son-in-law and to ply him, too, with schnapps. But on that count, Jonas was steadfast; from the time he was small, he had got used to rustic roisterings and was all too familiar with alcoholism in all its forms. Jonas took the schnapps bottle away from him. Still, Father got hold of more supplies. When he had reached the staggering, mumbling stage, he was carted off by Jonas and his able-bodied brothers and deposited in a bedroom.

The professor took over the role of father of the bride and made a short speech. Frau Schwab had dressed me up as prettily as could be expected in the circumstances. What touched me most of all was the fact that she presented me with a cutlery canteen full of family silver. The monogram of one of her grandmothers, M. D., was now just right for me, she said, because I was no longer Maya Westermann, but Maya Döring. Cora brought me a very chic pram; only later did she reveal to me that she had seen it standing outside a supermarket and had wheeled it home. The presents from many of the guests were of a practical kind, some of them cash. Also among them were five irons, two toasters and several hideous vases.

Late on in the evening, it was discovered that Father was no longer up in his room. Young and old joined the hunt. In the end, he was found in the cellar, bleeding from a head wound. On the hunt for liquid sustenance, he had tumbled down the steps. He had to have the cut stitched.

Not only Father, but the professor, too, had indulged in more than his customary sherry in the course of the festivities. He had always been very caring, though never familiar, towards me, but now he put an arm around my shoulders, and together we went for a stroll through the darkened vegetable garden. It was a rare thing for him to let his amiable aloofness drop and become confidential.

'It's going to be lonely for us, with Cornelia in Florence and you in the Black Forest; without your laughter and your machinations life's going to get boring.' What did he mean by 'machinations'? But he went on, 'I hope you'll come and see us often.'

My eyes filled with tears. This would have been just the right moment to thank him for everything. But I've never had the gift of finding the right words at times like this. 'The two years with you all were the most wonderful in my whole life,' I said. 'I can't get along with these people in the village here.'

'Maya, you're so full of prejudices. What you have here is neither the ideal world nor an absolute cultural desert. Jonas's parents, despite their seven children, can't abide each other, haven't you noticed? And haven't you heard the farmers chatting, not about the maize harvest, but about computers? Did you try the salad that some farmer's wife had prepared? That woman could hold her own against a top chef, h'm, yes.'

All that had escaped my notice. 'And what do you think of Jonas?' I blurted straight out, although I had a fair idea of what he thought of him.

'A good lad, Maya,' he said, steering me away because, at the corner of the cabbage patch, two guests were busy relieving themselves.

Saying goodbye to Cora and her family was painful. They were going to spend the night in the village inn, but would be setting off for home early the next morning. I lay, exhausted, next to Jonas in his youngest sister's room, while outside the guests carried on the celebrations, becoming noisier and noisier. Only once it was getting light did they gradually start taking their leave. Then the industrious brothers and sisters began clearing up.

At breakfast, contractions started up, six weeks too soon. I was spared having to stay at the farm up to the time when we moved into our own place, for I was taken into hospital and hitched up to a drip-feed that was to inhibit the contractions until, a fortnight prematurely, I gave birth to my quince-yellow son.

CHAPTER 8

Grey in Grey

Cora's psychologist once used the expression 'opulent neglect'. She forgot about it long ago, but the idea keeps haunting my thoughts. Ever since I've had a child of my own, I've dipped into newspaper articles on education and psychology. Some parents slave away, consulting educational guidance counsellors, in an attempt to do everything perfectly, and still their children turn into prime-specimen neurotics. Then you hear of parents who beat their children and in fact do everything wrong. Yet it can happen that these children grow up to be stable and even happy people. It's just like those centenarians who have spent their lives smoking, boozing and gorging themselves. I reckon it won't harm my child if, just now and then, I do a bit of thieving, so as to brighten up my own life. Naturally, always provided that I don't get caught. A child needs a contented mother, not one who is stuck in prison through her own lack of responsibility.

Marriage made me anything but the satisfied wife and mother. Between Jonas and me, there was a lack of common ground, namely shared tastes. Naturally, with my eighteen-year-old's arrogance, I considered he was a country bumpkin, and it was up to me to re-educate him.

It all started with the bitter quarrel over our child's name; in the first few days we had given him the pet name 'Canary', because we couldn't come to an agreement. In the end, we settled on a compromise: Jonas was allowed to register the name 'Bartholomäus', 'Barthel' for short, since the first son of the heir to the farm had, according to tradition, always to be called 'Barthel Döring'. Jonas did in fact have an older brother of that name, but when he took holy orders he managed to dodge out of passing on the Bartholomäus bit. As a compensation for the rigidity of this tradition, I was allowed to choose a second Christian name, which was to be the one he'd be known by. Craftily, I proposed Béla, after my favourite composer, so that the boy was then called 'Béla Barthel'. This combination caused many a smile; Jonas felt cheated.

Our furniture was, almost without exception, hideous. It had been borrowed from farm attics and had all the charm of cast-offs. But there could be no grounds for arguing on this count, since we had next to no money and just had to make do with it. What was at issue was our one and only exquisite possession, the celadon-green dish, which, after keeping it hidden for two years, I was at last able to display on our scratched synthetic-topped table. Jonas thought it looked awful and, without thinking, stated that, when he got his next pay-packet, that would be the first thing he would replace with a dish in Scandinavian glass.

We were living in a two-roomed flat in what had once been a village but was now populated by commuters. In their recently built semidetacheds, they would let out the granny-flat as a tax dodge. The houses were all the same, neat, small and with well-tended front gardens. Every fortnight, a board with CLEANING WEEK was hung on our front door.

Jonas worked hard. It took me a while to understand why he needed longer to get through his day's work than his colleagues. Whereas they cunningly managed, with a compliment on their lips and a free sample in their hands, to win over the receptionists and to slip discreetly in between two patients' appointments to see the doctors, he had to sit for hours in the waiting-room until it was his turn. He never got home till late.

In my early days as housewife and mother, I felt out of my depth. After all, I was still only a teenager. Whenever Béla caught a cold, I was terrified he would die on me. Fortunately, he lost his yellow complexion pretty quickly, and his eyes and his first hair turned dark brown. I was enchanted with him, thought he was fantastic and, at times, was beside myself with happiness. But my days also contained many grey hours, during which I was lonely, morosely cleaning, hanging up the baby's washing and perpetually looking desperately at the clock to see if, at last, it was time for Jonas to be getting home.

When he finally did arrive, in his smart suit with an ironed shirt and a tie, for he was expected to wear expensive and sober things, I would throw my arms round his neck, close to tears. I wanted to be hugged and comforted, wanted to laugh and talk about the day's doings. After a brief embrace, Jonas would push me off, change out of his good clothes and hang them up with great care, look in on his sleeping Barthel and then be ready to eat. Understandably, he was weary; he had had to spend the day talking to strangers, something that, by nature, he abhorred. At home, all he wanted was peace and quiet, the paper and a beer. If we could have exchanged roles, everything would have been simpler. I had never had any problem about making contact with people, and Jonas would have been perfectly content if he could have looked after his little son in his own quiet, capable way. As it was, we were both dissatisfied, yet unwilling to admit it.

Cora was living in Florence. She was a prolific letter-writer. Fat envelopes with sheets covered in her large handwriting reached me every week, rays of light in my lonely village life. I wrote, too, but what on earth did I have to tell?

One day, my mother announced she would be coming. Not once had I seen her since the death of my brother. I got into a real old panic. Fear mixed in with happy anticipation and left me hardly able to sleep.

In her military-style greatcoat, she looked so awful that I hardly recognized her. With Béla on my arm, I just stood looking at her and couldn't utter a word. From the way she looked at her grandson, she seemed to approve of him, and I passed him over to her. Maybe Béla was the one hope for building up a new relationship.

'A wonderful boy,' she said. 'You must be very grateful that it's a son. He looks just like Carlo.'

These words hit me like a bolt of lightning, and no doubt that was how they were meant to strike home. Béla didn't look the least bit like Carlo. I had pushed my mother's past barbed remarks out of my mind. Ever since Carlo's death, I had counted myself responsible for her unhappiness and her depression. But how was I to get her to see that, in the face of her total rejection, I was being made to suffer too?

I showed her round our flat, told her about the wedding (without mentioning my father), about the birth and even about my exams. Was she listening to me?

When Jonas got home, I was enormously relieved. I hoped that the presence of a third person would help to make things easier. There was, of course, just the possibility that she might reject him straight off for having got me pregnant. But it didn't turn out like that, and the two of them carried on a fairly normal conversation while I prepared the evening meal and changed Béla's nappy. Mother lay down early on the sofa and was ready for sleep. She was on sedatives.

The next day, she stayed at home alone with Béla while I nipped out to do some shopping. Some premonition suddenly stopped me from going on from the baker's to the chemist's and made me run home instead. At the corner of our street, I met Mother, complete with pram and infant, suitcase and coat. She had a crazed look about her.

'You took Carlo away from me. So now I've to get your son in exchange.' When I forced her bony hands loose from the pram handle, she put up no resistance. She followed me back home.

'Mother,' I said, sweat breaking out on my brow, 'you're ill and you can't stay here. I can't take on the responsibility. Please, go back at once.'

She shook her head. 'I'm not going back, I'm at the end of my tether. I've been planning my death for a long time now.'

'You're getting treatment,' I said, clutching the baby tightly to me all the while. 'They'll help you. Depression can be cured.'

'There's no cure for me any more. There's no point in my going on living, whether I'm well or I'm sick. The thought of dying is the only comfort I have left.'

Maybe it was a mistake, but I burst out angrily, 'All right then, do yourself in! Suicide isn't a crime!'

'Tell me honestly, Maya, whether you think it's right.'

'My God, Mother, before you try to snatch my baby, you should stop and ask yourself where all your hatred's coming from.'

She was silent, thinking things over. Then she said, 'My hatred is so great because my love was betrayed. All I can do is warn you – anyone who gives love always comes off worst.'

When Jonas came home, he drove her to the station, for I had told him on the spot that we couldn't leave her alone with the child for an instant.

Three days later, we received the news that she had killed herself by swallowing a pesticide.

In the weeks that followed, I sometimes felt I was going mad myself. Again and again I suffered from bouts of depression, floods of tears, even the beginnings of anorexia. I knew full well that it could all have a harmful effect on the child's development, and that thought just made things all the worse. I hadn't seen my father since the wedding; I had sent him word of Mother's death, but I had also added that she wanted to be buried without him being present. I waived my claim to my inheritance – my parents' horrendous furniture. Carlo's desk was the only thing I did have sent to me. But instead of the revelations I expected, practically all it contained was some men's magazines, a collection of unposted letters to Cora, a few of my father's sketches and a rosary.

One day, I took a good look at myself in the mirror: pale, thin, with poor skin and dark rings under my eyes. How different I had looked in Tuscany, when Jonas fell in love with me, and how intense our love life had been! On that count, too, I was dissatisfied, wondering why on earth I bothered taking the pill each day. It was just at that moment that our new telephone rang. It was Cora's mother. No doubt alerted by her daughter, she was worried about me. Recently, her husband had run into Jonas, in his smart suit and without the wild beard that he had grown in Tuscany. 'Maya, whenever Jonas is doing his rounds of the doctors in our area, he could bring you along and drop you off at our place. Will the pram fit into the car?'

From then on, I spent one day a week at the Schwabs'. In the mornings, I'd go for walks through the town with the pram and let passers-by and acquaintances stop me and admire Béla, in the afternoons, I'd sit with Cora's parents until Jonas came to collect me in the evenings.

These visits did me good; what helped me even more, though, was that I started thieving again. The way it began was when I was buying baby-powder and baby-oil in a chemist's, and, as I was doing so, I caught sight of the expensive cosmetics I used to use. I was sure that the bad state of my skin was a result of having nothing but cheap soap at home. With the pram, it was an easy matter to embark on pilfering expeditions. Everything disappeared under Béla's blanket. I never stole anything in our village, but whenever I came back from the town, I would always have some lovely souvenirs, things like perfume and stockings, music cassettes and art books, a silk blouse and an electric gadget for keeping the baby's bottle warm.

Now and again, Cora's mother would come along with me, and on those occasions shop-lifting was not on. But then she generally bought me something of my choice to wear, so I was able to tell Jonas that my other acquisitions were presents as well.

Above all, I stole nice things for my child. I couldn't bear to see Béla dressed in ugly things. While I had no objection to his great-grandmother's little hand-knitted jackets – rustic tradition did lend them a certain charm – I put aside the candy-coloured department-store stuff Jonas's sister handed down. I wanted to see my child in silk and lace. To Jonas, that was just absurd.

'Do you want to turn him into a prince?' he mocked. Yes, indeed, that's exactly what I wanted. After all, Béla was the son of a princess. I wanted to compensate for the fact that I myself was no longer the Infanta of Spain.

Quite surprisingly, the professor, who had taken little interest in his own children at the baby stage, absolutely doted on my son. Whenever he had the time, he would sit for a good hour at the tea table and insist on taking the child on his lap.

'Béla Barthel is a pure joy, h'm, yes. At the beginning, I thought it was a disaster that you, at only eighteen . . . But when I stop and think, in three years, Béla will get into a kindergarten, you'll still be in the full flush of youth and you can start studying. I've come across a lot of women who take their exams first and take a job, and in the end they're reluctant to interrupt their career to start a family. It never fits into their schedule, just like me with my gallstones. I'm supposed to have an operation at some time or another, but I can never find a time when it suits.'

Cora's mother quizzed me about her daughter, since all she ever got from her was greetings on a postcard, and that only rarely. She was worried about her. Cora had recently written to me with the news that she had fallen in love with a man older than her father. That was one detail I kept to myself.

When, one evening, I heard Jonas coming home and swung the door open to welcome him, I caught sight of a hunched figure behind him. In tattered clothes, looking like a tramp, my father stood before me. He said he was 'on the run'. What from? Debts, he said, his rent and his electricity bill were unpaid, and no one would allow him credit in the shops any more.

'And what about your job as a blood-courier?' I asked.

'I've lost my driving licence . . .'

'But you must be drawing dole money?'

He couldn't be bothered. In a rush of alcohol-induced befuddlement, he saw himself as homeless and had hitch-hiked all the way from Lübeck to us.

I ran a bath for him and told him there'd be nothing to eat until he had had a wash. Jonas didn't say a word.

Naturally, his suits were too tight for my father, so, after his bath, he sat at table in a towelling bathrobe much too small for him. He looked even more derelict than when I first went to see him in Lübeck.

I kept turning over in my mind how we could get rid of him. We had only the sofa for guests to sleep on, we had a baby, and we had little money. And after Father had used it, the bath was left with a black ring round it.

As I lay in bed beside Jonas and Father filled the living-room with his snores, I whispered, 'You've got to get rid of him tomorrow!'

'Why me? But anyway, you can't just kick a poor sick man out into the street.'

My voice rose as I became more agitated. 'What do you mean, poor, and what's this with sick? Lazy and drink-sodden, more like.'

'It's one's duty as a Christian to honour one's parents.'

At that, I exploded, 'I can't stomach him!' and I began bawling so loudly that Béla awoke and started crying along with me.

Father appeared in the doorway, without so much as knocking. 'Is all this yelling on my account? I'll be gone tomorrow.'

Day in, day out, it was the same story – I threw Father out and he grovelled and promised to leave the next day. The train ticket I had bought for him had disappeared. As for our child, he had hardly given him a second glance; when the little fellow cried, Father would screw up his face in a grimace, as if it was all done just to disturb his peace and quiet.

One day, when Father was caught in the act of stealing a bottle of schnapps, something he had taken up in a completely amateurish fashion, even the placid Jonas flew into a rage. With some interest, I observed that my husband had a boundless abhorrence of thieves. As for the bottle of beer I bought daily for Jonas, Father also managed to track it down, even in the most outlandish hiding places. I was well aware that you can't cure an alcoholic by sudden withdrawal against his will, so I always brought him back a bottle of cheap red wine. But a litre-bottle a day wasn't enough for him.

At the end of my tether, and never far from tears, I was beginning to feel like hitting the bottle myself, despite my youth. On that particular day – Béla and Father, each in his own ecstatic lethargy, were enjoying their afternoon nap – Cora phoned from Italy. 'We can have a good long chat, I'm not footing the bill,' she said. I poured out my heart to her. Cora then told me that her new boyfriend had, just the week before, bought a house, big and beautiful, and that she was living in it too. 'From the first floor, you can see green hills! I've made a great swop. My old room was a dump, and on top of that, it took me half an hour in the bus to get to Florence. Now I've got everything, just like home!'

'And a new daddy,' I said.

'That's the great thing about it! Young men have neither money nor houses, not even bath-salts.'

I envied Cora. She assured me I would be welcome to come to Italy right away. 'And what about Béla?'

'Well, of course, Béla too. You can't very well leave him with your father while Jonas is out doing his door-to-door stuff.'

That evening we all had a row, each one with the other, with the child crying all the while. I decided to leave the next day.

Once Jonas had left the house early in the morning, I packed the baby's bits and bobs, prepared several bottles of baby-food, hid the Chinese dish safely away in the cellar, wrote a lukewarm note for Jonas and ordered a taxi. Father would sleep like a corpse till midday, I could depend on that.

That journey, complete with an infant, a pram and two suit-cases, would have been impossible without other people's help in getting into and out of trains with the changes I had to make. In my haste, I had forgotten to look up the best connections, and so I had to make my way to my destination by various stages. What would Cora's rich old boyfriend say when I turned up with my baby, like some gypsy woman? Never mind, Cora would sort out the whole business.

In my compartment sat a ballet dancer, who was going off to a spa; he took a great shine to Béla. While he was in the toilet, I pinched money out of his wallet, so that, if the worst came to the worst, I'd be able to spend the first night in a hotel. This turned out to be a wise precaution, for when I arrived in Florence around midnight, there wasn't a soul to open the door to me at the house itself.

In a cheap hotel, I lay with Béla in a double bed. We were both exhausted after the journey. He went straight off to sleep, while I listened to the strange sounds all around me and ran a thousand thoughts through my mind. Jonas would be worried, but he would also look on me as a deserter. I had stolen his Barthel from him and left him my drunkard of a father in exchange. I had, of course, promised in writing that I would be back soon, but Jonas didn't have Cora's address and couldn't get in touch from his end.

Throughout that night, when I did more crying than sleeping, and learned the neon adverts on the building opposite off by heart, I drew my only comfort from the deeply slumbering Béla. The feeling of homelessness and alienation was alleviated by his presence. The professor had once jokingly referred to my son as 'Prince of Peace', because Béla's completely relaxed way of sleeping had such a calming effect on anyone looking at him. Again and again, I had watched how both men and women who were far from crazy about babies seemed attracted, as if by magic, to my child, going into raptures over him. There are nature-lovers who, at the sight of young kittens, blackbirds feeding and deer grazing, experience similar feelings of delight and euphoria. I was happy that I had this unplanned child, even if he had, superficially at least, thrown my own vague plans for the future into confusion.

Tomorrow, I would be able to show him to Cora. She had seen Béla only once, in his yellow state. Escape had been the principal motive for my journey, but of course it was vital for me to see my bosom friend again.

Cora's gentleman friend was two years older than her father, and I pictured him as an Italian version of the professor: his thinning hair pitch-black, maybe a moustache, thickening a little at the waist, intelligent and gracious, charming and witty. Whenever you build up such firm pre-conceptions, you're bound to end up disappointed. In fact, Cora's friend wasn't Italian at all, but half German, half Brazilian. He grew his fair hair long on one side so as to be able to spread it artfully over his nearly bald crown. No moustache, blue eyes and twice the normal ration of vitality and dynamism. However, it wasn't him who opened the door to me the next day, but an Italian domestic.

I asked for Cora, and the woman disappeared without asking me in. Although it was getting on for midday, Cora came rushing out, still in her nightdress, and we fell into each other's arms. By good fortune, her friend had gone to Ugolino for a game of golf, so we could have a long chat undisturbed. The maid brought espresso and became more friendly when Béla gave her a beaming laugh. Cora had him in her arms and was as delighted with him as I had hoped.

Before her inamorato got back, I wanted to hear all about him. We sat out on the sunlit verandah, drinking Campari and orange, with our legs propped up on a table made out of a millstone. Lizards darted about all around us.

Her lover was called Henning Kornmeier and was over fifty. As a young man, he had been sent to Rio by his Hamburg firm. A few years later, he had established a construction company of his own. Now he was rich enough not to have to work any more, but simply to enjoy life.

'Is he married, has he any children?'

'He was married to a Brazilian woman ten years older than him. They didn't have children. She died shortly after they divorced.'

'And then?'

'My God, I'm sure Henning has put himself about a bit, but that doesn't bother me in the least. You'll like him.'

'How did you get to know each other?'

'You'll never believe it. I was having money troubles.'

'Cora, you get enough from your parents, you surely don't need to go on the game.'

'Listen, I get enough to live on, but it doesn't stretch to

having a car. You can't be serious if you think I had to go on the game, after all you taught me about thieving.'

I laughed, rather flattered. 'Did you nick his wallet?'

'You can believe it if you like, but he caught me in the act. You know, there must be pick-pockets in Brazil that make us look like novices. When you come down to it, we never practised with live targets . . .'

I loved the story. I found it romantic for somebody to fall in love through theft. Cora hadn't changed a bit. Barefoot and in her nightdress, she danced across the stone floor with Béla in her arms, singing '*Azzuro*', then she fed my child with a coffee spoon.

'By the way, Henning will be back soon. We'll bend the truth a bit and tell him your father threatened you and the baby with a knife. Henning loves to see himself as a saviour of damsels in distress.'

I lay back in the sun and had the comforting feeling that the grey days were over, at least for the time being.

CHAPTER 9

Golden Calf

So far, Mercury, the god of thieves, has always held a protecting hand over me. Perhaps, as gods have the habit of doing in this land, he has assumed the shape of Cesare. While my coach-driver could hardly, in terms of age, be my father, he does have an extremely paternal streak. He probably approximates more closely to the ghost of the dream father that accompanied me through my childhood than my actual progenitor does. As a child, I saw myself as responsible for the disappearance of my father. I wasn't loving enough, not beautiful enough, to find favour with a king. The fact that Cesare finds me pretty makes me feel good, and occasionally I refrain from the odd little piece of mischief, so as not to incense him.

Cora, too, has problems with her father, but very different ones. Why else should she have taken up with Henning, if not because of some repressed Oedipus complex? She has never admitted that.

I can still remember very clearly how I met her ageing lover. If Henning was in any way peeved at my surprise visit, he certainly didn't let it show. He acted charmingly and boyishly, and together we selected a room for me. The villa was by no means a palace, but a respectable middle-class house dating from the previous century. It had been its solid fabric that had appealed to Henning's expert eye; from Cora, he had had a tip-off that both the previous owners had died, one shortly after the other. One of her many Italian friends had been talking about it, and so that was how she got to hear of this bargain before estate agents and property sharks had the chance to catch a sniff of the scent. Mind you, Emilia, the domestic, went along with the villa as a living part of the fittings, and in addition, no renovation work had been done since the war.

Henning, on first-name terms from the word go, showed Béla and me to a big, bright room with a balcony. The plaster was flaking from the ceiling, the shutters on the windows rotting, the terrazzo floor had holes in it – but I loved that room, with light coming in from two sides, beyond all measure. A wrought-iron bedstead, a chest of drawers with a mirror, and an armchair with worn upholstery comprised the entire furnishings. Emilia brought me some wire coat-hangers and strung up a cord between two metal hooks.

That evening, I phoned Jonas. He was every bit as talkative as the time I gave him the news of my pregnancy.

'In Germany, they still have to keep the heating on, and here we've been having our coffee out on the terrace. Béla slept for hours out of doors, it'll do him a world of good . . .'

Jonas was taking it badly. He wanted to know the address, intending to come down at the weekend and take us back. Cora's parents didn't know that she had moved out of her furnished room; he had already called them.

I refused to cough up the address, assuring him I would be back in a few days anyway.

'Don't you want to know what your father's doing?'

'Yes, sure.'

'He insists he's ill, but won't go to the doctor.'

Blackmail, I thought. 'Kick Father out!'

'How am I supposed to do that? He just lies on the sofa with a hot-water bottle, moaning all the time.'

I promised to call again soon, but had no intention of doing anything of the kind. Obviously, Jonas was trying to talk me into a bad conscience.

Cora had done herself up all very smart. She was going to the opening of an exhibition; she knew the artist personally. 'Can I have the car?' she asked. Henning drew the keys from his pocket. It turned out he wasn't keen on that kind of do. 'What about you, Maya, are you coming along?'

'I'm afraid not – Béla . . .'

'But he's sound asleep, and you'll be back before his next feed.'

Henning encouraged me to leave Béla in his care, and Emilia would hear him if he cried. I borrowed some glad rags from Cora, and we climbed into an enormous American limousine. 'Actually, it's his big chrome and green Cadillac that I like about Henning,' Cora said shamelessly.

'Aren't you the least bit in love?'

'Oh, hell, I suppose so. But he has his faults, and I'm not even talking about his age. If it hadn't been for me, he'd have bought himself a luxury modern flat. It's the solid construction of our villa he likes, nothing else; he's just got no nose at all for the charm and beauty of old houses. He loves golf and horse-racing.'

'And you?'

'Well, I'm not exactly the Queen, am I? Horses make me yawn. But the spectators are fun, you'll enjoy that.' Cora drove with panache, pointing out along the way her favourite church, Santa Maria Novella. 'This is the country for educating the eye,' she said. 'In the next day or so, I'm going to show you Ghirlandaio's frescos.'

Her American friend's exhibition was anything but an education for anyone's artistic eye, but it did provide the pleasure of meeting people. As the time for Béla's next feed drew close, I grew rather impatient and suggested we should be getting back.

'I'd like to stay on a while,' said Cora. 'Sandra can drive you home.'

When I entered the pink villa, slightly late, I was met by a picture of family bliss: Henning was holding the baby on his lap, while Emilia had made some semolina for him. Feeding was well under way. I offered to take over from Henning, but he was throwing himself into the job. Seemingly, Béla had aroused his grandfatherly instinct with his cries.

'The things you miss out on in life,' Henning said to Emilia. He always talked to her in Spanish, which he adapted from his Brazilian Portuguese. Most of the time, she could understand him. And, thanks to Herr Becker's Spanish lessons, even I could catch the gist of the conversation.

It was hard to imagine a greater contrast than these two would-be grandparents. Emilia was younger than Henning, had never married and always acted the matron lady. Her apron, her hair and even her canvas shoes were black. The fair-haired Henning, on the other hand, favoured white, or at least bright clothes, golden bracelets and chains and braided shoes, and looked much younger than Emilia. Any encyclopaedia could have used them as illustrations for prototypes from northern and southern Europe. Emilia's round face bore a proud expression; she didn't exactly feel she was a maid, even though she put her all into scrubbing the stone floors. She had lived here since she was a girl and had been granted lifelong tenancy rights (as opposed to Cora or, for that matter, me). Henning's aggressive features I liked rather less, they reminded me in a way of Klaus Kinski, although Cora could never go along with that comparison. In unsophisticated adventure movies, the baddies always wear black, the goodies white; where Emilia and Henning were concerned, it seemed to me the roles had been reversed.

That was the start of a very pleasant period for me. Whenever Béla was hungry early in the morning, I could rest assured that Emilia would slip into my room and lift him out of his pram. In her spacious kitchen, he would be bathed, fed and petted until he went back to sleep. So I could rise late and breakfast with Cora. Most days, Henning was already on the golf course at the crack of dawn, and he would usually have his morning coffee in the clubhouse. In the course of the day, my son would be snatched from my arms by Henning, Emilia and Cora in turn.

Every day, Cora and I would drive out in Henning's car to do the shopping, coming back with a car load of Pampers, jars of baby-food, grapes, ham and cheese, chocolate and bunches of flowers. Emilia made a constant supply of minestrone, which stood on the stove for anyone to help themselves, but we went out for a meal most evenings, leaving Emilia alone with Béla and her minestrone. Within a week,

I had browned nicely in the spring sunshine and had been transformed from the hassled, frazzled mother into a happy young woman. As for my loved ones back home, I had almost forgotten them.

'Would you call Henning a playboy?' Cora asked me. I didn't have to think long before answering. 'Absolutely.' She was pleased at that and looked positively impish.

I hadn't bothered to phone Jonas a second time and my bad conscience had been suppressed.

One morning, even Cora said, 'You really must get in touch again, or else Jonas will end up getting the police to look for you, or he'll start my parents wondering . . .'

'All right, this evening. He'll be on his rounds just now anyway.'

'And another thing, Maya, you've really landed me in a fine mess.'

'I'm sure your parents will take it all with good grace.'

'No, that's not what I mean. It's to do with Béla. Henning is daft about him. Yesterday, he came up with the bright idea of asking me, not for my hand, but for a baby.'

I was staggered. 'And what did you say to that?'

'I just laughed. But that hurt his feelings. He really meant it.'

That made me think. All right, Béla hadn't been wanted at first, far less planned, but all the same he was my everything. Cora read my thoughts. 'A sweet little thing like yours is an exception. Have a child by an old man, and you can expect a monster.'

'Cora, that's rubbish. And anyway, the prenatal check-ups can tell if there's anything wrong.'

Henning came home earlier than usual, just so as to enjoy Béla Barthel before bedtime. I was well aware that his liking for me was limited – I was welcome merely as the child's mother. Maybe he was looking to me for an ally. In the rare moments when he was alone with me, he tried to sound me out about Cora's past and her family. I was very chary. Apparently, Cora had spun him a tale about how she had fallen out with her parents and been cut off without a penny.

'I just can't understand a father like that,' said Henning.

'A professor he may be, but not even an academic has a right to be such a stranger to reality. A young girl, alone in Italy without a penny to her name, that can soon go very badly wrong.' He saw himself as a saviour, who had rescued Cora from a life of thieving and jail, prostitution and drugs.

I felt sorry for the professor, who continued to finance his daughter's studies, paying an adequate amount directly into her account, which she wasn't drawing on at the moment, but leaving it to appreciate. Henning was very generous and we lacked for nothing, not even spending money. He was planning major renovations for the villa, and Cora did all the running to tradesmen and architects, because she was afraid he might ruin the look of the place.

When I phoned Jonas, I heard a deep sigh of relief. 'At long last!' He had taken my father to hospital for observation, as his liver-function readings had given grounds for concern. They'd probably have to do a scan. And he would take steps to ensure, said Jonas, sounding very masterful, that Father would not come home to us from the hospital, but would go into a home. 'So when are you coming home, then?'

In the end, we arranged that Jonas would take a week's holiday and come and fetch Béla and myself.

From that moment on, the happy days were numbered. When Jonas arrived, tired out after driving all through the night, I was unable to raise the proper enthusiasm the occasion demanded. Of course, I was happy to be wrapped in my husband's arms, but the prospect of our poky flat and the greyness of everyday life made me miserable.

So we spent that final week together. Jonas slept with me in the narrow wrought-iron bed, we drove out to the race-course, called in on Henning at the golf club and wandered through Florence. Jonas shed his pallor just as quickly as I had done, he got handsomer and even a little jollier. Henning and he couldn't find much in common, although Jonas did take an interest in past escapades in Rio. As for me, I could hardly stomach those macho tales.

On the last evening, as the four of us sat at dinner in our favourite ristorante, Henning announced that he was going to marry Cora and that he wanted a child. Jonas could appreciate his point of view. So, the men were agreed; as for us women, we looked at each other and weighed up the advantages and disadvantages.

Once everyone was in bed, I quietly got up again and, as I had anticipated, came across Cora in the kitchen. It was still too cold to go out on to the terrace at night. The air smelt of the basil that Emilia was growing in tin cans on the windowsill. We moved closer to the coal-fired stove, which was still giving off heat, and put our thoughts into words.

'Maya, here's the way I see it: Henning wants a child, which is understandable, at his age. For him, marriage is only a means to an end. With me, it's the other way round – I don't want to have a baby, but getting married to a rich man is far from a bad move.'

'You never so much as mention the word love, Cora. Just imagine, if you were suddenly to fall for a young man.'

'Could happen, of course. If it came down to it, I'd get a divorce. In twenty years I'm bound to be a widow, then I can help myself.'

'But that's a long time! Do you only think of the money side of it?'

'If I'm honest about it – it is important to me. Just think, as his wife, I could do this house up after my own taste, have a studio put in and paint whenever the mood took me. I wouldn't bother tormenting myself with the language test and with studying, but take private lessons in painting instead. This house would be great for having marvellous parties and inviting interesting people.'

'So what about Henning?'

'So, what about Jonas?'

We had to admit that we hardly made the perfect wives. 'Right then, accept him, Cora! And if I were you, I'd have the child into the bargain, otherwise you're not being fair.'

'Good God, is Henning being fair, wanting to start a family with a nineteen-year-old?' Cora reckoned she had a perfect right to go on taking the pill, secretly as before.

Just as we were about to slip back into bed beside our men, we met Emilia in the darkened hall.

'Sometimes I get the feeling she's eavesdropping,' said Cora, 'but then again, she only speaks Italian.'

'That may well be, but she's no fool. I get the impression she knows all about every one of us.'

On the following day, we said our fond farewells. Béla, who throughout the whole time in Italy had hardly cried at all, turned downright rebellious and yelled his head off. Henning cuddled the child, Cora hugged me, and Jonas was left with Emilia, whom he shook by the hand while assuring her of his gratitude. Then we drove off towards the grey north, leaving the couple alone with their plans for the future.

We had gone about half way, with neither of us having uttered a word for a good two hours, when I announced firmly, 'One thing I must do is learn to drive.'

'Yes,' said Jonas.

With the sleeping child on my arm, I went up the stairs to our flat, while Jonas struggled to unload the pram and the cases from the car. I opened the door and knew at once from the smell: Father hadn't gone. Either that, or he had come back again. He lay asleep on the sofa, surrounded by empty bottles. The window was tightly closed and you could have cut the air with a knife. I went back downstairs with Béla.

'You can drive us straight back to the station,' I raged at Jonas. 'Father's upstairs.'

Jonas was so shocked he dropped one of the baby's bottles. 'I swear he wasn't supposed to be discharged from the hospital for another week. I arranged everything, so that he'd be transferred from there to a home.'

Obviously, the home was an institution for drying out drunks, and, faced with this prospect, Father had taken off. Jonas took Béla from me and went upstairs to take a look at the whole mess for himself.

'After you left, I had to let him have a front door-key,' Jonas said by way of an apology. 'Otherwise, he wouldn't have been able to leave the house. But of course I should have taken the key from him when he went into hospital.'

We were both dead tired, and it was late, so we went

straight to bed after I had changed ‚Béla. This is a great start, I thought angrily. I'm not stopping here.

The next morning brought no happy dawn. Jonas went off to work, I had to take care of Béla on my own, and Father lay on the sofa, impossible to wake. In the end, I poured cold water over his face. He leapt up in such a fury that he dealt me a slap across the face. He wasn't going to get away with that, not with me; I gave him such a kick on the shins that he fell back on to the sofa, moaning and groaning.

'Father, things can't go on like this. If you're going to sprawl about here as if you owned the place, I'm going back to Italy.'

'Go ahead, then. It was fine and comfortable here without you and that bawling brat. What did I ever do to deserve such a nagging bitch for a daughter!'

'Father, are you seriously trying to ruin my marriage? Do you want me to leave my husband because of you?'

'A good marriage will stand up to strains. If it can't, it's no good anyway.'

I didn't waste another word on him. More than anything else, I would have loved to throw him out with the rubbish. I hoped the people at the hospital might have discovered some incurable disease. But Jonas phoned them and heard that Father had fled before they had been able to complete the necessary diagnostic tests. They were furious at his behaviour and didn't want him back. Besides, he had pestered the nurses with indecent suggestions. That was the last straw, even for the patient, good-as-gold Jonas. He grabbed Father by the collar, bundled him into the car and drove him, without so much as a word, to the 'home'. When he arrived back, he was quite proud of himself. 'Everything's going to be all right again now,' he told me, fully convinced that we'd once again be the 'happy little family' we had never been.

There followed a few peaceful weeks, during which I did the cleaning and cooking and took my turn at doing the stairs. Not that I enjoyed it one bit. I was keen to take driving lessons, but Jonas was always so late in getting home that there was no time for that; after all, it was then his turn to look after Béla.

One day, Jonas's mother phoned, a sensation for such an uncommunicative woman. His father was in a bad way. The doctor had said he should take things easy and pass the heavy work over to his sons. Jonas felt duty bound to help, and I could see he was turning something over in his mind.

A week later, it all came out. 'Maya, what do you think of us moving in with my parents? We'd have two rooms to ourselves and wouldn't have to pay rent. There'd be a lot of advantages for you, for there are always a lot of women about our house who could help out with Barthel – Mother, Grandmother, my sisters. You could take your driving lessons and maybe even take up a course of study. I really would like to help my father out, and anyway, I'm not exactly enjoying being a pharmaceuticals rep.'

That was the longest speech Jonas had ever made. I felt like throwing the sticky noodle-strainer in his face, but I kept a grip on myself. Some aspects of this plan did have advantages for us both that were worth thinking about. But the prospect of living on the farm, of sitting down to meals every day with the whole Döring family, of sharing the bathroom with other people and, finally, of having to go through the motions of lending a hand in the cowshed and in the fields gave me the shudders. Then I pictured Béla in lederhosen. I cried a little, trying to use feminine wiles to get through to Jonas that I was not best pleased with the idea. Then, for some days after, we skirted round the subject of life down on the farm.

Cora's parents phoned, very concerned. In her latest postcard, their daughter had mentioned something about getting married, and did I know anything more about it? I went to see the Schwabs and tried to choose my words carefully to hint to them that Henning was no spring chicken. They looked at me in consternation. No, I said, I didn't know exactly how old.

'If we had her new address, h'm, yes,' said the professor, 'we'd be off tomorrow.'

Naturally enough, Cora's parents expected me to help them out. With some reluctance, I coughed up the desired address and telephone number. The professor went into action right away and dialled the number in Florence, fortunately without success. Emilia hardly ever answered the phone, Cora and Henning weren't at home.

Frau Schwab spoke up: 'In my youth, parents used to get hot and bothered about an unmarried couple living together; nobody objects to cohabitation these days. Instead, it's marrying rashly or too soon that's not on.'

Since I had married too young and without due consideration, I sat shamefaced and said nothing.

'Well, yes, but when something as lovely as Béla is the result' – the professor tried to be conciliatory – 'then I could put up with anything.' And he kissed the little fellow.

Back home, I rang the Florence number every ten minutes to try to reach Cora before her parents did. When I finally got to speak to her, she flew into a rage. 'That's all I need, my old folks suddenly turning up on my doorstep!'

'But, Cora, it was you yourself that wrote to them about the wedding; they deserve better than for you to tell them nothing more about it.'

'I suppose you're right, but I know that, whatever happens, they'll start bellyaching.' I was well aware of that, too. 'We've fixed to get married in four weeks. Naturally, you and Béla are invited, but I really don't want any other guests there. But if my parents find out about the date, there'll be no stopping them.'

The next day, everything went wrong. Béla developed a temperature and wouldn't eat a thing. I struggled with compresses for his legs, and, for the first time, it struck me that my mother had done the same for me. In the meantime, Cora's parents had found out how old the bridegroom was. They were beside themselves. To cap it all, Jonas came home early, looking, himself, like an old man. He had had news that his father had suffered a stroke and was now in hospital.

It was assumed that he'd get home right away to lend a hand. 'We've got to pack,' said Jonas.

'Béla's ill, we can't go off with a child that's running a high temperature.'

He rushed into the bedroom and picked up his feverish son. 'Barthelkins, soon you'll get to play with little pussycats, soon you'll be able to help Grandma to bake cakes and breathe good country air all day.'

'Will you be able to take some leave?' I asked.

'If they chuck me out, it won't bother me. The family comes first,' he replied.

Did Jonas mean by that his farming family, or Béla and me? It still didn't seem to have sunk in with him that I thoroughly detested a life in the country, however fresh the air might be. And anyway, what were we supposed to live on if he wasn't earning a wage, but slaving away in the cowshed and out in the fields instead? The reek of pig-dung, the kitchen swarming with flies, the coarse dialect, the unheated bedroom and the communal meals on wooden benches full of splinters, the very thought of it all made me feel physically sick. Was that where Béla was to grow up? His native heath might be paradise to Jonas, but for me it was hell. My paradise was Florence, and I resolved to take myself off there again. Cora was right, marrying a rich man. And his age was even an advantage – she'd outlive him three times over.

CHAPTER 10

Grass-Widow Green

At Easter time in Florence there is a procession, which I never take part in, and a fireworks display, which I always enjoy watching. On the occasion of the Festival of the Grass-hoppers, on Ascension Day, we head, like all Florentines, for the park and have a picnic, or, to be more precise, we buy bread and sucking pig at the stalls. Many children carry little cricket cages with them; Béla doesn't like that, but prefers a balloon instead.

I can't remember ever having gone to a public festival with my parents. When I was at last big enough to go with my brother Carlo, he did his systematic best to ruin the fun of the fair for me. He fixed it so that he was given my money as well, to buy the tickets for the dodgems for both of us, and then he ran off with it. When I think of it, I wouldn't like Béla to have brothers and sisters; he'd only be bound to end up coming off worst among them. But I am glad that he is growing up in Italy; it always was, and still is, the land of my dreams.

Once I had returned to Germany after my first sojourn in Florence, I no longer fancied my chilly fatherland one little bit. The child was ill, Jonas had to go to his mother's. Hardly had he left, than I was on the phone to Cora. She was in a state; her parents were on their way. So I announced that I, too, would be turning up as soon as I could.

'Thank God for that,' said Cora. 'You seem to have a positive effect on my parents. And anyway, Henning is constantly asking after Béla; with the child on his arm, he looks more like St Joseph than a playboy.'

There was certainly enough space in that big house, with even a room for Cora's parents.

'Have you started the renovation work yet?'

'You bet! The bathroom's turning out a dream; I've managed to get hold of Art Nouveau tiles! On top of that, we've bought some furniture, and in your room there's a wickerwork chair and the cushions are in a rose pattern. All right by you?'

I was delighted. Henning's money was being put to good use.

The doctor was very reassuring, Béla had nothing more than a cold. His temperature subsided as quickly as it had risen. Inside three days, the feverish, apathetic little bundle had turned back into a hungry and lovely little person. Béla was starting to talk, although no one would believe me. At six months, he was making an effort to say 'Dada', but only I had ears for that.

Jonas phoned, full of complaints. There was an enormous amount of work. Apparently, apart from himself, only two sisters were lending a hand. His youngest brother was only fifteen and still at boarding school, while the eldest – the Brother Bartholomäus who had taken holy orders – seemed to consider it beneath his dignity to climb on to a tractor in his monk's habit. I insisted that Béla was still too sick to travel, which worried Jonas no end.

As on the first occasion, I left a note for my husband and headed south with our child. This time, Henning came to meet me, Cora having stayed back at the house with her parents. They were all at the door to welcome us, all happy to see us. Emilia was almost in tears as Béla reached out towards her. My room had been lovingly done up. Henning had indeed invested in a cot, no doubt reckoning it would not be long before he needed it for a baby of his own.

It was very quickly obvious to me that Henning was bending over backwards to find favour with his future in-laws, and also that it wasn't doing a bit of good. All the same, the

Schwabs were not totally unimpressed: they had taken a real shine to the house. Cora's mother took great delight in discussing colours for painting the shutters for the windows. She was all for bluish-green, Cora for white, while I favoured olive. The professor, who had no inclination for gardening whatsoever, wheeled Béla from one shady tree to the next as he picked bay leaves for seasoning or pulled tough weeds out of the dry earth. In my mind's eye, I could see him spending his declining years in that garden. Whenever they had the chance of a quiet chat amongst themselves, the couple tried to talk Cora out of the idea of marriage.

One day, we were all sitting in the garden drinking Chianti. Henning had Béla on his knee. Suddenly the miracle occurred: my son said, clearly and distinctly, 'Papa'. Tears welled up in the old playboy's eyes. That apart, Béla came out with not another single intelligible word in the months that followed.

Emilia tried hard to teach my son Italian. She didn't like his name. Often, she would call him 'Bellino', or, when his nappies were full, 'Bel Paese'. But I also listened in admiration as she got her tongue round the jaw-breaking German term of endearment, '*Schätzchen*'.

The Schwabs left – after all, the professor did have a job to do. Cora had to promise her parents that she would think everything over and at least do the language examination first.

The couple had scarcely left the house when the wedding preparations began. In this respect, Henning had just as few scruples as Cora. I couldn't help feeling uneasy, but at the same time I wanted to play my part as witness. I phoned Jonas to ask whether he would like to come to the ceremony. In a huff, he demanded, 'Is that all you've got to worry about? Why don't you get in touch more often? Don't you think I want to know how Barthel's getting on?'

So there were just a few close friends at the celebrations. Some acquaintances from the golf club, some students from Cora's class, that was the lot. But when we returned to our pink villa after the wedding supper, we found a ragged figure leaning against the wrought-iron gate. My father.

'Who in all the world is that?' asked Henning.

I very much hoped he wouldn't let my father in, but when Cora answered, 'Maya's dad,' he went into raptures and shook him by both hands.

I didn't so much as greet my father. He obviously had some sort of instinct for knowing where a wedding was being celebrated, probably because there was always plenty to drink at such occasions. Glowering, I followed Cora, Henning and my father into the house. Emilia brought Béla to me, full of how good he had been.

Henning asked Cora to bring something to eat for our guest. We all sat at a round table, and Father talked about how he had given his minders the slip and managed to escape. He had then asked the professor for Cora's address, claiming he wanted to write to me. In two days, he had hitchhiked his way to the house, no trouble at all.

I had to give Father a good grilling before he admitted that he had gone to our flat first and then, when he found no one there, the farm. Everyone had been out in the fields, all except the old grandmother. With a shout of, 'This is no place for scroungers!' she had chased him off with a broom. I had the feeling the old woman was furious at me and all my tribe. How she would have loved to be able to show off her great-grandson in his little saffron-yellow jacket!

Henning was greatly taken with my father, who immediately started to play the fool when he saw how well that went down. Once the wine and the grappa were on the table, the inevitable booze-up followed. Henning, too, had his fair share and more. On her very wedding night, Cora needed Emilia's help to haul her inebriated husband off to his bed, while we left my father lying where he was on the carpet.

We were back sitting in the kitchen again. Astonishingly, Cora was not in the least put out, whereas I was boiling. 'I come here to try to find some peace, and he's right at my heels.'

'Maya, you're just so like him. When something doesn't suit you, you both simply clear off.'

'Well, even Goethe did a runner from Frau von Stein and came to Italy,' I said defiantly. I thought of another parallel: Father and I both had someone on our conscience.

'I'll have a word with Henning in the morning,' said Cora. 'He's not such a wimp as Jonas; he'll have your father on his way back to Germany before you can blink, maybe even with the strong arm of the law behind him.'

I had my doubts. My father was impossible to shake off and would cling tenaciously to his chance of a place in the sun.

Henning was a strange character, and we really couldn't fathom him. He loved the adventure stories of Karl May, and he loved babies – the latter only since he had met Béla. He had a marriage to a boring woman behind him, and no doubt any number of bits on the side. On the one hand, he had had to struggle hard in life and could tell a tale or two about crooks and blackmailers, and yet he could be sentimental and loved to play the benefactor. After only two days, he was doting on my father; he bought him a suit and took him along with him to his very posh golf club. Cora's warnings went unheeded. As long as Father and Henning were out and about, we couldn't complain. But they no sooner arrived home than the drinking started. This side of Henning, which is nothing unusual in the building trade, had been hidden from us up till now. Cora cursed. 'If there's one thing I detest, it's drunken men.'

She started humming quietly. 'Do you remember that sad wedding song by Béla Bartók that we learned in school?' I sang along:

> 'Thus sent the mother her little daughter
> Into a distant land,
> Sternly she bid her: "Follow thy husband!
> Never return to me!"
>
> "Lo! I shall change me into a blackbird,
> Shall fly to Mother's home;
> There I'll be waiting, perch'd in her garden
> On a white lily's stem."

Out came the mother: ''Who is this blackbird?
Strange is her song and sad.
Forth and begone now, thou little birdling,
From my white lily's stem!''

''To a bad husband, Mother, hast sent me
Forth to a distant land.
Hard 'tis to suffer such bitter pining,
In an ill-mated bond.'''

Cora took up the tune and improvised:

'With a playboy, old and raddled, Mother,
Hast sent me to a distant land.
Ah, dear Mother mine, now must I weep
Far from my own dear land.'

We decided we had to put a spanner in the works of this
new pals act between the two men. It was easy enough to
stir them up. 'Henning said . . .' we began, and made it clear
to my father that his host didn't take him seriously. We went
about it with Henning more or less the same way: Father
regarded him as a washed-up, randy upstart. We had a great
deal of fun, but unfortunately it didn't produce results right
away.

The whole thing came to a head only when Henning, the
worse for drink, tried to lay down the law to his young wife
that he expected to have a son in exactly nine months' time.
The stink on his breath nauseated Cora and she slipped into
the iron bedstead beside me. Henning beat a tattoo on my
locked door and kicked up a shocking racket. In the end,
Emilia woke – if, that is, she had been asleep at all – and,
with soothing words, led her master back to his bed.

'Here I am, only a few days married, and already I can't
stand him any more,' Cora sobbed.

'It's all Father's fault, he has to go. It used to be that
Henning would drink only two glasses of wine with his meal.
When we get rid of Father, everything will be all right again.'

But Cora was inconsolable. As she saw it, Father had

brought Henning's true nature to the surface, and for that we should be grateful to him.

Our new tactics involved staying away from the house as much as possible. With Béla, we would go and visit all the friends Cora had in Florence. We would sit in the Boboli Gardens, rummage about in the shops around the Via dei Calzaiuoli, spend hours staring down from the Ponte alle Grazie into the Arno, and we eventually did go into the Uffizi galleries. But, sooner or later, we had to go home, where at least one of them would be completely smashed.

As a rule, Father would have nothing to do with his grandson, whom he regarded as a nuisance. But it almost pained me more whenever he stood, pie-eyed, by the cot, coming out with the most nauseatingly sentimental 'Diddle-diddle-dum-dum'. And my stupid son would be cooing with delight.

Henning, for his part, was not to be underestimated. For one thing, he had found out from the professor that Cora was indeed receiving a study allowance every month, for another, he didn't believe my father had threatened Béla and me, and thirdly, he had discovered that his wife was carrying on taking the pill as before. To forestall any excuse she might try to make, he had been checking, over a week, her daily intake against the number of missing tablets. If there was one thing he couldn't stomach, it was being taken for an idiot. There was a row. Against that, though, he said he 'couldn't give a tinker's fart' that Cora was after his money, and that he had got to know her when she was in the act of trying to rob him. In his youth, he claimed, he himself had pulled every trick in the book to get rich.

Whenever Cora was going upstairs in front of Henning, he had the habit of pinching her backside. Cora would just nip him back. Sometimes Henning slipped up and mistook Emilia or me for his wife. Thanks to my sharp reaction, that happened only once with me.

On her twentieth birthday, Cora promised to lay off the pill. There were other means to the same end, she reckoned. There was a very noisy reconciliation in bed, something that, in that house, escaped the notice only of Béla. The next day, Henning was very considerate, bringing a bunch of white roses in from the garden, and, in the time that followed, he drank nothing but mineral water. He referred to my father, the child and myself as the 'refugee family', with a mockery I didn't like in the least. I had an uneasy feeling that my days there were numbered.

Cora assured me, 'His money belongs to me, and so it's your money too.'

Even Father was off the drink in the days that followed. However, Henning's efforts to motivate him towards some light work in the overgrown garden met with no success whatsoever. Father was too far gone, past it. One morning, he had to be taken, in a state of shock, to hospital, with sirens blaring and blue light flashing. His bout of vomiting blood was put down to a dilation of the veins in his gullet, the result of long-standing cirrhosis of the liver, the doctor in the intensive-care unit informed us. I hoped my father wouldn't regain consciousness.

But some days later, when, on Henning's urging, we went to visit him, Father said, 'You can't keep a good man down.' They were going to operate on him with lasers. With a wink, he asked Henning not to bring flowers the next time, but something drinkable.

Without Father around, life became much cosier again. As in the old days, Henning wanted no more than two glasses of wine with his meals, and we enjoyed lots of laughs. Sometimes he would talk about earlier women in his life.

'The two of you remind me of one of my first girlfriends. In those days, I was young and inexperienced, I hadn't made my fortune yet and was still single. I got to know this Chinese girl who had only recently come to live in Rio. Mary Wang came from Shanghai, she spoke pidgin English and was really sweet.'

'And what are we supposed to have in common with her?' Cora asked.

'Your fondness for *dolce far niente* and your lust for money,' said Henning with singular lack of gallantry.

'I always thought the Chinese were supposed to be busy

little bees,' I said, more than a little put out, since I had spent that very day painting all the garden chairs.

'Mary Wang had a special motto, I'll tell you what it was: "Me no savvy . . ."'

'What does "savvy" mean?' Cora interrupted him.

'It comes from the French, from *savoir*, to know. So it went like this:

> "Me no savvy,
> Me no care,
> Me go marry
> Millionaire.
>
> If he die,
> Me no cry.
> Me go marry
> Other guy."'

That got a laugh; the maxim appealed to us, but not Henning's expression as he delivered it.

And anyway, we weren't as lazy as Henning believed. All right, when he was out on the golf course in the mornings, we would have a long, leisurely breakfast, but after that we had an extremely busy schedule. Almost daily, there were tradesmen around, with whom Cora carried on a running battle. She was having a studio built. And as for me, well, I had a child to look after. On top of all that, since I shared Emilia's company for so much of the time, I was having great fun learning vocabulary from Cora's Italian course-books. Emilia would test me and correct my efforts, feeling very important in her role as teacher and child's nurse.

'So what became of Mary Wang?' I asked Henning over dinner one evening.

'Prostitute. No grass widow her, not like you.'

Cora didn't like answering the phone, having no desire to talk to her parents. Usually, I had to invent excuses for her not being there. 'Has my daughter Cornelia finally put all ideas of that dreadful marriage out of her head?' the professor

124

would ask every time. Hesitantly, I would suggest he'd better ask her that. Frau Schwab was full of how Cora's brother had sat his exams and broken off with his fiancée. Very soon, he'd be coming back to Germany and would certainly want to visit his sister.

Only on rare occasions did Jonas phone, since he regarded international calls as a luxury he could ill afford. However, since I was not in the least interested in listening to his reproaches, it was entirely up to him if he wanted to have news of his Barthel.

Sometimes Cora and I would talk about our future. In her case, it was all clear cut: as soon as the studio was finished, she was going to paint every day, perhaps even take private lessons and finally become famous. Henning no longer got even a mention in her plans.

It was a different matter for me. Would I be able just to stay on in Florence, with Cora and Henning? Was I not every bit as much a parasite as my father? Was it right for me to dump Jonas, without so much as a by-your-leave? He had never done me any harm. If he could live in Florence and continue his studies – that would have been marvellous. As far as a career was concerned, it was my dream to stay here and study Italian, and finally to get a job as a translator.

'Do you know who I sometimes feel is standing in my way?' asked Cora. 'You'll hardly credit it, but it's Emilia. Sure, it's very handy having her to do the housework and the cooking. But, against that, her two attic rooms would have made a much better studio than the north-facing one on the first floor. But I know you're very fond of her because she does such a great job of looking after Béla . . .'

That wasn't the only reason I liked Emilia, but also because she would catch the spiders in my room and deposit them outside in the garden. I often went up to see her in her apartment. She had hauled a pine chest down from the loft, unscrewed its lid and transformed it into a bed for Béla. Nowadays, he slept up here more often than in my room. In the evenings, Emilia was in the habit of going off early up to her room, where she would lie on the bed watching television. Béla would lie, perfectly content, in his chest next to her. Since I went out for a meal with Cora and Henning most evenings, I'd often look in on Emilia quite late on, to gaze on my sleeping child. Sometimes I was almost jealous of this self-appointed grandmother who had struck up such a perfect symbiosis with Béla. She would sing for him, *'Ma come balli bene bella bimba,'* and, at the word *'bella,'* he would slap his hands on the table.

The Tuscan summer was approaching, it was getting hot. Henning talked of going off to the coast with Cora; obviously I didn't figure in his plans. We bought a plastic sandpit and filled it with water, so that Béla could splash around in it, while I could cool my feet. Cora's parents sent word they would be paying us a visit; her brother was expected back from God's Own Country and they were going to have a holiday together in Colle di Val d'Elsa – did we fancy joining them? About their daughter's marriage, they were blissfully ignorant. Cora turned down their offer and begged me to break the news gently to them.

In the meantime, we had learned that Henning was prone to going on a binge every now and then. He had admitted he suffered from periodic bouts of alcoholism; in his youth, these had occurred every three months, but now they came at irregular intervals.

'You know,' she said, 'he's really been conning me. Never mind, though, what you predicted has happened.'

'What do you mean?'

'You know – a young man . . .'

'You've fallen in love?'

'Not exactly. Now don't go all moralistic on me! I've been cheating on Henning.'

'But who with? We've always gone everywhere together.'

'Ruggero.'

I didn't know any Ruggero. She explained he was the glazier's apprentice, seventeen and gorgeous with it. Unfortunately, the work on the studio windows was nearly finished.

A deceptive peace prevailed. Cora was being unfaithful to

her husband, I was expecting the return of my convalescent father, maybe even of Jonas, who wanted to take me and his Barthel back with him, and now Henning was acting at times as if Béla was his own son. He would go for walks with us in the cool of the evening, pushing the pram and insisting Cora and I walked on either side, like decorative accessories for him to show off. We always had to do ourselves up. Although he was friendly enough towards me, I was growing to like him less and less. I became jumpy and was suffering from the heat. Nothing had been decided about when anyone was going away, or even if they were, and who was going with whom. Emilia, up in her stifling attic, seemed to be the least affected by the heat. One day, she sang to me the song about thoughts being free – '*Die Gedanken sind frei*' – and in German at that.

'Where did you learn that song?' I asked in amazement. For my part, I was now able to carry on a conversation in Italian.

Emilia dug out an old-fashioned song book and read from it. When she was still young, but already working in the house, a German archaeologist had lived there, renting a flat, and he had taught her some sad songs to ease the homesickness that was plaguing him. She knew all the words of the songs in the book. There had probably been some romantic affair involved, but I didn't dare ask such personal questions. Whatever it was, Emilia knew a few bits of German, perhaps more than we had assumed.

'So what?' said Cora. 'We've nothing to hide from her.'

Once Emilia had revealed her secret treasury of songs to me, she got into the habit of working in a few German quotations. When Henning heard this, he barked at me, 'Why do you have to go and teach her such an antiquated kind of German? It suited me just fine that she couldn't understand a word of our conversations. If you're wanting Béla's first words to be German and not Italian, then it would fit you better to look after him yourself.' That cut me to the quick.

Emilia also had a special knack in her choice of presents. For his birthday, Henning got an antiquated Swabian coffeepot with the inscription: 'Where coffee's served, no harm will you befall; it's evil folk who turn to alcohol'.

One sweltering August day, Cora and I decided we would get up early the next morning and drive to Marina di Pisa on the coast. Henning didn't want to come, as he said he had arranged an important golf match. 'It's really that he's afraid the sea breezes will uncover his bald patch,' said Cora, and we drove off in the car with Béla, while Henning was left to take a taxi.

At the seaside, it was noisy, busy, dirty and wonderful. We hired a parasol and laid out our things near a surfing school. Béla was in his element, crawling all over the place as to the manner born. There was so much for him to see and grab at, that by midday he lay down on our mat and fell fast asleep. Cora had a try at surf-boarding, getting in tow with some handsome young Romeos, who kept helping her back on to her board. But she did take her turn to sit by my child and look after him while I went for a splash about in the water. In between times, we fetched takeaway pizzas to eat with our fingers. Things like mineral water, fruit and baby-food we had brought with us. It was a fantastic day, and I felt quite young and carefree again. 'This is the way it should always be,' I said to Cora.

'A teensy-weensy little yacht wouldn't go amiss either,' she added.

Lazing about had made us tired, and it was quite late when we headed for home. If we had known what was waiting for us there, we'd have stayed all night at the seaside.

CHAPTER 11

White as Alabaster

Sometimes the clouds look like crocodiles. When my tourists are getting a crick in the neck from gazing up at the cupola of the cathedral and I'm saying for the hundredth time that the name 'Santa Maria del Fiore' refers to the lily in the city's coat of arms, I'm usually not looking at Brunelleschi's masterpiece at all, but at the changing patterns formed by the clouds instead. I discover more than just alligators in the sky; there are also angry hunters, angels with trumpets, devils with three-pronged pitchforks and other figures from the Last Judgement cavorting around above me. Sometimes it frightens me. At the moment, my life is running along what you might call orderly lines, if you disregard my little swindles and thievery. I'm earning good money and I look good, I have the most darling son and good friends – but my faith in the future is none too great. There are things in my life I have not yet come to terms with. Among them, that night when Cora and I returned, with our sleeping child, to the pink villa after our outing to the coast.

All was amazingly quiet in the house. I carried Béla into my room, so as not to disturb Emilia. Cora headed straight for the bathroom. A few minutes later, we went into the kitchen together to rustle up something to eat.

Both my father and Henning were lying bleeding on the terrazzo floor, with cuts on their faces, lacerations on their heads, smashed bottles and broken glass all over the place. There was a stench of vomit. Both of them were blind drunk, and badly injured as well. Their snoring sounded more like a death rattle. We stood speechless with revulsion. In the end, I went over to the sink and filled a bucket with water, intending to throw it over my father.

'Wait,' said Cora, almost inaudibly, 'this is a chance we'll never have again.'

I looked at her, puzzled. Cora took a kitchen towel and wrapped it round the neck of a bottle. Gripping this weapon and with a determined look on her face, she stepped over towards Henning, drew her arm back, and then let it drop again, the heavy bottle hanging by her side. 'I can't do it. After all, I've slept with the man.' Her face distorted, she held out the Chianti bottle towards me.

I took hold of it with both hands and brought it straight down on his head, three times, with all the force I could muster. There was a distinct sound of something cracking. But somewhere deep inside of me, too, a dam burst: all that pent-up, unbelievable rage at all those people with a better life than mine was released in a sudden discharge like a thunderstorm breaking.

Cora watched me with rapt concentration. Then we heard a quiet 'Bravo', and looked up to see Emilia standing in the doorway. Now Cora took the bottle from me and, trembling, turned towards my father. 'Get out, both of you,' she ordered in Italian.

'You're out of your minds,' said Emilia. 'Give me the bottle!'

I staggered out of the kitchen. What on earth was Cora intending to do? Only once she was standing by my side and we could hear strange noises coming from the kitchen did I realize she had wanted to beat my father to death, and now Emilia was carrying on the job for her.

Emilia came in. 'You'll have to call an ambulance. You'll tell them you've only just come home – I'll back you up on that – and found the two of them in this state.'

Cora and I lit up cigarettes. It was one of the very few I had smoked in my life. Cora went unsteadily to the phone.

'How long has Maya's father been here?' she asked Emilia, who said she didn't know. She had been watching television and had paid no attention to the racket downstairs on the ground floor. I very much doubted my father had been discharged from hospital. More likely, he had run away again.

The ambulance was not long in coming. They lifted the two bodies on to stretchers and loaded them in carefully. Apparently they were not dead.

Cora, Emilia and I sat in the kitchen shivering in spite of the heat of the night. We were rid of those troublesome men, for the time being at least, but could feel no triumph at our victory. We were terrified out of our wits.

'Henning's face was as white as alabaster,' Cora said in a whisper.

Emilia took my son up to her room, so as to find some peace by his side, while I slipped into the empty double bed beside Cora.

'Wouldn't it be the right thing to do,' Cora said, 'if I were to go to the hospital and sit in tears, waiting for news from the doctors? How is it going to look, us not going along with them? Come on, we've got to get dressed again and drive in.'

I found it a struggle to get back out of the soothing comfort of the bed. We told Emilia we were going to the hospital. She nodded. 'Clever girls.'

At the hospital, we were treated with every consideration and taken to the senior doctor's room. From the look on the sister's face, every patient in the place had died. But that, it turned out, was not the case. We learned that Henning had a double fracture at the base of the skull, with a discharge of brain matter, and was to be operated on at once. While my father was unconscious, his condition was not critical. They knew all about him already, because he had only that day done a vanishing act from that very hospital. There were no signs of broken bones on his x-ray. There was nothing we could do there for the moment, said the duty doctor, so we should get off home. They would be in touch by telephone if necessary. Much relieved, we drove off.

As we lay in bed for the second time, Cora, in a sudden panic, said, 'Do you think your father was able to see what you were doing?'

'I hardly think so. The two of them were absolutely dead to the world.'

Our sleep was a brief one. There was a phone call from the hospital to tell us that Henning had not survived the operation. We were still pulling on our clothes again when the police phoned, too. We were not to shift anything at the scene of the crime, and they would be there shortly. 'I'm going to take this green dress off again,' said Cora. 'This calls for black. Give me your linen dress, would you?'

Before we had even finished dressing for mourning, the doorbell rang; the police were there. Emilia, with the crying Béla in her arms, opened the door. On the stairs, Cora, still struggling to pull black tights over her tanned legs, strained to hear what she was saying. 'I hope Emilia doesn't bugger it up,' she said, and hurried down.

When we came into the living-room, Emilia was talking like a torrent. But the policemen stopped listening as Cora made her entrance. So young, so beautiful, and yet already dealt such a blow by cruel fate! The guardians of the law leapt to their feet, apologized for having to be there at such a time and tried to find adequate words for their sympathy. Cora sank into an armchair and was brought a glass of water. After a brief pause, Emilia started talking again. She told them of the terrible excesses on the part of the two drunks, of the misery suffered by the two young ladies and of how everyone had breathed more easily when my father had been in hospital and Henning had gone over to mineral water.

Now the scene of the crime was inspected. She had cleaned things up a little, said Emilia with all the innocence of peasant cunning. The policemen gathered up bottles and broken glass, photographed the bloodstains and marked out with chalk the presumed positions of the injured men on the bloodied floor. We gave our versions, too, telling of our horror when we arrived back from the coast the previous evening. Cora had pulled herself together and was able to tell them exactly which surfing school we had set up our things next to, where we had bought our pizza and which filling station we had stopped at. I just kept backing her up on everything, but my role was of no interest to the officers.

Once the police had left, we drove to the hospital. My father, we heard, was improving, but would be unfit for questioning for some time yet. They had done everything they could to save Henning, but, with such severe injuries, his death had been inevitable. Did Cora want to see him? She said she didn't feel up to that. She had to fill out a form giving her consent to a post-mortem examination. At last, we were able to go home. 'We must have a talk with Emilia right away,' said Cora. 'I hope you realize she's in a position to blackmail us. Besides, I didn't hear everything she said to the policemen. Anyway, I'm rich now; we can start making plans, but outwardly we have to act very restrained.'

Emilia was waiting for us; Béla was asleep. She reached for Cora's cigarettes without stopping to ask. It was clear she had sized up the situation. But as soon as she started to speak, we were reassured. Emilia had covered us from all sides and was making no demands. 'Every cloud has a silver lining,' she said. We sat drinking espresso and grappa and smoking, and then at last set about cleaning up the kitchen. When Béla woke and demanded to be fed, some kind of normality returned; we tried to hide our trembling nervousness and our distractedness from the child, playing the usual little baby games.

In the heat of midday, we all went for a lie-down, but sleep was beyond Cora and me, and we talked on in a whisper.

'I've got this weird feeling we're far from out of the woods yet,' said Cora. 'It has all gone too smoothly. Your father will come back, unless they stick him in jail. And I don't trust Emilia one little bit, she's much too crafty for an old servant. Right from the start, she's been able to understand any amount of German without letting on; what reason could she possibly have for helping us if there's nothing in it for her?'

'True. We'll have to make her an offer. Have you any idea how much you're going to inherit?'

'No. I've never talked straight out with Henning about how much he was worth. But I do know he owns apartment blocks in Rio. And I also know that Emilia always wanted a dog, because her previous employers wouldn't allow it. Henning wouldn't let her, either. Now she shall have one, even if it's only as a sweetener.' I pictured Béla romping around with a dog, which was certainly preferable to cows and pigs. Cora went on, 'Maybe it was some kind of premonition, but recently I finished with Ruggero, so that means, thank heavens, he'll not be showing up here.'

'I thought it was so terrific with him?'

'It was, twice, but then it wore off. The poor kid had fallen in love with me, and I can't be bothered with adolescent infatuation.'

'Sometimes I get the feeling you've never been in love.'

'Clever girl! Maybe I'm not like you. As a matter of fact, I find women much more lovable than men, although, mind you, I'm afraid I don't have any lesbian leanings.'

'But there are lots of wonderful men. Just think of your father, for one!'

'Maybe that's exactly the trouble. I'll never find one like my daddy anyway.'

'Good God, you've got an ideal father and you're all screwed up, so who am I to talk, with a shambles of an old man like mine?'

At that, we were able to raise a laugh, and now we made fun of our long-forgotten psychotherapy. When we went back to the kitchen and came across Emilia, all three of us fell upon the stocks of ice-cream in the freezer.

Emilia sat rocking Béla in her arms. '. . . by morning, if God wills, you will waken again,' she crooned.

Suddenly, I no longer liked the sound of these words from her lips. Was it right for me to entrust her with my child so casually? Had she realized that I had killed Henning, or did she think we were just wanting to teach him a lesson? Obviously, she hadn't laid into my father as I had at first thought. After all, she was so much stronger than us, and it would have been no problem for her.

Cora went off in the car to buy herself some stylish widow's weeds, taking Emilia with her, to drop her off at the supermarket. In the days that followed, we intended to eat at home. As she left the house, Cora was snapped by a photographer. Next morning, there was a large picture of her in the paper: *Brazilian millionaire clubbed to death by German drinking companion. Beautiful young widow carrying his unborn child.* Not a word of it was true.

I was alone with my child when the bell rang. My first reaction was to ignore it, because I didn't much fancy any dealings with the police without Cora around. But in the end I did open the door; it would be a mistake to act as if we had a guilty conscience.

There, before me, stood Cora's brother, Friedrich.

I had lived so long without a man, always alone in my bed. At least in this respect I missed Jonas: after all, I was young and at this time more than ever in need of loving support. Without warning, I threw my arms round Friedrich's neck.

Cora's parents had sent him as a mediator, since they were extremely worried. On the one hand, they had the distinct feeling that their daughter would allow no interference in her love life, yet, on the other, they were suffering, out of a sense of responsibility, under the impression that they might not have intervened soon enough.

But at this moment, that didn't come into it. Friedrich, who, back then in Tuscany, had distanced himself from Annie and fallen for me, couldn't believe his eyes. In my state of agitation, I was thirsting for familiar male company like someone in a delirium in the desert. We made love as if we had been waiting ages for just that moment. Only after that did I tell him what, in fact, had to be said sooner or later: his sister had married and had today become a widow. Her rich husband had been killed by my father in a drunken brawl. By now, I almost believed this version myself, since after all it wasn't the first time Father had behaved in such a way.

It was a good thing that Friedrich was there now. He was a great help with all the formalities that were about to confront Cora; he dealt with the legal matters and went with his sister to the notary and to the consulate. He was able to break the news gently to their parents and yet fend them off.

Friedrich and I made up for all I had had to go without in the last months; I never gave Jonas a thought. For all the stress in the house of mourning, I was happy, slightly hyped up, unable to think of what the future might hold. Cora looked on our loving bliss without envy, even with approval; she had always known, she said, that we'd 'click sooner or later'.

Emilia, for all that she knew Jonas as well, still took Friedrich to her heart. Obviously she wasn't one of those pillars of morality, for it couldn't have escaped her notice that Cora had relinquished the use of the double bed to me. So there we were now, three young people, a small child and an elderly lady, all living together here and getting along like a house on fire.

Cora's studio was finished, and straight away she began painting. Her brother asked, 'Who are you trying to outdo this time? Michelangelo or Giotto?'

Her answer came with great seriousness. 'I'm going to be a modern-day Artemisia Gentileschi.'

Both Friedrich and I gaped at Cora in bafflement. 'And who's that supposed to be?' I asked, and her brother added, 'Stop showing off.'

'I don't hold the gap in your education against you, because you haven't seen the exhibition. Artemisia was born about four hundred years ago, and her favourite subject was Judith chopping off the head of Holofernes. She's helped by a maid who holds the fellow down on his bed.'

'The only one like that I know of is by Guido Reni,' I said, trying to sound knowledgeable, although the topic was not altogether to my liking.

But worse was to come. Cora said, 'I want you to sit as my model for Judith, Maya. Maybe Emilia will be willing to take the part of the maid. Friedrich, will you be Holofernes for me?'

'No, thank you. Now you've gone right round the twist,' he said.

And sit for Cora I did, for there was practically nothing I could have refused her. While she painted, she told me how she identified closely with the Gentileschi woman who had become well known as the result of a rape trial. 'It was through her art that she overcame her neuroses,' Cora said, 'and perhaps that'll work for me too. Neurosis is the wrong expression by the way, what I mean is trauma.'

'And how am I to get rid of mine?' I asked. In the studio, which was bathed in light, Cora was standing in a black mourning bikini, while I had to hold a heavy blue curtain draped around me.

'Don't natter so much, you're supposed to look heroic,' Cora ordered. 'But not like on the stage. Put everything into being a she-elephant!'

Emilia did the job better than I, but then she didn't have to brandish a sabre. She felt flattered at being immortalized in a painting that she dubbed '*Il trionfo*'.

Friedrich had helped her to buy a young puppy at the market, which was now forever peeing all over the place. We had to keep a constant lookout to stop Béla crawling through the puddles.

It was impossible to overlook the fact that Emilia was taking her duties less seriously now. She spent most of her time amusing herself with her dog, Pippo, and Béla in the garden. Since the last thing Cora and I wanted to do was to incur her displeasure, we began to do the cooking ourselves.

When Friedrich asked me whether I fancied going to a summer-evening concert in the Pitti Palace, she took the invitation to include her as well. She had had no difficulty in understanding our conversation, and made no secret of the fact. Cora, who still didn't want to appear at public entertainments, stayed home as babysitter. Emilia thoroughly enjoyed the music.

The post-mortem had, as expected, revealed that Henning had died as a result of severe injuries to the skull, but also that he had consumed an incredible amount of alcohol. By this time, my father had been interrogated, through an interpreter, in his hospital bed; he admitted he had struck out while under the influence. He could not recall any details. Since he was not yet fit to be moved, far less imprisoned, he remained in the clinic for the time being. Henning had paid the bills regularly, now it was Cora who did it.

Henning's funeral was held in private, and we managed to keep the date and time secret. Cora had no desire to appear again in the newspaper as the pregnant widow. At the cemetery, Emilia pointed out to us the grave of her German archaeologist, who apparently deserted her by dying, and not through an act of unfaithfulness. Dr Albert Schneider was the name on the stone.

The formalities surrounding Henning's estate proved to be more complicated. While Cora did gain access to the bank account fairly quickly, what was in it was going to cover our lifestyle for only a few months. The tradesmen's bills for the studio conversion were hefty. Henning had a few stocks here, some property there, he had a share in a transport firm and still had his construction company; but everything was widely spread and it was difficult to get a clear picture of all his investments. It was just as well that Friedrich had his exams in the USA already behind him and he hadn't yet found a position in Germany. He was considering writing his doctorate thesis first. Anyway, he had both the time and the inclination to concern himself with Cora's fortune. There was no will, and no legal heirs had come forward. In actual fact, Cora was perfectly capable of looking after her affairs herself, speaking as she did much better Italian than her brother. But, for the moment, she was painting as if possessed, and it suited her fine if Friedrich took the disagreeable work off her shoulders. She was fully aware that he was actually staying on because of me, but was using the alibi of helping her to suit himself. I was now beginning to find Cora's paintings less and less attractive, but where aesthetic points of view were involved, there was just no talking to her; her taste tended towards the morbid, mine towards the highly sensitive.

Once, Jonas phoned. He was up to his neck in work on the harvest, was missing Béla Barthel and me, and he begged me to come home. I was able to draw him a convincing picture of how Cora needed me much more urgently – just think, her husband had been killed by my father! Jonas was horrified and asked whether he should come down. I declined magnanimously, saying the harvest was more important.

I spent a while wondering whether Jonas himself wasn't quite content to be rid of me. Was the harvest work really as vital as all that? Wasn't Jonas's mother being selfish in placing him under such an obligation that he had to sacrifice his own family life? But for her it was probably only right and proper that I should fit in with where Jonas happened to be living, and not the other way round.

We rejigged our daily routine. In the mornings, I took driving lessons and attended a course in Italian at the university. Cora took private lessons from a teacher of painting who came to the house. She was painting with such passion that she developed a sizeable callus on her right middle finger, at the pressure point of the brush. Friedrich busied himself with the 'family fortune', as he called it, and between times he did some odd jobs around the garden and put in several ventilator fans. Emilia looked after Béla and Pippo. In the afternoons, I was there for the little one, and all the time Friedrich never moved from my side. Cora did the cooking, while Emilia did the housework when she felt like it, or just loafed around. It was a pleasant life and, after about four weeks had passed, we began to put the incident in the kitchen out of our minds.

Nevertheless, I sometimes had the feeling that my whole life had been one long exercise in suppressing things. I never went on my own to visit my father in hospital; I didn't have the strength to face him without someone else being there. Cora and Friedrich would come with me once a week, but these visits were an embarrassment to all, even Father himself.

When I had passed my driving test, we had a little party. We had other successes to celebrate too: Pippo seemed almost house-trained, Béla took his first steps, Friedrich had got what seemed a good price for an apartment block in Rio, and Cora had found a male model for Holofernes, a taxi driver who took on the job with great enthusiasm. On top of all that, Emilia cooked a superb meal of rabbit in thyme and lemon, with tomatoes and onions. To accompany it, we drank a Tuscan white wine.

In the past, Emilia had eaten her meals in the kitchen, but now it was taken for granted that she should sit with us at table. At this meal, she went easy on convention, but heavy on the rabbit. Then she said, 'I want to learn to drive, too!'

We were speechless with amazement. She was easily old enough to be our mother; could anybody possibly want to take driving lessons at that age? Cora said, affably, 'Why not? And yet, mind you, we do drive you wherever you want to go, don't we?'

Emilia agreed, but felt it would be nicer for her not to have to ask all the time.

'That's true,' teased Friedrich, 'and then you'd be able to drive to the supermarket early, while we're still in bed.'

'It's not just a matter of the shopping,' said Emilia. 'I've a notion to go and see my cousin in Falciano.'

We gulped, because that would mean we'd probably have to go without the car for some days. In the end, Cora said, 'Actually, I've been wondering recently whether we couldn't do with two cars. The money's there, after all.'

So Emilia enrolled in a driving school, and I tested her on her theory. She was grateful for the support and encouragement, and now and then she would tell me more about her past. For five years, she had had a relationship with the archaeologist, until he died. They were happy years, for that was the first time anyone had tried to take her seriously as a person. They used to go to museums and concerts together, he taught her German and a little French, he would talk to her about the book he was writing, and he was grateful for her companionship. As a result, Emilia had broken with the Church and developed not only a weakness for all things German, but also a yearning for a repeat of that idyll. She had always wanted a family, she said, but it had never worked. Now she was happy, here with us.

*   *   *

Cora's parents had spent September on holiday in Colle di Val d'Elsa, and, on the journey home, they dropped in unannounced. No doubt, they wanted to see at first hand what Friedrich had told them about. Their little daughter had become a rich widow overnight.

Cora had to put up with her father now wanting to have a look at the books, and her mother having words with Emilia about dirty windows, as well as constant reminders not to spend money like water. Cora flew into a temper. 'That's exactly why I don't want you around here! After all, I'm old enough to know what I have to do. What have I treated myself to so far out of all the huge amount of money? A black mourning dress, a wreath for the grave! Not so much as a second car yet! Compare that with when Henning was alive – we'd go out for a meal every day, and for weeks now I've been doing the cooking with my own fair hands!'

She was right. She wasn't planning on throwing the money away on senseless luxuries. All Cora wanted to do was what she enjoyed, to paint, to own a beautiful house in a beautiful city, to have her friends around her. She had no interest in valuable jewellery, journeys to distant parts, model clothes, and even the second car, she considered, would be necessary only when Emilia had learnt to drive properly.

Nor was Emilia proving presumptuous, far less outrageous, in her demands. In silence, she cleaned the windows, scrubbed the kitchen floor and made the beds, so that Frau Schwab would have no further grounds for complaint. But she did sit at table with us; no professor was going to take that privilege away from her again.

While I did nothing to parade my intimate relationship with Friedrich before his parents – in fact, I was slightly ashamed – they had recognized the lie of the land. They didn't like my cheating on Jonas. Friedrich and I were very close, laughing and fooling around like big kids, but he never mentioned Jonas. I considered getting a divorce. But we had been married in church, and for Jonas, marriage was something sacred and indissoluble.

When, after four days with us, Cora's parents left for

Germany, we heaved a sigh of relief, even though we liked them. 'Everything's hunky-dory,' said Cora.

And the Schwabs, who had expected to find a daughter in deep depression and desperate for comfort, could bring themselves neither to approve of, nor even understand, the happy atmosphere that met them, with a pair of billing and cooing lovers, a crowing infant who was constantly being nibbled at by a pup, a self-assured maid and a widow painting as if in a frenzy.

CHAPTER 12

Pink Cloud

There are certain activities which give people their own particular kind of thrill. Emilia enjoys kneading dough with her hands; she would never have a food-processor in the house. Even more, she just loves cutting meat. She claims that taking a long, sharp knife to slice up a fresh leg of lamb into pieces for a stew gives her a unique frisson of sensuality.

I can't understand what she sees in this, but then she, for her part, only shakes her head whenever I gaze raptly out of my window on to the neighbour's wilderness of a garden. I have a weakness for grass that is burnt brown; for me, waist-high, dried-out stalks, withered shrubs, a lawn that looks like the steppe or wilting reeds are the very epitome of beauty, especially with the late-evening light or the early-morning sun falling on them. If a cat should be hunting mice in this wilderness, then my happiness is complete. I could sit there transfixed and forget the world altogether.

Cora has different quirks. Like so many people who love holidaying in the south, she likes to look out over old roofs clad with Roman tiles, and that is a pleasure I can share. Swallows float in the blue air, there is a scent of pines, crickets chirp – that's one of the reasons why we love to live here. However, Cora does not just collect impressions, but objects as well: brightly coloured feathers, kaleidoscopes, perfumes I can go along with, but I cannot share her penchant for dead animals. She would love to have Galileo's finger, which we can go and see, pickled in a museum; but I want no part of that.

There was a time when I used to obey without question

whenever Cora wanted something from me. Not only where money was concerned, but also in emotional things, I was utterly dependent on her. In those days I would probably have wrapped Galileo's finger in greaseproof paper for her without batting an eyelid. Since I started earning for myself, I think very carefully about exposing myself to danger for her sake.

Right after Henning's death, I began discreetly making myself useful. I gave German lessons to a young Albanian refugee. We had got to know him while we were shopping at the market, where he helped his uncle by weighing out vegetables. Twice a week we would sit together in the garden, and I would get him to repeat phrases from an old-fashioned textbook, *German for Waiters*. '*Winschen Sie gefillte Teigtasch mit Gemies?*' he would ask in his tortured accent, and I would explain that every tourist knows that ravioli is 'pasta envelopes filled with meat or vegetables'. '*Mechten Sie Rechnung?*' would always be his final question, very pleased with his progress. Admittedly, there was no bill for this service, but my pupil always brought along a basket of fruit. I was as delighted with it as if I had stolen it with my own fair hand.

During our latest visit to the hospital, the doctor in attendance had wanted a word with us. I knew anyway that my father was in a bad way. He was losing weight and his resistance to infection was greatly reduced. The doctor said he had suffered another haemorrhage of the gullet. They would allow Father out to spend a few hours with us every now and then if we came to collect him and brought him back by car. The doctor gave us to understand that he had been in touch with the public prosecutor's office and that they were aware that it was extremely unlikely that the patient would live to see the opening of proceedings. His head injuries were of no significance. Father was dying as the result of decades of alcohol abuse.

I had no intention of going to collect Father. I was sorry for him, of course, but then he had never lifted a finger to help me, and I couldn't see why I should do any more for him than pay the occasional brief visit. Friedrich couldn't agree with me on this point, while Cora kept out of the discussion. Nobody asked Emilia what she thought.

One day, as autumn approached and we could once again enjoy sitting out in the sun, Jonas appeared on the doorstep. Béla didn't recognize his father and, crying, reached out towards Emilia. Jonas was disconcerted. The harvest, it seemed, was still going on, but was nearly all in. He couldn't stand it any more. Now he had come to collect us, he said, although his voice did not have a very confident ring. At first, I said nothing, holding Béla on my lap, merely smiling at Jonas and hoping that Friedrich and Cora would move my things quickly and discreetly out of the master bedroom while we sat there. But Cora was one move ahead. 'Jonas,' she said, 'you can sleep in my room with Maya tonight, I've moved everything already.'

Friedrich left the room in a hurry; I hoped that he, too, would have cleared up all his things. More than that, he didn't show his face again that evening.

While I sat facing Jonas and he told me the news about his parents, it struck me that, just like him, my father, Friedrich and I myself had all landed unannounced on this doorstep; the only real refugees, however, had been Father and I. The other two could be counted as guests.

'My father's now in need of constant care,' said Jonas. 'Mother has to dress and feed him, but of course she can't lift him. I've got to do that.'

I could still hear the professor's words in my ear, about how this same couple, despite having had so many children, couldn't stand each other. 'Wouldn't it be better if your father went into a nursing home?' I asked. Jonas was horrified.

After dinner, he was eager to get off to bed. In contrast to myself, he had been starved of love. I would far rather have slept with Friedrich, as was my wont, but I could think of no plausible excuse for denying my husband this right.

Jonas was all tenderness, and I was ashamed of myself. But when he started off about how we all belonged together and he was going to take Béla and me back home, it all blew up into a row. 'I could just as well demand that you stay here with me,' I argued.

'You can't be serious,' said Jonas. 'Do you expect me to put up with a life as a scrounger? To live off Cora's money and run the odd errand or trim the laurel hedge for her in return?'

'So that's what you think I am, a sponger?'

'I'm not judging you. But I can tell you from experience that a day's hard physical work can make you feel really good. Certainly it's more satisfying than just lying in the sun.'

'There are other kinds of work than physical labour.' And I told him about my work as a German teacher and my Italian studies. In Jonas's book that was neither one thing nor the other. In the end, I suggested we should get divorced. At that, of course, out came the Catholic arguments, against which I was powerless.

The next morning, I awoke late. Jonas was no longer lying beside me. I cleaned my teeth and, still in my nightdress, went downstairs. Cora was apparently still asleep, and Friedrich was nowhere to be seen. But Emilia rushed to meet me, wringing her hands. Jonas had just driven off with Béla in the car! For a few seconds, I thought he had kidnapped him. Emilia seemed to have the same idea: 'I'd kill him rather than let him take our baby to Germany!' As she said this, she had such a wild look that I was almost afraid of her.

At that very moment, Jonas pulled up outside and got out with Béla and a large white loaf. 'I was going to make breakfast for all you lie-abeds,' he said brightly, 'but there wasn't a crust left in the house.'

Later on, Jonas came up with another decision. 'Come on, Maya,' he said, 'let's go and visit your father.'

'I was there only a week ago,' I protested.

In the end, he went off without me. An hour later, he was back and leading Father into the garden. That was all I needed. Neither Jonas nor Father understood any Italian, but there was a nurse who could speak German, and she had given her support for this visit. Father was very weak and could hardly walk more than a few steps at a time. He didn't talk much either, just sat gazing up into the trees and the sky and sighing. He took nothing to eat or drink.

By this time, Jonas had become friends with his Barthel and was trying to coax the word 'Papa' out of him. All my obstinate child would say was, 'Mila, Mala, Béla, Cola'. The pair of them sat in the back garden, leaving me on my own with my father. At last, Cora came in, and, seeing my help-lessness, persuaded Father to come and have a look at her studio. It took a long time for him to manage the stairs.

When Father caught sight of the half-finished painting, he shook his head. *Giuditta decapita Oloferne*, Cora had written below the picture in gothic lettering.

'That's not what Holofernes looks like,' said Father. We had to admit he was right. While the taxi driver had been an enthusiastic model, he didn't make a convincing villain in distress. 'I'd be much better,' Father suggested, stretching out on the couch. 'Take up your sabre, Infanta!' he com-manded. Hesitantly, I picked up the weapon. What was that last word he said? Cora was watching us both closely. 'Well, go on, strike,' he said, 'then you'll be shot of me at last.'

I let the sabre down slowly, looking him in the eye. 'It's not worth it any more,' I said and left the studio.

Cora made a lot of sketches of Father. Even though he looked a dying man, there was nothing else about him that came close to my vision of Holofernes; most of all, the wild beard was missing.

Three hours later, Jonas took Father back to hospital. Emilia cooked the meal, while Cora and I sat in the garden, smoking. Pippo was gnawing at Friedrich's abandoned shoe. I was so morose that I couldn't be bothered doing anything to stop him. Cora took my son in her arms. 'Bella, bella, bella Marie, hang yourself high, I'll cut you down in the morning,' she sang.

'How can you sing crap like that to a child?' I rounded on her.

'My God, but you're touchy today. Anyway, the only thing he understands is "bella",' she said.

'Oh yes, I forgot, it's a time to be jolly: my father wants me to stab him, Friedrich hasn't been seen since yesterday

– no doubt he doesn't want to disturb my domestic bliss – and Jonas is hellbent on carting Béla and me off, back to his little empire. Mind you, I can even see his point. If it were the other way round and Béla was being brought up by Granny and Great-Granny in the Black Forest, I'd have only one thought in my mind – to snatch him.'

Cora was thinking. 'It'll all sort itself out. Your father's not going to last much longer. Jonas isn't capable of baby-snatching, he's too sweet and too boring. In three days, he'll be back tilling the good German soil, and by then at the latest Friedrich will be back here.'

I calmed down and took the chewed-up shoe from Pippo. When Jonas arrived, it was time to eat. Emilia strained to keep up with the German conversation. The telephone rang and, for once, she rushed to answer. 'Maya,' she called, 'Papa dead!' An hour after his outing, my father had died of another haemorrhage.

Shortly after that, Friedrich phoned. Cora talked to him. He just wanted to put our minds at rest, he said; he had spent the night in a hotel.

'Well, we didn't assume you had thrown yourself under a train,' said Cora coldly. 'Maya's father has just died.'

Friedrich was shattered at the news. All he had wanted was to find out how long Jonas was going to be staying in Florence; now he promised to come back in the morning and give me his support.

'Do you know something,' Cora said to me, 'Friedrich's call gives me an idea. After all this uproar, you deserve a bit of rest and enjoyment and not yet more stress coping with two men. Tomorrow morning, first thing, we're going to the seaside, you and I, Béla and Emilia. We'll leave the lads to sort out the funeral. We're off out of it.'

We didn't say a word about our plan to Jonas, but let Emilia in on it. She did the packing and seemed beside herself with anticipation of the trip. The next morning, we sent Jonas off to get fresh bread and hurried to load up the car.

'I must buy another car,' said Cora. 'A Cadillac isn't exactly the right thing for a family runabout.' Cora had left a note for Jonas and Friedrich: *Maya is absolutely at the end of her tether and needs a few days' rest. Sort out the funeral between you.*

Just as we were driving off, breathless and in a wild fit of giggles, we saw Jonas approaching in the distance. We nipped up a narrow side-street and were able to make our getaway without him seeing us.

That little trip, which ended up lasting two weeks, compensated generously for all the hassle I had been through. We took two rooms in a little hotel right by the sea and spent our days as happy and carefree as if we were sixteen again. It was still sunny, and warm enough even for bathing, but the hordes of tourists had already left, and we had the beach to ourselves. Emilia was blissfully happy. Barefoot, she ran about in the sand with Béla and Pippo, hunting for seashells.

'We've earned this,' Cora reckoned. 'After all, we've got to get something out of our hard-earned fortune.' It was obvious that, through my energetic assistance, I deserved some claim to it, too.

Now and again, my conscience made its presence felt in a dream. I really ought to be there to lay my father 'in his last resting place'. But what good would that do him? Friedrich was very conscientious about carrying out that kind of duty, so let him get on with it! Would he try to find us? I assumed that Jonas would have headed straight for home, no doubt pretty bitter about it all. I could have had no idea that everything was much worse.

One afternoon, we were slowly gathering our belongings together on the beach because it was getting cold. Emilia said, as she shared out some biscuits between Béla and Pippo, 'You know, Cora, you're a widow, and Maya has just lost her father. Yet neither of you would dream of sticking to black. I've been wearing mourning clothes ever since Alberto died. Do you think that's right?'

We were unanimous in our reply, 'Not at all.' And went on munching our sandwiches.

Emilia ran an envious eye over our white jeans and brightly coloured cotton tops. 'I'm sure I couldn't wear that sort of thing, I've got too much of a belly on me, but a summer dress . . .'

Cora laughed. 'Emilia, you're getting quite daring!'

We all went off to a boutique where the last of the summer stock was on sale at reduced prices. In high spirits, we made Emilia try on everything they had in her size. She wasn't exactly fat, but rather stocky, and short in the leg, so slacks wouldn't suit her. In the end, she stood there in a girlish pink dress and looked great. Her swarthy complexion, her black plait and heavy dark eyebrows stood out against the pink dream, positively old-fashioned and romantic. 'You remind me of the painter Frida Kahlo,' said Cora, and Emilia was quite flattered, without the faintest notion of who she was being compared to.

We tried to drag Emilia along to a hairdresser's to have her pigtail cut off, but we had no luck there. Anyway, she was having second thoughts. 'In Florence, I couldn't cross the street in this dress, but nobody knows me here.'

We bought her some white shoes that she could wear to go shopping, even in Florence. Cora and I had a good giggle at our pink cloud, but Emilia was not at all put out. She found it great fun being one of the girls now.

Only once did Emilia and I fall out with Cora, and that was because she wanted to load into the car a pig's head that had been washed up on the beach. 'We should take *nature morte* literally,' she insisted. But even she gave in because of the stink off it.

Our influence over Emilia was only superficial; bare-legged, in her pink dress, she lay on the beach, smoking. But there was also a current flowing in the opposite direction: Emilia was trying to educate us. Whenever we casually said, 'Give me the paper,' she would not react until she had heard the required 'please'. As far as cheating, marital infidelity and manslaughter were concerned, she was very broad-minded, but woe betide Cora whenever she came out with 'Shit!'

A few days later, it started to rain. Sitting around in our hotel room, we decided to head for home. The weather forecast for the next few days was looking none too good. At first, Cora did the driving, so that we could make good time, with me beside her and Emilia in the back with Béla and Pippo. After a while, Emilia began to feel sick, because Cora's driving style belonged rather to the breakneck school. We swopped around; I drove, Emilia was allowed to take the passenger seat, and Cora tried to get some sleep in the kiddies' nest in the back. But suddenly I heard her call, 'Pull over!'

Out of the rain loomed a figure in cut-off jeans, loaded down with a rucksack. A thoroughly drenched young man clambered happily into the back seat. I hadn't a chance to look closely at him, but the fleeting glance up and down that I did get reminded me in a way of Jonas. Not the Jonas in his medical rep's suit, nor the hard-working farmer Jonas either, but the dishevelled Jonas from the caravan days, with his beard and stinking training shoes, the one I had fallen in love with.

In the back, they were talking English, or at least something approximating to it. I pricked up my ears. The young man was called Don and came from New Zealand. He had been on the road a long time and had already 'done' Asia.

Emilia sat shaking her head and grumbling quietly in Italian; I just hoped Don couldn't understand. After a hard hour's drive in the increasingly heavy rain, I glanced in the driving mirror to see Cora leaning cosily on Don's chest, sound asleep. Pippo was draped over her lap, while Béla had long since succumbed to the monotonous sound of the engine and the clicking of the windscreen wipers. Don was tenderly stroking Cora's red hair. Maybe it was that small gesture which awakened in me for the first time a new, and yet at the same time age-old, sensation – jealousy.

Emilia's experience of life told her right away that this strange man enjoying the warmth of the car, wet through and filthy, was going to be a source of discord. Cora didn't make any move to offer to swop places with me, even though she was normally most reluctant to hand over the wheel and laid no great store by my driving ability. For all that, I drove better than she did, more smoothly and without the mad urge to try to overtake every other vehicle on the road.

When we arrived home, late in the day, I was exhausted, Emilia grumpy, and the rest of the company refreshed and bright. Emilia got busy right away, warming the stove, putting water on to boil, unpacking and getting something to eat for the baby and Pippo, muttering curses and imprecations the while. Cora showed Don round the house. I came across a letter from Friedrich. Neither he nor Jonas was about, which was really no more than I expected anyway.

Friedrich's letter was written to both Cora and me. It tone was reproachful. He had gone to Germany because he had had replies to various job applications and had to present himself for interviews. Well, that had to come sooner or later. But then it got trickier. On the first evening after we had decamped, he had had a good man-to-man with Jonas, which had apparently ended in a piss-up.

Anyway, Friedrich had pulled no punches with his fellow boozer, enlightening him as to his relationship with me. Jonas, drunk as he was, had driven straight off home in the middle of the night. I was furious. That wasn't the way Jonas was meant to find out; I owed him an honest explanation.

Finally, Friedrich went on to say that my father had not yet been buried. Firstly, that was my business, and secondly, he had neither the legal authority nor the money for it and no precise details as to where and in what way it was to be done. The deceased had been put into temporary deep-freeze storage, for which, however, rent had still to be paid. On top of that, a pretty steep hospital bill had come. I was being spared nothing. Among the mail there were other letters that needed dealing with – settlement of the estate, forms and the like. I gave a loud groan.

Emilia had little sympathy with me, simply telling me to let the dog out into the garden and to dig the cigarette lighter out of my son's mouth. At last, Cora came into the kitchen, looking pleased with herself, but without Don. She said she had packed him off to the bathroom. 'So is he supposed to be staying for dinner?' demanded Emilia angrily.

'My God,' said Cora with some disdain, 'in weather like this we'd hardly throw even our pink cloud out on the street.'

Emilia was hurt.

'Read this letter, will you?' I asked Cora.

'Later. I'm starving just now, and then I want to do some painting. I'm just dying to sketch that Don.'

When the pasta was ready, a spick-and-span Don put in an appearance, too. From his rucksack, he pulled out bits of Indian craftwork and spread his treasures out before us. He presented Cora with a silver ring with a moonstone in it, and I got an imitation ruby. Did we have girlfriends who might be interested in buying such fine things? he asked in all innocence. During the summer season he had made some cash moonlighting in Greece, but that was running low now. I could hardly make him out, and even Cora was having some difficulty.

'Can you Australians not speak decent English?' I demanded irritably. Now it was his turn to be offended; he wasn't Australian. As he spoke, he gave me a look of such bitterness that I could almost see my wounded Jonas before me.

'He's a Kiwi,' Cora corrected me.

I don't know what impulse made me do it, but I gave Don a hug. 'Thanks for the lovely ring,' I said.

Cora shot me a warning look: hands off Don! Emilia was taking it all in as she heaped our plates. She couldn't understand English and wanted to put us in a peaceful frame of mind with good food. While Cora chatted on with Don, who ate with indecent haste, Emilia started a lengthy discussion with me about whether it wasn't high time Béla got his first pair of sturdy shoes. Then I heard that Don's parents owned an apple plantation, which he would take over at some time or other. Not another farmer!

What exactly was the matter with me? Did I really like this character? Don had come to an agreement with his parents that, next year, he would dutifully take up his work as a farmer, but until then he was going to travel the world. Whenever he was a bit short of funds, they sent him a small amount. After the meal, he gave a demonstration of Chinese shadow-boxing, which made Béla laugh more than anybody. Don had eaten his fill, but even that did not put him in Emilia's good books. She went off early to watch television up in her attic and, contrary to her usual habit, did not take Béla with her.

Cora said to me in German, 'I've got a lot of new ideas for pictures. Variations on my theme. Naturally, you'll still be Judith, but, as a change from your father and the taxi driver, Don could be Holofernes . . .'

When I took Béla upstairs, I found that my things had been shifted out of Cora's room. Everything was piled on the rose-patterned basket chair. So, she was intending to share the double bed with Don. She wasn't wasting any time about it, I thought; did he know of her plans? I laid my son down in his cot and decided not to go back downstairs. I was in a foul mood.

Only at first sight did Don look like Jonas: brown hair and dark eyes with that sad, trusting teddy-bear look in them that had once got to me. It was probably some kind of appeal to the mothering instinct. Was it the same with Cora? I wondered. Yet she hadn't fallen for Jonas. Don was thinner than Jonas, with a receding chin that even his beard couldn't quite hide, and his brown hair was naturally curly. You just wanted to run your fingers through that undergrowth and come across a pair of little horns. Yes, that was it, there was something faun-like, which was missing in Jonas.

I thought for a while about Cora, too, which was something I seldom did. For me, she was just there, a necessary part of my life, yet she was the most unsettling person I knew. Was she selfish? Well, so was I. I loved her courage, her nerve, her happy disposition, her wit and her generosity. She was streets ahead of me in all respects. Shouldn't I just be happy for her with this Don? I had only just rid myself of a husband who had become tiresome, and taken up with Friedrich, although he was away for the time being, too. Why did I want this stranger, whom I could hardly understand, who was in all probability no great shakes, who was going to be a farmer like his father and who would in any case be moving on again soon? Why couldn't I just sit back and let Cora lay claim to him? I had no idea.

Late in the night, I woke with a thirst. On my way to the kitchen, I passed the studio. The door was wide open, Don was asleep on the sofa, his clothes scattered all over the floor. Had they done it or hadn't they?

At breakfast, Cora, in a particularly good mood, it seemed to me, announced, 'Don needs new shoes. Anybody coming with us?'

Emilia's eyes followed mine towards Don's battered sandals, which were too light for the time of year. 'I'll come,' I said at once. 'Béla's needing new shoes, too.'

Emilia scowled. 'I'm not coming,' she said. 'And if I were you, I wouldn't go buying shoes for any ragbag who just happens along.'

'What dinky white shoes our pink cloud has on her pretty little feet,' said Cora. 'Did she really need these shoes so desperately, I wonder?'

With a snort, Emilia cleared away the plates. Quite by chance, the milk jug toppled over right in front of Cora, pouring its contents all over her new woollen skirt. As cool as you like, she peeled it off and sat there on the bench in her black briefs. Emilia had no option but to put up with this brazenness in the presence of a strange man, and to clean the skirt with damp kitchen cloths. I felt Cora was pushing things a bit far. Even Don seemed to think that. He looked at me with a conspiratorial smile which I wasn't sure how to interpret. I simply smiled back.

In the shoe shop in the Via Tornabuoni, Cora bought herself a handbag in Korean eel-skin, while I struggled to put Béla's first strong shoes on him. Like a baby monkey, he kept curling up his toes.

'What kind of shoes would you like, Don?' asked Cora.

He didn't mind. She picked out black gent's shoes, elegant and expensive, which didn't suit him at all. Don put them on, nodded and threw his scuffed sandals in the wastepaper basket.

'Maybe we should take something back for Emilia,' I suggested. 'When we have visitors in the house, it's more work for her.'

'You didn't say that with our other visitors,' Cora remarked, but didn't object to my buying a bunch of asters and some white-chocolate truffles.

On the way home, Don was allowed to drive the Cadillac. No doubt he was more accustomed to the wide open spaces of home than to Italian traffic, because even Emilia after her first fifty driving lessons couldn't have made a worse job of it. Rather impatiently, Cora reminded us it was time we were home, since she had work to get on with. Don was prepared for his task of representing Holofernes. My Albanian pupil would be waiting for me, and then I had to get on with my own studies.

'Before you do anything more to your great daub,' I said, 'perhaps you would be so good as to read your brother's letter. I don't know if you've noticed, but neither Friedrich nor Jonas is around any more.'

'I can imagine Friedrich is a bit peeved.'

'Peeved or not, they haven't buried my father!'

'And where is he now?'

'In some deep-freeze or other.'

Cora laughed. 'In that case, there's no hurry. Leave him there for another few days.'

'Did he ever bother his head about me? Would he have shelled out for a funeral for me?'

'I do remember him turning up beside your brother's coffin.'

Usually, we tried to avoid any mention of Carlo. Angrily, I said, 'If there was a chance of getting a drink out of it, no doubt he would even have stood at my graveside.'

I couldn't hold back the tears. I had learnt from Cora to talk coolly and callously about the dead, but that was a gesture to please her, and it hurt me.

Cora read the letter through. 'That was only to be expected,' she said. 'For the moment, you're well rid of both of them. Anyway, it's my turn now!'

That was a warning to me. 'I've no idea what you mean . . .' I said.

There were sounds of laughter coming from the studio all day long. I couldn't bring myself to go in. Emilia kept shaking her head disapprovingly. There was a new central-heating system being installed, tradesmen were leaving dirt all over and Emilia squabbled with them.

Where was my father to be buried? I hadn't the faintest idea. One thing I didn't want was for Cora to lay out a lot of money on it. At lunch, I brought the subject up again.

'OK,' said Cora, 'that's very noble of you, wanting to save my money. I can't see any point in expensive graves either. With Henning, it was different, it had to be, since the general public was interested. Tell you what, let's simply have your father's urn buried in Henning's *grand lit*, quite anonymously. Murderer and victim in the one double bed.'

She had been speaking German, but, at the word 'murderer', Emilia had given a meaningful laugh, and strangely enough, so did Don. I thought Cora's idea was excellent and decided to take care of it in the next few days.

Cora had run out of paints, so she drove straight into town. I was left on my own with Don.

CHAPTER 13

Incarnadine

All the same, I suppose it is thanks to that damned Don that these days I can sit here as queen of my coach (the princess has grown up) and hold a score of subjects under my sway. After the differences of opinion with Cora which first surfaced as a result of Don's two-timing, I made up my mind to extricate myself at least from my financial dependence on her.

Only very rarely do types like Don sit in my bus, because they despise organized tourism and prefer to sprawl about on the pavement in front of some fountain or other, with their bottles, guitars and rucksacks. If, however, one of them does happen to wander by mistake on to my air-conditioned coach, I don't even need to waste so much as a smile on him. My trim tailored suit acts as an effective barrier, it is supposed to please my normal clientele, as indeed it does. I would have no trouble at all in reeling in some top-ranking German civil servant, but then they're not my type either. The only thing that might interest me in that kind of gentlemen is their wallet.

I did once go out with a fancy big-shot like that. He wanted to go for an espresso in a 'typical' café. I steered him into a bar. We sat on incredibly hideous plastic-and-chrome barstools, as if on horseback, and followed the lead of our neighbours by hooking our heels on to the rail that ran all the way round the bar like an umbrella stand. Nearby, some people were playing a kind of *boccia* on billiard tables; the next room was a kind of amusement arcade, and there the noise was even worse. VIETATO AI MINORI DI 18 ANNI seemed to attract a lot of youngsters, drinking and lounging against the walls in shoddily veneered alcoves. Everyone was quite casually dropping litter on the imitation marble floor. Now and then a girl would come in and buy an ice-cream. The owner of the establishment, a small, fat man with a rather roguish charm, pointed out for us the German football results in his *Sportsman* newspaper.

It's a place I enjoy frequenting, but my escort found it spoilt his appetite both for me and for his coffee. It's just that tourists' taste differs from mine. In the Baptistry, I'm fascinated by the floor, which most of them never give a second glance. And on wonderful June nights, they sit and knock back Chianti while, in dewy gardens – including ours – unnoticed by the philistines, the most enchanting summer night's dream is being enacted. Thousands of glow-worms dance out a soundless, fairy-like fireworks display, and any-one who has experienced it realizes that the best things in life are indeed free.

Sometimes, when I sit of an evening in the garden, with bats sweeping around and the trees giving off an intoxicating fragrance, when a 'gentle zephyr wafts from azure skies', I am gripped by a yearning to be loved. And amazingly it is Don who comes into my mind, that creep who foisted himself on us.

When Cora left that day to buy paints, we had been sitting in the kitchen, warming ourselves at the stove. Emilia was washing up, Béla was banging a metal dish with the whisk. Pippo was lying next to him, shredding a newspaper.

'Come on, let's have a grappa,' I said to Don, and we went into the living-room. It was pretty chilly there; the workmen who were replacing the boiler had switched off the heating. The stove in the kitchen was fired with wood and coal, but I had had enough of the family idyll.

Don shivered. 'It's warmer upstairs in my room,' he said, meaning Cora's studio, where there was a little electric heater.

'Where's she gone anyway?' he asked.

'To buy paints. She needs red and white, to mix incarnadine.'

'What's that?'

'The colour for skin, for flesh,' I said, because I couldn't think of the English word, 'complexion'.

'You have a fantastic incarnadine,' he said, reaching out to take my hand.

I withdrew it, rather too feebly. Don said, 'She's the one with the cash, isn't she? The house and everything, it's all hers, right? What do you have to do to get to live here?'

'I'm only visiting, we're old friends.' What business was it of his anyway? I was getting annoyed. But he was getting bolder.

'What would I have to do to be allowed to stay with you both?'

'I thought you wanted to see Europe . . .'

'Sure, but you've got to take your time over Florence, isn't that right?'

Cora came in and, none too pleased at finding us sitting together on the sofa, barked out the order, 'Come on, let's get to work!' Don had to lie down and offer his head to an imaginary sword. I went back into the kitchen.

Emilia, noticing my sullen expression, said, 'Get rid of him!' Again and again she muttered, '*Diavolo*,' and crossed herself, even though she never went to church.

To cheer her up, I sang some German songs to her. Béla accompanied me on his drum.

'Alberto,' said Emilia, letting a tear roll down into the washing-up water.

'Come on, now,' I said. 'Let's go for a breath of fresh air with the little fellow.'

Emilia quickly changed out of her pink dress and into a black one and then we set off on our laborious child-and-dog-walking.

When we got back home, I had to give my expert opinion on Cora's sketches for an oil painting. Don's head, which she had caught well, lay in a basket that hung on a housewife's arm as if she had just got back from the market. Don

160

was dropping hints about having expected to sit not just for his head, but as a nude model.

'Well?' Cora inquired.

'Your pictures have one crucial weakness,' I said. 'You're hardly going to be able to exhibit them.'

She reckoned that material success should not be a criterion for the true artist. 'The pictures where your father or Henning can be recognized, now these ones I'll certainly keep secret. But who knows Don?'

'I find it just as out of place if I'm identified as Judith or Salome.'

The evening meal went off quite happily. Emilia retired with Béla and Pippo, we drank beer and Don talked about Nepal. I went to bed fairly early.

I was awakened from a deep sleep by someone touching me. Don was lying in bed beside me. I couldn't think of the right swear-words in English. 'Beat it, you ratbag,' I said, or something like that. He kissed me on my parched mouth, and that really woke me up. 'Piss off, I said, go back to Cora and leave me in peace,' I hissed.

'She doesn't like me; she's kicked me out,' he insisted. I'm ashamed to admit it, but my resistance was not convincing, and in the end he stayed.

When I opened my eyes next morning, Cora was standing by my bed, watching us with an expression that bode no good at all. 'You take them in and feed them, and this is what you get,' she said. Don, too, awoke, and fled naked from the bed and into the bathroom.

'He said you didn't want him.' It sounded pathetic.

'The bastard's lying,' said Cora. 'Why do you believe everything he tells you?'

'I didn't invite him in; he took me by surprise in the middle of the night. Best thing would be, we throw him out right away.'

'We can't do that now; I need him as a model.'

The next day, he was in Cora's bed. I know that for a fact, for it was my turn to get a look at that still life the following morning.

How did we come to fall for such a miserable little rat

anyway! Don took great delight in playing us off one against the other. From that time on, there was nothing but strife in the house, with us hurling terrible accusations at each other. The whole business with Carlo was dragged up again. If Cora hadn't egged him on so blatantly, I said, it would never have got as far as the attempted rape, and my brother would still be alive. She argued that, if only I had been there at the time, that would have been enough to prevent the attempt, and she never asked me to kill him anyway.

And what about Henning, then? There, too, she had made sure she kept her hands clean and left the dirty work to me instead. She yelled back at me: I was the one who stood to gain the most from it, and now, here I was, living in the lap of luxury.

'You're always putting the blame on me! All right, I'll go. That's what you really want, isn't it? Don means more to you than all our years of friendship.'

'No.'

Don was present during most of our squabbles, sprawled out lazily on Cora's sofa, snoozing or smoking a joint. We were sure he couldn't understand a word of what we were saying.

In fact, we should have learned our lesson from the 'Emilia incident'. It was the same sort of thing with Don. He had grandparents from Hessen, with whom his mother always spoke German. While '*Auf Wiedersehen*' really was all Don could say, he could understand more than enough.

I first found out about that when he started to chat me up and tried to put the squeeze on me, hinting that he knew a few things, so that gave him as much right as me to scrounge off us for the rest of his life. I didn't take him seriously at first, but, as usual, Emilia had pricked up her ears, had watched Don's reaction and put two and two together.

I slept with Don only the once, and I was made to pay for it. From that time on, Cora did it on a daily basis. Nevertheless, she wasn't to enjoy the pleasure for long, since her lover fell ill a few days later. Probably he had caught some infection, she supposed, and she wanted to call a doctor. But Don wouldn't hear of it; in India, he said, he had often been plagued by bouts of diarrhoea and had always got over it without the help of any doctor. He just had to fast for one day and then, on the next, to live on water biscuits and Sprite and everything would be fine. After his day's fast, Emilia made him some camomile tea and fed him dried white bread; she also charred some coffee-beans on the hotplate of the stove and made a kind of charcoal tablet out of them, which he swallowed gratefully. He was a great one for natural products.

All the same, he was poorly, the therapy didn't work, he became listless and wasn't a bit of use, either as a lover or as a model. Cora and I got on better together. We had to eat and sleep without Don; he would lie on the studio couch or hang about the warm stove in the kitchen, seeming to have lost all interest in what was going on around him. 'If things are no better tomorrow, I'll have to call a doctor,' said Cora. 'Who knows, maybe there's some kind of tropical disease at the bottom of it. How are we supposed to know about these things?'

It never came to that, though. The freshly mixed incarnadine was left to dry up.

Cora wanted to drive me in to the Galleria Palatina, to show me a painting by Gentileschi. 'You know, I've looked at this picture before, but I can't remember the details any more. It's called "*Giuditta e la fantesca*".'

'You'll think I'm showing my ignorance again, but I don't know what a *fantesca* is.'

'Emilia's one. If you were my *fantesca* – my maid, that is – I'd call you Elefantesca.'

The painting made a profound impression on us. Judith was shown holding the sword casually on her shoulder, like a hiker's staff, while her *fantesca* had the basket with the chopped-off head in it propped against her hip like a laundry basket full of damp washing. The two of them were turning to the right, looking at something out of sight for the viewer. They were both magnificently dressed, although the *fantesca* had wound her headdress rather untidily. Judith's elaborate coiffure was pinned up with a golden brooch. The light fell on her beautiful profile, which bore a slightly crazed, wildly determined expression. What disturbed me was her enlarged thyroid gland.

'Now that's painting for you,' said Cora, taking a deep breath. 'Just look at Judith's skin; I'll never manage an *incarnato* like that.'

I twisted my own head round to have a close look at Holofernes in the basket. He really did look like the ailing Don with his almost greenish complexion.

'What are you going to do when Don is fit again and you've portrayed him from all angles?'

'Then he'll have served his purpose,' Cora said brightly and put her arm round me.

We looked at some other pictures, getting along together just like in the good old days, then we went for an ice-cream and got home pretty late.

'Béla has to be fed,' said Emilia reproachfully, although, up till now, she had seen to that often enough without me. We went into the kitchen. Béla was crying, the dog was howling. In one corner, Don was propped against the wall. 'What's up with him?' Cora asked, horrified, for he looked like a corpse.

'Dead,' said Emilia. There was a strangely bitter smell in the air.

'For God's sake, why didn't you call a doctor?'

Suddenly, Emilia looked just like Giuditta. '*Non voglio nessun dottore*,' she sang in a shrill voice.

Cora took Emilia by the shoulders and shook her. 'What happened?'

Emilia burst into tears. 'It had to be,' she sobbed. 'It couldn't go on like that. He had a hold over us all.'

'What had to be?'

'I put poison in . . .'

We looked at each other, completely at a loss. 'She's gone mad,' said Cora.

'We'll have to call the police and a doctor,' I said to Emilia. 'We can't help you.'

'A doctor can't help him either,' she remarked.

'He has to make out the death certificate, don't you see?

164

Don can't just go on sitting here in the kitchen!' I took my son protectively on my lap.

Emilia wiped away her tears and said, 'You just don't understand a thing. This guy was going to blackmail you! And so, by the way, could I, if you'd just cast your minds back! I could tell the police quite a nice little tale.'

I froze, but Cora said, levelly, 'Nobody would believe a word you said. But let's hear what you plan to do with this stiff.'

At that, Emilia cheered up. 'I've worked it all out already. It really isn't a problem at all.'

'Out with it,' said Cora.

'No,' I said, 'I just don't want to know. If Emilia goes around bumping off our visitors, then it's up to her to answer for it, thank you very much.'

'I thought you were my friend,' said Emilia, 'but you're a snake in the grass. I watched you beating Henning to death on her orders, I saw it all! I forgave you everything, because I love you both, because I'm happy here with you and I want to stay that way. I did away with this swine out of loyalty to you. And what thanks do I get?' Emilia was wringing her hands over the parmesan cheese, a picture of sheer misery. Then she went on: 'It was so lovely at the seaside! That's the way I always wanted my old age to be: two sweet daughters, a grandchild, a little dog. I almost felt young again. And then along comes a fiend like this and ruins everything. My children can't stand each other any more, there's nothing but screaming and quarrelling.'

'We're not your children,' said Cora, 'so you can save all your dramatic performances for the public prosecutor!'

'Right,' said Emilia, 'you're in for a big surprise! Do you think there's anyone else who'll dance attendance on you from morning till night, who'll clean, cook, wash, look after the child and forever iron your blouses? Not even a mother would do that, you thankless, selfish pair! And just think for a minute; if this creature had become known hereabouts, it wouldn't have been so easy to shut him up. As it is, he won't be missed by a soul.'

We were stunned into silence. She was right, of course,

but then she was doing quite nicely out of our little ménage herself, unfair or not.

'. . . and anyway, he kicked Pippo and peed on my little marguerite bush,' she said, flushed with rage.

Cora tried to pacify her. 'Are there no depths to which he didn't sink! Maybe you'll be so good as to tell us what you're proposing to do with the corpse?'

'Whenever I go to see my cousin,' Emilia began, brightening, 'I always give a hand when they have pigs to slaughter. I could cut this swine up, say into twelve pieces, put them in the deep-freeze and get rid of them gradually.'

I was flabbergasted. 'There'll be no dismembering of corpses done in my house!' yelled Cora. 'They can find the tiniest traces of blood even years later. And anyway, I'd never allow any such disgusting goings-on. What are you – some kind of pervert, or what?'

'And what about you?' Emilia demanded. 'You're forever painting stabbed men and chopped-off heads. What do you call that, then?'

I asked, tentatively, 'How would you go about disposing of the twelve bits?'

'That's easy. I'd just go for a walk with Béla and put a parcel in the pushchair. If a little child's sitting on top of it, no one will suspect . . .'

Now it was my turn to scream. 'My Béla is not going to sit on any corpse!'

But now Cora was showing some interest. 'Purely hypothetically – where would you take the parcels?'

'I could drop them into the litter baskets in the park.'

Cora shook her head. 'That might work the first time, maybe even twice. But then they'd be sure to be on the lookout, and every litter bin in Florence would have a policeman watching it.'

Emilia had plenty more bright ideas. 'I could go and visit Alberto and throw the parcels into an open grave.'

'A bit better,' said Cora, 'but someone is bound to notice any strange objects lying in the hole. Quite apart from that, I've told you before, there'll be no dismembering here.'

Not to be deterred, Emilia said, 'Well, you'd have all the

time in the world to paint the severed head ... But I've another suggestion. When Maya's daddy is cremated, we could all go to the crematorium to say our goodbyes. Each of us takes along four parcels, two in each hand. When we're alone with the dear departed papa, we place the parcels under him. Then Don and Daddy are pushed into the oven together ...'

'Emilia's certainly not short of imagination,' I admitted in admiration.

But Cora was not satisfied with this ingenious plan either. 'How on earth would it look if each of us turned up with four heavy parcels! It's not something you can camouflage with bunches of flowers. I reckon each of us would have to lug along forty pounds. And anyway, I stand by what I've said – there'll be no cutting up! Never mind anything else, my freezer would be contaminated beyond recall.'

By this time, I had fed Béla and put him to bed. When I came back into the kitchen, they were packing the silent Don into two plastic bags, starting from his head and his feet, because one wasn't big enough. So Cora had finally decided not to call the police. 'What we need is one of these gadgets for sealing plastic,' she said. As usual, Emilia knew of a clever way out. With the iron, she welded the two plastic sacks together round about Don's chest. As she did so, she kept pressing the air out of the parcel, as if she was preparing a large roast for the deep-freeze.

'So what now?' I asked.

Emilia said, 'That way, nothing can seep out. Now, let's get to bed, and tomorrow we'll see what's to be done next.' She closed all the shutters on the windows. 'Probably the workmen will be round tomorrow,' she remarked.

Cora shook her head. 'That's not on, Emilia. Either you think of something tonight, or I'm going to call the police.'

'I've already had another idea,' said Emilia, 'but it won't work till tomorrow. And besides, it's not cheap. You'll need to buy a jeep. Cora, you wanted a second car anyway ...'

I wasn't having that. I didn't like jeeps at all. 'If we really need one, then I'll pinch one for you,' I proposed. 'We don't have to buy one, just for the sake of one day. So what do we do once we have the jeep?'

Emilia enjoyed being the focus of attention and she certainly knew how to hold her audience as she outlined her plans. 'Up in the mountains, where my cousin lives, there's a whole lot of deserted buildings. I know one where hay is stored. So we drive Don out there in the jeep – you couldn't get up the steep tracks with any other kind of vehicle anyway – then we lay him in the hay, as if he had been spending the night there. We'll put his rucksack beside him. Then we put a lighted candle by his bed and buzz off . . .'

'What kind of poison did you use anyway, and where did you get it?' I asked.

'There's a whole medicine cabinet full of Alberto's stuff still there. At first I only gave Don laxatives.'

'He can hardly have died of those!'

'I told you once before that Alberto was an archaeologist, if you have any idea what that is. From his expeditions, he brought back things like potassium cyanide capsules, I don't know exactly what for, maybe wolves . . .'

'And I suppose our Don Cossack swallowed those quite happily?' Cora asked, with renewed interest. 'After all, he wouldn't have anything to do with orthodox medicine, but put his trust in nature healing!'

'I coated the tablets in soot; he had no objection to charcoal.'

I went to fetch Cora's coat. 'I'm off to steal a jeep right now,' I said excitedly.

'Do you know how to do that? With a piece of wire? Or what else do you have in mind?' Cora asked.

Unfortunately, I was not very well up in technical things. I couldn't so much as change a wheel and was even scared to drive a strange car. 'I'm going to our disco,' I said, less than sure of myself. 'There's always a jeep outside. Somehow I'll have to find out who it belongs to and then swipe the keys.'

Cora was back to her old self again, not averse to a bit of adventure. 'Leave it to me,' she said, 'I've a better idea. I know a bloke from the university who owns a jeep, or at least something of that sort. This rich mummy's boy drives a sports car as well as the jeep. He fancies himself as a sculptor and sometimes needs the jeep to carry blocks of marble. I'll just call in on him and steal his keys.'

Emilia and I were all for it. 'Come with me,' said Cora. 'You can drive and wait in the street outside. If the bloke's not at home, I won't manage to get in. Then we'll have to go on to the disco together.'

We set off. It wasn't far, and if need be, Cora could walk back home. Emilia stayed behind with the plastic parcel and the sleeping Béla. 'If I don't come straight back out, you drive on to the filling station and fill up both the spare canisters,' Cora ordered. I waited five minutes, saw the hall light come on in the flat upstairs and then drove the Cadillac to the Esso station.

When I got back, Emilia had already dragged the bundle close to the front door. 'It's a good thing he's not all that heavy,' she said. 'We could have managed quite easily with the twelve parcels.'

'If it does work out with the jeep tonight,' I asked, 'how far do we have to drive? And what am I to do with Béla?'

Emilia hedged a little. 'Five hours, maybe,' she said.

'Then we'll have to take Béla with us,' I decided, but I didn't like the idea one little bit. Couldn't I simply wait here? Emilia had to navigate, one of us had to do the driving – but did all three of us have to be involved in the operation?

Cora came in, dangling two keys. 'It was almost too easy,' she said. 'The twit went to get a bottle of wine, I dipped his coat pocket, a kiss, a quick drink – and that was it. Luckily the jeep was in the underground garage. He couldn't have heard it driving away.'

'But what if he needs the jeep again today?' I asked.

'No way. He always takes the other car in the evenings. Besides, he wasn't planning to go out again at all. Tomorrow morning his jeep will be back in its stable and he'll wonder how the key came to be in the ignition.'

'Cora, can I not stay here – or you? I don't really want Béla to have to come with us.'

'Either everybody goes or nobody,' said Cora.

Emilia took a peek out of the window. It was still only eleven o'clock, but the weather was bad and it was pretty quiet outside. 'Let's go,' she said. 'We've got to make a start now. Reverse the jeep up to the front door.'

Cora manoeuvred the vehicle, I dressed Béla in warm things, while Emilia shut the whining dog in the bathroom. Then we heaved our bundle out to the car and waited till the street seemed completely deserted. Cora opened the door of the jeep. We had to strain once more to hoist the body and push it on to the floor at the rear.

'Girls,' ordered Emilia, 'you've got to put on something else – trainers and dark things.'

In the bathroom, Pippo was howling like a young wolf. 'That's no good,' I said, 'the neighbours will hear him and realize right away there's no one in the house.' So Pippo was liberated again, despite Cora's mutterings, because by now Béla was screaming, too.

At last, we drove off, complete with child, dog, warm blankets and corpse; Don's rucksack lay under the front passenger's feet. I took the wheel first, because Cora wanted to take the difficult stretch on the mountain track. 'So what story did you spin your sculptor when you paid him such a brief and unannounced call?' I asked.

'I used to stay with him often, long before I met Henning. He was after me for months on end. He's a bit too much of a coke freak for my liking. The last time I saw him was at the Gentileschi exhibition. So I asked him first if he had a copy of the catalogue, but he's so tight-fisted he hadn't bought one. But he was so overjoyed to see me again that he's going to get a hold of the catalogue and says he'll bring it round in the next few days.'

'Holy Madonna!' groaned Emilia. 'Not another young man in the house!'

'Listen,' I rounded on her, 'he won't be the last young man in Cora's house, so don't think you can do away with them all. And anyway, just tell us the truth: what did you have against Don? After all, he didn't do you any harm.'

Cora, too, chipped in. 'The story of him bringing discord

170

into the household doesn't hold water with me. He would have gone off on his travels again, and the problem would have been solved by itself.'

Emilia said, 'You two are more stupid than I thought. Don's German was better than mine, he read Friedrich's letter and had a good laugh. He understood all your drivelling about your bloody past. Besides, I couldn't be sure whether the cyanide would still work at all.'

Suddenly, in the distance, I saw a blue flashing light. All the vehicles in front of me were braking, and behind me, too, a line of traffic was quickly building up. 'Police! Shit! Sorry, Emilia,' I said. 'What do we do now?'

Cora spat out her chewing gum on to Don's rucksack. 'Get out, let me take the wheel, and play dumb.' We quickly changed places. The cars were being checked one by one. Turning on this narrow road with oncoming traffic was an impossibility. We were trapped.

In the end, Cora had to wind down the window; two young policemen wanted to see our papers. One of them flashed his torch over the rear seat. Cora was suddenly speaking very broken Italian. She handed over her driving licence. The policemen asked for the registration documents. Cora pretended not to understand a word at first, then she burst out in a nervous giggle – she had left the papers at her boyfriend's, on the bedside table, how stupid of her! Before the policemen could ask any further questions, Emilia stuck her head out of the window and asked the gentlemen not to talk so loudly, otherwise they'd wake the baby. I turned my head and saw, to my utter horror, that Béla was lying on the body. Emilia had shifted him around. Pippo started to bark. 'For heaven's sake, the little darling's going to start crying; how can you be so cruel!' Emilia scolded, and the policemen waved us on. As we pulled away, we could just catch them saying that, after all, it wasn't three women, but two jail-breakers they were looking for.

As soon as the tailback began to ease, we lit up. When we had calmed down somewhat, Emilia inquired, 'Just how old are you two anyway?'

'Twenty.'

'I'm nearly fifty-five,' she said, 'and at your age I still didn't even have a boyfriend. But I'm not sure I envy you.'

'Better not to. We've got a much harder time of it than you. In your youth you were spared the sort of thing we're doing today, you lucky devil.' Emilia nodded and picked dog-hairs off her skirt.

'Are we actually going to douse him in petrol?' I asked.

'No,' Cora said. 'They're supposed to believe he fell asleep with the candle still burning.'

'Then I'd better put his identity papers back in the rucksack,' I suggested, 'because I took them out, as a precaution.'

Cora asked, 'Was there anything else in particular among his things?'

'Nothing that would point to him having come from New Zealand, but, curiously, there was a Gideon's Bible. Not a single letter from home, not even from his mum. But here's a surprise for you – he was married.'

Cora said, 'Oh yeah? But then, so are we.'

Emilia reckoned that this revelation vindicated her dislike for him. 'I told you right at the start he was a devil. Roaming all over the world and his poor wife left in the lurch.'

I pretended to be offended. 'Don't be so old-fashioned, Emilia, that's really no big deal these days.'

For a time, we drove in silence through the dark, deserted countryside. Emilia had long since removed Béla from his lifeless palliasse; now Pippo was sleeping on top of Don. Cora was driving more slowly than usual, so as not to attract attention. Emilia was watching out for the fork in the road where we had to turn off.

Suddenly, Cora said, 'I'm starving!' It occurred to me, too, that we had had nothing to eat for hours on end, except for an ice-cream.

'Work before pleasure,' said Emilia. 'I've packed some nice sandwiches, but you're not getting them till we're rid of him.'

'You do think of everything, don't you?' I said, not without a trace of genuine admiration.

Emilia beamed. 'I've got hot tea as well,' she said, modestly. 'We'll be there in an hour, and then we'll have deserved a rest.'

Cora pulled over to the side. 'Come on, out with your picnic. I'm hungry now; in an hour I'll probably have lost my appetite.'

With the delicate touch of the proud cook, Emilia took out the Thermos flask of tea and the sandwiches. We wolfed them down.

Emilia massaged her varicose veins. 'What kind of person was this Don anyway?' she asked, all innocence.

'Like today's weather,' I said. 'Wet and windy, hardly what you'd call a devil.'

Emilia laughed and passed round the salami. Pippo jumped on to her lap to snatch at a piece, causing Emilia to spill hot tea on our bundle. She cursed, now Pippo was a devil, too. Fortunately, nothing could disturb Béla's sleep.

At last we moved on again. Half an hour later, we came to the village where Emilia's cousin lived. We had to turn off on to a narrow hill-track, and now the driving turned into torture. More and more, the track resembled the dried-up bed of a stream, with great lumps of rock lying in our way, while to our right the land fell away steeply. At first, Cora steered with care and concentration, but after a while she lost the notion. 'This is an elephant track,' she said. 'You drive, I'm sick of it.'

We swopped places, and I had to plough on with dipped headlights in the unfamiliar jeep. 'What if we meet something coming the other way?' I asked.

'There's little chance of that in the middle of the night,' replied Emilia. 'Even in broad daylight, it's only once in a blue moon somebody drives up here, maybe to bring down some hay.'

All at once, the jeep stopped, and my heart with it. Cora knew at once what was wrong. We had run out of fuel, but then we had brought along two full jerry cans. Cora held the torch while I filled up. 'You're good at that,' she commended me. 'We'll make a useful chauffeuse out of you one of these days yet.'

When we finally reached our destination, we found there was even room to turn the car next to the dilapidated building. The windows were smashed but the roof was still partially intact. We got out, stretched for a bit and then, armed with our torch, went into the building. I let out a shriek – a mouse had jumped right on to my hand. The hay was piled up in large bales, and together we soon cleared a nice little bed for Don. 'Right then, sleeves up and let's get on with it,' said Cora. We hurriedly hauled the bundle out of the jeep. Béla started to cry.

'What's that infernal stink?' grumbled Cora. 'I thought a respectable corpse did that only after a few days.'

'That's not Don,' said Emilia, 'that's our Bel Paese.'

'So how come I only got salami?'

'I'm not talking about cheese; it's our little darling that's making such a smell. Béla's filled his nappies.'

'Then go and put fresh Pampers on him.'

Emilia was really sorry, but she hadn't bargained for such an emergency.

Cora reckoned we ought to get a move on, since it would be getting light in a few hours. So we dragged the heavy bundle along the stony ground, shredding its plastic skin as we did so. But since we would have to take it off anyway, we didn't bother about it. My son was still screaming. He was afraid of the dark and wanted to get out with us, but I had only put socks on him. We shut him in the car. To make matters worse, it was starting to rain. Once we had got the dead man into the building, we laid him in the hay. I ran to the vehicle to liberate Béla. Pippo was sniffing around after rats.

'And now for the lighting of a candle for the dear departed,' ordered Cora. We looked at each other. I didn't have a candle on me.

'Emilia, the candle!' I demanded.

She shook her head.

Cora got nasty. 'Do you know, Maya, why people actually keep a *fantesca*? Apparently it's only so that they can do away with our lovers!'

'What did you call me?' Emilia was offended.

'So it'll have to be petrol after all,' Cora reckoned.

I shook the contents of Don's rucksack out on to the dusty

174

ground. 'Pity about those nice rings, though,' said Cora.

I rummaged around in Don's belongings. 'Look, joss-sticks,' I said, relieved, 'maybe we could manage it with these.'

'Hardly,' said Cora.

I rooted around some more. His Indian loincloth would do for a nappy, which was some reward for my search. Then I did in fact find a stump of a candle. 'Well, thank God for that,' I sighed. 'The clever lad thought of everything.'

Emilia changed the baby, while I pulled off the plastic sacks. We had forgotten to close Don's eyes. That was not the way it was meant to be – he was, as it were, supposed to have passed away in his sleep.

Cora lit the candle, and a cigarette as well. 'Come on, let's all have a smoke. Then we'll throw the fag-ends into the hay. Make doubly sure, in case the candle goes out.'

Even Emilia smoked, while Béla fell asleep in her arms. When at last we had wrapped the dirty nappies in the plastic and were about to leave, the dog was missing. We whistled, Emilia yelled, 'Piiii-poooo!' but he didn't come.

'Shit, that's the bloody end, begging your pardon, Emilia,' said Cora. 'We've got to go. If he doesn't want to come with us, he'll just have to stay here.'

'Please, Cora,' Emilia begged. 'In that case, I'll have to stay here too. What's to become of a poor little doggie out here in this wilderness!'

'Yes, you're quite right, soon there'll be a huge blaze here, and we've got to get down that damned gravel track before then.' We got in, with Emilia still yelling 'Pippo!' When Cora started up the engine, the dog appeared with Don's shoe in his mouth and, for the first time in his young life, he was given a good thrashing by his mistress.

The downhill run was even more dangerous than the way up. With the rain now settling in, it was becoming slippery. Cora drove more calmly and carefully than she had ever done. Emilia was sitting beside her, while I lay in the back with my son and closed my eyes. How good it was to have two friends you could depend on.

By the time it was getting light, we had the stony path

and a fair stretch of the main road behind us. The rest of the trip was no problem at all, we weren't stopped, and the jeep didn't fall apart. Once we were finally back in Florence, the borrowed vehicle still had to be returned. We shoved child, dog and blankets into Emilia's arms, I jumped into the Cadillac and raced behind Cora to the underground garage where she had picked up the jeep the evening before. With enormous relief, she parked it in its rightful place.

'Cora, we should have washed the car!'

'Nonsense. For one thing, it was filthy anyway, and for another, that mummy's boy is so dumb he won't notice a thing.'

CHAPTER 14

Bolt from the Blue

If you are always travelling along the same route in your bus, you discover things that would never occur to the newcomer. I notice that the pink phlox has blossomed overnight, I notice an old man clearing spiders' webs from that whitewashed house with a scythe, I notice that my French colleague has steered a group made up exclusively of ladies towards Michelangelo's *David*. She'll not be very pleased with the tip that brings her.

Unnoticed by the swarm of tourists, Cesare and I wait daily for the strange little girl to get better. For weeks now, this sick child has been sitting at her window, looking down on the street with sad eyes. Every time we pass, we give her a smile or a wave, Cesare even pulls funny faces. The little girl gives no obvious sign of response, but all the same, she does seem to be waiting for our bus to pass. One day, when we ignored her, just as a test, I quickly looked round from farther on and saw that she was crying.

As a little girl, I practically never cried, because unhappiness was a permanent and all-pervading companion. Somewhere, deep down, I still am that poor child, but I have, in the meantime, learned to look after myself. Anyway, the next day, Cesare stopped his bus, despite the no-stopping sign and the protests from the other drivers, and placed a small parcel for the little girl on her windowsill; out of our tips, we had bought a few toys, and Cora had contributed one of her kaleidoscopes. Cora is a very generous person, I can't emphasize that enough, but now and again she tends to lay stress on her generosity herself, which unfortunately spoils the whole effect.

Cora never fails to amaze me. When we had at last rid ourselves of Don, and had more than made up for lost sleep, she said, in that cool way of hers, 'There's always one mistake, somewhere.'

Startled, I asked, 'And what would that be?'

'That was a once-in-a-lifetime chance to do a portrait of a dead man, and in all the excitement, I clean forgot. I'd really love to go back and put that right.'

I listened to her in horror.

'You might just as well scratch together a pile of ashes from Emilia's stove and do a black-and-white picture of that.'

'We can't be absolutely sure there was a fire; it was windy. Candles and cigarette ends can go out . . .'

'All right then, on you go, get the jeep and drive away, but count me out! If you need a stiff as a model, get yourself one from the anatomical institute, the way your famous predecessors have always done.'

'Which reminds me, your father's still available. We'll really have to have him cremated soon.'

'Leave my father out of this.'

Once we finally had managed to have Father firmly planted in the ground (in Henning's roomy grave, as agreed), that was a load off my mind.

After the funeral, which passed off smoothly without priest, headstone, speeches, flowers and all the rest, we were sitting cosily in the kitchen, drinking tea and eating Emilia's delicious panettone.

'Would you actually like to have married?' I asked Emilia.

She hesitated. 'When I was young, it was my dearest wish, but I was very choosy; I turned down two young men. Later, I fell in love with Alberto. After he died, I was much too unhappy to think of that sort of thing. Then, somehow, I was too old.'

'But supposing someone was to come along now?'

'For one thing, nobody will come along, and for another, I don't want to any more. I'm past having children. If I had a husband, I'd have to wait on him hand and foot and do everything his way.'

'I can understand that, Emilia,' said Cora, 'you're absolutely right.'

But she hadn't finished with the subject. 'If I were to be perfectly honest – and I can with you – I don't need a husband, but I wouldn't mind a boyfriend.' She blushed, and we burst out laughing.

'Bravo, Emilia,' I said. 'Once you've finally passed your driving test, then you can go tearing around Florence and chat up the pensioners.'

'Rubbish,' she said, 'this is all purely theoretical. I can't very well start walking the streets. But it would be nice to be able to go for walks with a man friend, or to go to cafés or concerts. Can't you understand that?'

'We'll help you,' said Cora. 'Listen, I'll get one for you.'

'Your taste is not the same as mine,' said Emilia with great dignity. 'A skinny little scrap like Don, or a playboy like Signor Henning – that's not my style.'

'The choice will be entirely up to you. I'll put an ad in the paper: *Wanted: sturdy pensioner for occasional gardening work.* You look the lads over, and we take on the one you fancy.'

It was Emilia's turn to laugh now. 'Maybe I won't fancy any of them!'

'In that case, we won't take any of them on.' Cora was all fired up with the idea and went straight to the phone and called the newspaper to put in a small ad. In the next few days, three men applied by phone, while a fourth got someone to call for him. We set appointments for a Sunday, in our pink villa, at hourly intervals.

It was Cora's plan that, for the time being, none of the candidates should either be appointed or turned down. We would take their photograph and observe them carefully, and afterwards we'd discuss the pros and cons of each in detail.

'You can't very well photograph a gardener without good reason,' protested Emilia.

'I'll insist that for this job they've got to be fond of animals and children,' I suggested, 'and, just to try them out, I'll put

179

Béla and Pippo on each applicant's lap. Then Cora can exclaim, all delighted, ''Oh my, what a lovely picture that would make!'' and reach for the camera, which will just happen to be lying handy.'

'I'll die laughing, I know,' said Cora. 'But you're on.'

The first to come reached straight into his pocket and pulled out a small slate. On it, he wrote, in chalk, *I have a speech handicap, but can understand you.* That shortcoming aside, he was a nice elderly man, strongly built and friendly. He had clumps of black hairs growing out of his ears. He looked a bit like some ageing Easter bunny. Of course, we didn't fall about laughing as we took his picture, since he would have thought it had to do with his speech problem. He had hardly left when we asked Emilia, 'How would you fancy a boyfriend you can chatter away to incessantly, and all he does is smile and say nothing?'

Emilia wagged her head from side to side. 'It does have its plus points, if a man can't talk back. On the other hand, I'd have to make all the moves, and that would be the end of being courted.'

'Well, let's wait and see what the others are like. The next grandad should be here any minute.'

The next one was so disagreeable we didn't even have to bother with a photo. Dirty, unkempt, with rotten teeth and very pushy. I had no desire to put Béla on his lap. Emilia, too, gave us a look to say that we could write this specimen off straight away. Cora did it very skilfully.

'Well, thank goodness he's gone,' said Emilia. 'I wouldn't even have trusted that one with my dog.'

Next, there appeared an ex-seaman with a rolling gait. He admitted he hadn't much idea about gardening, but said he was willing to learn; without beating about the bush, he started off telling us about some hair-raising adventures, with the odd wink towards Emilia. Entertaining as he was, he made no impression on her.

The last one was, by contrast, a keen gardener. He examined our trees and explained how the apple tree urgently needed pruning and the cherry tree was rotten and should be chopped down. He had no doubts that he'd be starting right away.

Once we were alone, Emilia said, 'I want the mute.'

'Why?'

'He's the only one I could maybe fall in love with. Number two is right out, and the other two just don't interest me.'

'OK,' I said, 'we'll take him on tomorrow. We'll keep our fingers crossed for you.'

I had got to know a girl who was a tourist guide and was about to give up the job to get married. If I was interested, she told me, I could learn the work. It involved collecting German parties from their hotel in the coach and, in the course of a three-hour excursion, with several stops for taking pictures, giving them a rundown on Florentine history and art. There was a certain amount you had to learn by heart, you had to be prepared for some specific questions that always cropped up, and be able to weave in the occasional flowery or racy anecdote. I started right away on getting the guide book on art treasures firmly into my head. My instructress gave me some tips: 'There's almost always some smartarse among them who'll want to know the year of construction of even some outside toilet. The only thing you can do then is to put on a snooty arrogance and witter on that, "that must have been in November 1935, when all the sanitary installations in the city were renovated or, as the case may be, put in for the first time", even if it is a load of absolute crap. The show-offs soon go quiet if you're convincing and serious enough. But then there are also the intellectuals, who know a lot more than we do. There, you have to flutter your eyelashes and say sweetly, "There is some disagreement about the exact date. Which would you tend to go along with – as someone with inside knowledge?"'

I rather liked the idea of drawing both the know-alls and the art freaks out on to thin ice, and I sensed that here was the ideal job that would leave me time for other things. Later on, I earned quite a fair living during the tourist season.

*   *   *

We were busy, and we were happy. Cora painted, I studied, and Emilia fell in love.

The dumb gardener, as it turned out, was not a mute after all. He had a stutter, especially when he found himself in unfamiliar situations and among strangers, when he preferred simply to whip out his slate as a means of self-protection. Once he felt at ease in alien surroundings and had gained confidence in his new acquaintances, he would cautiously begin with his stammering. Emilia had quickly twigged that she had to treat him gently and not be too demanding.

She talked to him about herself and accepted his stammered responses without any trace of impatience or surprise. We found it very touching, watching how the two of them would often sit together, enjoying a laugh at Béla and Pippo and, in their own quiet way, growing closer.

'That's coming along fine,' said Cora, 'but it won't be as soon as it would be with us before they're hopping into bed with each other. If they ever do.'

Sometimes I tried to sound Emilia out. 'Does Mario always stammer?' I asked.

'No, only when he talks.'

A few weeks before Christmas, Cora's parents phoned. They were fully expecting us to arrive any time, to celebrate a real German Christmas with roast goose and a tree. And of course, Friedrich would be home, too. 'No,' said Cora.

Jonas, too, got in touch, rather sheepishly, with a similar proposal for the Festival of Love. We immediately got into a quarrel over the phone. He could forgive me my adultery, Jonas stated. His piousness made my hackles rise. 'My God, don't make such a big deal of it, it can happen to anybody, even you!'

'Not me,' said Jonas.

When I told her about this, Cora said, 'I've almost a good mind to invite the whole family – Father, Mother, Fred and Jonas – and then seduce your faithful Jonas right under their noses. What do you bet I could pull it off?'

'You wouldn't get very long odds on it. Nobody doubts you could do it. But is it worth the effort?'

'I don't know,' said Cora, 'it would probably be better for us to have peace and quiet and celebrate a Florentine Christmas in our own way. For the moment, we'll leave the little seduction ploys to Emilia.'

Three times a week the gardener rolled up, even though at this point in the winter there was nothing to do other than pruning the trees and digging over the flowerbeds. He would sit, in his unobtrusive way, in a corner of the kitchen (exactly where Don had sat), smiling benignly, and slicing onions, peeling tomatoes or chopping herbs, occasionally lighting up a cigar and now and again laying a chapped brown hand on Emilia's plump forearm. At moments like those, they looked like something off the top of a wedding cake.

Emilia had talked on the phone to her cousin, who invited her over for the holiday period. Emilia asked pointedly whether anything had been happening in the village, you know, like a fire. It was only at the end of their conversation that her cousin remembered that, yes, there had indeed been a fire somewhere. 'Was anybody hurt?' asked Emilia.

'No, of course not, there was nobody living out there. It was too late to try to put it out; it just blazed up like tinder.'

Wasn't that just typical sloppiness, Emilia said to us, a disgrace that Don hadn't even been found yet. That could only happen in her sister's village. It was fine by us.

Mario, the taciturn gardener, had his roots out in the country, too. While Emilia was not so stupid as to blab about Don's charred presence up in a mountain village, she did talk to him occasionally about her cousin and about country life, something our gardener enjoyed hearing about. By this time, he had, however laboriously, managed to convey some details about his previous life. The son of a large farming family, he had left home while still a boy – no doubt because he was made fun of, on account of his stammer – and earned a living as a storeman in a factory. Later, he had worked for the city council, driving the tanker that went round watering the municipal green spaces, emptying the litter bins in the parks and carrying out similar tasks with conscientious care. He had been in receipt of a modest pension for some months now. In his younger days, he had several times been keen on getting married, but nothing came of it.

In the meantime, Emilia had struggled through countless driving lessons and was beginning to lose faith in her abilities. Mario practised with her at weekends, especially the dreaded reverse parking, on deserted factory car parks. Since he was incapable of passing critical comments, but only smiled or gave an admonitory shake of the head, he achieved more than the driving instructor. Emilia applied for a test, and passed. That day was undoubtedly one of the high spots of her life.

Emilia's success just had to be celebrated. But on that very day, when I was in fact intending to go shopping with Cora and to do the cooking, I fell into a severe depression.

I had had bad dreams during the night. I couldn't remember exactly how it happened, but in the dream someone had murdered Béla. I awoke bathed in sweat, reeled up the stairs to Emilia's room and lifted my sleeping son out of his pine chest. Emilia scolded me. With Béla in my arms, I tried to get back to sleep. In the darkness, my brother, my mother and father, Henning and Don all stood in front of me, reaching out towards my child.

As I said, I was completely useless the next day. Emilia's celebration dinner was postponed, and she went to the cinema with Mario instead.

I lay in bed, incapable of doing a thing. Cora came in, leading Béla by the hand. 'If you're running a fever, we'd better send for a doctor,' she suggested. These words reminded me of Don when he was ill, and I burst into floods of tears.

'My parents have made up their minds they are coming to spend Christmas here with me. My father said if the mountain won't come to Mahomet, and so on,' said Cora. 'But I don't really want to have my family here. They'll be telling us what's right, rapping us over the knuckles and trying to turn us into respectable citizens. And most of all they'll want me to take some élitist course of study, like my brother, for instance. They've always thought architecture was the bee's knees.'

'Doesn't it ever occur to you that they love you and that's why they like to be with you?'

'Well, sure, and I love them too. But supposing we just took off over Christmas and left my folks to celebrate on their own here. What do you say?'

'And where are we supposed to go?'

'Somewhere warm. Sometimes I find Florence too noisy, too dirty, too busy, nowhere to park, everything so expensive . . .'

'And do you reckon it would be any better elsewhere?'

'We'll go to the sea, to Malta or North Africa or Sicily, then you'll soon perk up again!'

'Oh, Cora, do you really believe travelling is a cure for everything? Mind you, Emilia would love it.'

'Emilia would be staying here; and Mario would stay in the house, too, to help her with the work with three visitors for Christmas. Wouldn't I make a good matchmaker?'

The thought of Mario acting as butler and Emilia grabbing her chances with both hands cheered me up no end. But the prospect of luring Cora's parents, loaded with presents, to an empty house, seemed to me contemptible.

'Put your parents off,' I advised her. 'Tell them we're going away. Mario can still stay here with Emilia, to scare off burglars or something.'

Emilia was late getting back from the cinema. Rather embarrassed, she admitted that Mario had shown her round his little flat. 'Have a look at this, Cora,' she said, unwrapping a heavy paving stone from a piece of newspaper. 'What do you think of that?'

Cora's response was immediate. 'Where did you get that? That's a pretty old piece. Have you any more?'

Emilia went all confidential. Yes, Mario did have more of them. If Cora was interested, he could pave her whole patio with them.

'And what would that cost me?' asked Cora.

Not a lot, Emilia considered, since after all Mario had close and respectful ties with the household.

Once Emilia and Béla were in bed, Cora said, 'Have you any idea what that bit of stone is?'

'A very fine one, I'm sure.'

'It's a piece of paving stone from the Piazza della Signoria, which, after the Campo in Sienna, is the most beautiful square in the world.'

'So how on earth does a poor soul like Mario come to be in possession of stones like that?'

Cora then told me how the paving had been removed from the piazza because excavations were to be carried out. Two years later, they wanted to put all the paving back neatly, but the original stones had disappeared. There was a huge scandal! Apparently, Mario, who was working for the city authorities, must have taken away a load on his water wagon, perhaps with the innocent intention of flooring the cowshed on his brother's farm with it. But he could have no more than a small slice of the whole cake in his possession if it would only just be enough to do our patio.

'Well now, isn't this our lucky day?' said Cora. 'Paving that, in the eighteenth century, grand dukes would have had laid, and soon it'll be on my terrace!'

Cora's delight was beginning to infect me. And now, into the bargain, this gave us the perfect excuse for billeting Mario here over Christmas: he would have the job of laying the paving stones for us, all carefully arranged to recreate their beautiful pattern.

'But hold on, Cora, there's one snag. Just by looking at one piece of stone, you recognized where it came from at once. Don't you think that people coming to visit us in the future might also identify our patio right away as the Piazza della Signoria in miniature?'

'Oh, go on, this is an old house, it's only natural there would also be old stones around. Anyway, our visitors aren't as smart as me.'

'Don't you be so sure. What about your friend with the jeep, the sculptor? He's bound to know something about art history.'

186

'I won't let him farther than the kitchen.' Cora remained obstinate and impulsive, but I have to say in her defence that everybody who did visit us actually seemed convinced that the patio had always looked like that.

Cora's brother Friedrich was the next to come on the phone. He would not admit that his reproachful tone was the result of his own hurt feelings, but instead made the point about his poor parents who could not see what they had done to deserve being cold-shouldered by their daughter.

'To be honest with you,' I told Cora, 'I've always envied you your parents. You have this fantastic good fortune, and all you do is kick it around.'

'You idealize my parents, Maya. As a child, I would have loved to have a mother who stood in the kitchen in a white apron baking cakes, instead of one that dressed up in the latest fashions to attend the openings of exhibitions.'

'Emilia spends her days standing in the kitchen making dough for ravioli.'

Cora ignored my remark. 'And I could have done with a father who could mend my bicycle or build me a cage for my hamster; what good did all his eloquent speechifying ever do me?'

'Mario can't talk, and he's busy building a kennel for Pippo.'

At that, Cora laughed. 'You're right. We've just got ourselves a new set of parents.'

Emilia asked whether she might have the car for a few days before Christmas. She wanted to take Mario and Pippo on a visit to her cousin.

'So long as the quiet man does most of the driving, I've no objection,' said Cora, 'but don't get up to any nonsense!' And she wagged a warning finger at Emilia.

Loaded up with cakes of her own baking, all sorts of Christmassy kitsch from the city shops as well as useful presents, the two of them set out on their trip. We waved them off.

It took us only an hour to appreciate how lucky we were to have Emilia. When you came down to it, she was on the go all day long, and when she wasn't actually working she would be attending to Béla, patiently and fondly showing him ways around his all too precocious contrariness.

Cora got on with her painting, I caught up with my homework and looked after my child. Now and again I wondered whether I should, once and for all, write Jonas off as a bad job and give Friedrich the come-on again. What I was really hoping was that other opportunities would present themselves, so I ducked out of making any decisions for the time being.

Two days later, the pair of holiday-makers were back. It was Cora who heard the Cadillac pulling up outside. 'They can hardly have spent a full day at her beloved cousin's,' she said, amazed. 'They'll have ended up falling out with each other. You just never know what's coming next!'

We went out to meet them. It was only half past four, yet it was already dark. Pippo jumped all over us for joy. Emilia and Mario got out of the car looking grim-faced.

'What's up?' I asked.

There was no answer from Emilia, and I hadn't been expecting one from Mario in the first place. We went into the kitchen and Cora put the kettle on for some tea. Mario and Emilia huddled round the stove, looking dejected, and held their hands out over the hotplate.

All of a sudden, Emilia said, 'We've brought Don back with us.'

Cora's jaw dropped – and I dropped my cup. 'What did you say?' I asked.

'Don's lying in the car; we wrapped him in a blanket.'

'I thought he was incinerated in the hay, wasn't he?' Cora asked.

Emilia regained some of her composure. 'There was nothing else I could do. I drove out with Mario to see everything was all right. This time we borrowed my brother-in-law's four-wheel drive; I told them Mario was so fond of the mountains. The fire hadn't caught at all, my cousin had been talking about a different building. The candle must have gone out right away. Everything was exactly the way we left it, the rucksack lying on the ground and Don next to it.'

'So Mario knows the whole story?'

'Well, I had to explain everything to him. It seems they can find traces of poison in a corpse even after months have passed, and even in charred bones, so he told me.'

I glanced at Mario. He was watching Emilia with an anxious, yet at the same time happy, look in his chestnut eyes. 'But you could have started the fire again, couldn't you?'

'And what if it had gone out again? We couldn't very well hang around to make sure we got a good blaze going. The fire brigade would have turned up and caught us at it!'

'Why didn't you just leave him lying there?'

'Cora, I thought of something – those expensive shoes of his! They would have seen right away that they were Italian, they would have found out where they had been bought. The shop assistant would have remembered you both.'

'So why didn't you simply bring the shoes with you, instead of the complete Don? Did you pack him into the four-wheel drive and then transfer him to the Cadillac?'

'Yes, something like that. On a lonely stretch down in the valley, we hid him in a ditch and picked him up on the road home.'

'So what are we supposed to do with him now?'

'Well, first we'll have to bring him in here.'

I looked at Cora, indescribable disgust in my eyes. What must Don look like now! Emilia guessed what I was thinking. 'Don't get all upset. The cold, dry mountain air has preserved him almost as well as a Parma ham.'

In the meantime, Mario had been scribbling away on his slate and now he held it up for us to look at. *A grave under the paving stones*, it read.

Emilia nodded proudly. 'Mario's going to work all through the night. Fortunately the ground isn't frozen. In a few hours, he'll have dug out a hole for a grave. I'll just go and set up the standard lamp for him outside. When you get up in the morning, it'll all be taken care of, you can fly off to Sicily and have fun. By the time you get back, the beautiful new patio will be finished.'

Mario got to his feet and shook us by the hand, presumably as a gesture to assure us our secret was safe with him. Then he went out into the garden and got straight down to work.

'Have you been phoning Jonas in the last month?' Cora asked.

'He called me once. Why do you ask?'

'Look at this. The phone bill is twice as high as usual. I mean, I'm not really bothered, but I've got a sneaking suspicion Don might have been making calls to New Zealand.'

'Oh, he was much too ill for that. I hardly think so.'

Emilia came in, looking for an extension cable. 'Don didn't make any calls,' she said.

'How can you be so sure of that? Just look at this bill!' said Cora, clearly worried.

'That was me,' Emilia admitted. We were surprised, but once we heard that she had talked to Mario daily, we got the point: long distance calls to someone who stutters were bound to be long-drawn-out affairs.

'Well, thank God for that,' I said. 'We were scared he might have passed our address on to someone in New Zealand.'

Emilia stood smiling like some conjuror who has just pulled a white dove out of a top hat, and handed us a postcard and a letter. Don had indeed written home, and had given his mail to Emilia to post. The card to his parents was boring: Italy's lovely, and so forth. The letter, which Emilia had already opened, would have been disastrous for us. In it, Don reported to his wife that he was on the trail of something very interesting. *It's all to do with a German widow – neither young nor good-looking – who has apparently had her rich husband murdered.*

'How did you hit on the idea that there might be some touchy subject in this letter? You don't understand a word of English, do you?' I asked.

Emilia gave a shrug. '*Intuizione*,' she said modestly.

Mario carried Don into the kitchen unaided and laid him, still well wrapped up, in a corner. 'No, take him straight outside!' I yelled at him, holding my nose as a precaution.

But Cora came back in, armed with camera, drawing pad and charcoal pencil. 'Nice to have him back!' she said. 'But if your nerves aren't up to it, maybe you should go and see to Béla.'

As she drew the blanket off Don, I couldn't help it, I just had to look. I shall never forget that gruesome sight as long as I live.

CHAPTER 15

Crystal Clear

I know some Italian cemeteries which are fully wired up, because the relatives want to have an everlasting electric light bulb burning like a sanctuary lamp next to the photo of the deceased. Because of the heat, nearly all the flowers are plastic ones. The colour green, which predominates in German cemeteries, is hardly to be seen here. To be sure, a few cypresses border the kingdom of the dead, but when I think of the birdsong that comes twittering out of the trees by the graves of Carlo and my mother, then my father and Henning have been accommodated in more peaceful surroundings. If you subscribe to the theory that the dead can still derive some pleasure or other from their resting place, then you have to say my father gets more sun than my mother, whereas she has more greenery.

Don's grave lies, unfortunately, right under our sensitive noses. I would much prefer it if, as a foreigner, he were buried in the historic Cimitero degli Inglesi, a cemetery which, like its occupants, is crumbling and decaying. Every time we have coffee out on the patio, our former lover intrudes into our thoughts in a most unpleasant way.

Mario had promised to lay Don to rest overnight, and he was as good as his word. Where the old paving had been removed, a very suspicious shape had been left. But the thick laurel hedge blocked the view for any inquisitive neighbours; and besides, Emilia assured us that the house next door was occupied only in the spring and autumn.

Cora and I were delighted that we were still able to get a

booking on an Alitalia flight to Sicily. Béla, sitting on my lap, was thoroughly pampered by a stunningly handsome steward, and he proved himself a very good-natured little travelling companion.

At the terminal in Catania, that town dominated by black lava, a throng of press photographers and paparazzi was lying in wait. 'They've rolled out the red carpet for us,' I joked and went to find a luggage trolley. Then we heard that some politician was expected from Rome, coming back to his native heath to spend Christmas as he always did, at his Mamma's.

When I had wheeled the trolley back to where our luggage was, Cora, holding Béla by the hand, was being snapped by the photo-mafia. She flashed her teeth like some hungry dog and the press boys, who had been bored stiff up till now, shouted for more – '*Ancora! Ancora!*'

We asked our taxi driver for a hotel he could recommend. He could take us fifty kilometres farther along the road, to Taormina, he told us, and there we'd have the choice between posh – in a former monastery – mid-price, and plain but respectable.

'We can afford a posh one,' Cora reckoned, 'but would it be much fun spending Christmas with nothing but a set of Henning Kornmeiers, I wonder? Let's go for plain but comfortable, then at least we might have the prospect of pleasant company!'

Our hotel was charming, but not exactly cheap, for all its plainness and respectability. We had a spectacular view out over the sea to our left and Mount Etna to the right. The weather was mild, with almost a threat of rain. We settled into what they called our 'junior suite', and then all three of us hit the hay for a short nap. After that, we went for a stroll along the Corso Umberto. At dinner, we ordered stuffed pig's trotters with lentils, followed by delicious *Torta di Mirtilli* – tiramisu with blueberries.

As we were enjoying a late breakfast the next morning, the waitress rushed excitedly up to our table waving a newspaper. Cora's picture was splashed over it, with the caption: *The widow of the murdered Brazilian millionaire Kornmeier on a visit to Sicily with her small daughter.*

'How stupid can they get!' said Cora. 'If they reckoned I was pregnant the last time – the day Henning died – then I should be going around now sticking out to here or maybe even carrying an infant in my arms, but certainly not a child that can walk and talk.'

I felt quite flattered, for, as far as Béla was concerned, he hadn't yet made that much progress in those departments. 'But where do they get the daughter from?' I asked.

'Because they're stupid, that's what I'm saying. They probably think Béla's a girl's name.' We had a good laugh at this and then attached no further importance to the whole thing.

After a few pleasant days' holiday, I phoned Emilia. Everything was fine, she said, Mario had worked so busily, despite a cold snap, that he would finish laying the new paving stones the next day.

'And how are you getting along with each other?' I asked.

'Famously,' she said and then, after a pause, 'Maya, I'd like to ask a favour. Without you, and especially without Béla, it's boring here. We'd love to come and visit you, at our own expense, of course. We thought we might drive right down through Italy. Do you think Cora would let us?'

I promised to put in a good word for this plan.

'Then I'd have my Cadillac here,' said Cora. 'That would be quite handy. I'd love to go and see the catacombs in Palermo. Tell them to come.'

On the day we were expecting the enterprising couple to arrive, we went for a post-Christmas shopping stroll. In the front entries of all the houses, there were little wooden boxes with Christmas stars. Cutting out all sentimentality, we had spent Christmas Eve in the hotel lobby, where a big nativity scene, complete with manger, had been set up. Now, though, we decided to treat ourselves, at our leisure, to some presents of our own choosing. We picked up some ethnic silk scarves, necklaces made from polished lava, brightly coloured marzipan fruits and silver hearts and feet, which had once served as votive images.

Loaded with parcels, we finally sat down in the Café Wunderbar and warmed ourselves over mugs of hot chocolate, and Béla was allowed to join in. Cora slurped the disgusting skin off all three mugs. Afterwards, we also indulged ourselves with one more *Tartufo*, a delicious icy truffle. After this great orgy, I left Béla and Cora and went to look for the ladies' toilet.

In five minutes, I was back at our marble-topped table, where only Béla's empty pushchair stood. I gazed around, looking for them. Cora was at the cash-desk, paying the bill and chatting to the cashier. 'Where's the baby, where is my little poochie?' I asked her.

Cora turned round. 'In his pushchair,' she said, but noticed at once that the baby-buggy was empty.

Up till that day, Béla had never been able to climb out by himself. We looked all around – not especially worried yet; no doubt some Sicilian mamma had taken the little fellow on her lap and was stuffing him with fruitcake.

'Look – what's this?' said Cora, picking up a letter from her plate.

At that moment, my heart almost stopped. I slumped on a chair, Cora ripped open the envelope, and together we read:

Signora Kornmeier, we have your daughter in our power. If you want to get her back alive, on no account call in the police. You are being watched! Act naturally and go back to your hotel room with your companion and wait for further instructions.

Cora took my hand. She felt responsible because she had left Béla alone for one minute, which I would have done myself in any bustling café. She turned to two elderly ladies sitting at the next table to ours. Keeping her voice as calm as possible, she asked, 'Did you see who lifted the child out of his pram?'

'Of course, signora. You've no need to worry. It was the little one's uncle. I think he's waiting outside.'

In spite of the letter, I thought for one brief moment that Emilia and Mario had arrived and taken Béla in their arms.

I shot Cora a warning glance: we mustn't do anything to make the women suspicious, or they might end up calling the police.

'Oh well, that's all right, then,' she said, and we beat a hasty retreat. As soon as we were out in the street, pushing the empty buggy, I went completely to pieces; I could neither speak nor cry, but broke out in a cold sweat and my heart was pounding.

Cora waved down a taxi, and we drove the short distance back to our hotel in silence. Only once we were up in our room did Cora start talking. 'They think Béla's a millionairess's child, so they're going to try to squeeze a juicy ransom out of us. It's all a misunderstanding, and we'll soon get it cleared up, I'm sure.'

'Cora, these are professionals. If they don't get any money, they'll murder Béla!'

'You know I'm prepared to shove every penny I have down their throats if need be. I look on Béla as if he were my own. But maybe it's not absolutely necessary. We've got to drive as tough a bargain as we can.'

At last, my tears started to flow. I lay face down on the bed, with the tears streaming on to my neatly folded nightdress. 'Cora, I've messed up everything in my life. If only Béla comes to no harm, I'm going to be a good person, I'll go and look after lepers or become a social worker in the slums of Rio.'

'Now just hold your horses. They're not going to harm a hair on Béla's head. And besides, it wouldn't do him much good if his mum turned into a second Mother Teresa, would it?'

'Just what are we waiting for? A messenger, a phone call, a letter – what?'

'Could be anything. It's also possible that somebody on the hotel staff is in cahoots with them. Cast your mind back to the waitress with the paper! We've got to be patient.'

An hour passed, during which we worked our way through various strategies and possible ways of getting the money together. Then there was a loud knock. Cora flung the door open. There was no messenger there, no kidnapper, but Emilia and Mario, standing beaming on the threshold. They noticed immediately that something had happened.

'Where's my little treasure?' demanded Emilia, who, thanks to her tried and tested intuition, was on the right track at once.

Through my tears I told her of the whole catastrophe. Pippo ran through both rooms, sniffing all over. Mario got so worked up that he started stuttering wild nonsense.

Cora was the one who kept her cool. 'I've already told Maya I'll put up my whole fortune if that's what it takes.'

'It's a good thing Béla can hardly talk,' said Emilia. 'He can't tell anyone where he's been and what these people look like. That means there's a good chance they won't do anything to harm him.'

When the phone rang, Cora practically pulled it out of its socket. I pressed my face against hers to try to hear everything that was said. It was the reception desk, to say that a Signor Dante wanted to talk to her.

Dante had hardly managed to say that the child was all right, before Cora was yelling at him. 'You idiots! No doubt even you will have discovered by now that the kid isn't a girl. If you had one brain cell among you, it would have struck you that, after a pregnancy of six months, I could hardly have an eighteen-month-old son already! I've never been pregnant, I neither have children nor am I a million-airess; if I were, don't you think I'd be in some top-class hotel? So hand over the child and don't make things worse for yourselves!'

Obviously, she had given Dante quite a fright, for he hung up. I was furious. 'Oh, great! You've done it now!' I screamed. 'That's exactly how not to go about it. Now they'll never get in touch again and my child is going to die!'

Emilia took me in her arms. 'Of course they'll ring again. They've got to talk things over now, and check whether Cora's telling the truth. No doubt one of the swine is getting a right thumping now for messing up his research. When they call back, I'll talk to them. After all, they're my com-patriots, I know how to handle them! But you've no need to worry about me being undiplomatic; far from it – I'll butter them up.'

I wasn't convinced butter was exactly what was called for here; in fact, I wasn't sure about anything. Cora and I didn't altogether see ourselves as greenhorns when it came to criminal activities, but, in this situation, I was as helpless as my poor child.

'Emilia,' I said, 'you can suggest to them that I'll offer myself as a hostage in exchange for my baby.'

Everyone shook their head. 'Not a good idea, and you know that yourself,' said Cora.

'I wonder whether Jonas has anything to do with this?' asked Emilia.

Two hours later, Dante called again. Emilia answered and claimed to be Béla's grandmother, a poor woman who had no money for a ransom. 'The child can speak two words of German and three of Italian,' said Dante. 'If it was your grandchild, it wouldn't know any German.'

'How clever you are, Signor Dante,' said Emilia amicably. 'It's true, the little lad is the son of a German woman, in fact, of a friend of Signora Kornmeier. Unfortunately, she has no money, because my son – the child's father – left her and went off to America, and hasn't been heard of since.'

Dante was a chivalrous type, and expressed his regrets. But the rich signora, he reckoned, would undoubtedly be able to cough up for her friend's child.

'I'm sure that's true,' said Emilia. 'We love the little fellow, and we're all sitting here crying over him. Have you no feelings for children?'

Dante assured her he was fond of children and no harm would come to Béla, but they could hardly be expected to give him back without any kind of ransom being paid.

Cora murmured, 'That sounds a bit more promising already.'

Emilia now asked about the price. We couldn't catch the reply, but, judging by the cry she let out, the figure was out of the question. We could never get that kind of money together, she said, that was quite impossible. At that, the mild-mannered Dante grew rather more forceful: no money, no child, it was as simple as that. 'Do I have to send you a finger or an ear before you get the picture?' And that was the end of the conversation.

Mario wrote on his slate: *Emilia = Grandma. Mario = Grandpa.* Cora smiled, 'Right enough.'

Mario wiped it all off with the heel of his hand and started writing again: *Emilia = negotiation. Mario = action.* I was deeply moved. Did I really deserve having all these people who loved me so much? For all my terrible fear, I knew I wasn't on my own. Cora was prepared to hand over her money, while the other two were, in their own way, doing everything they could to help me. I was determined I would never forget what they were doing for me.

'What do you mean by that, Mario – action?' Cora asked.

He was unable to reply, so he wrote: *Handover of cash.* There was no doubt that when it came to that point, it would be a dangerous situation. But was Mario the right man for it, since he wouldn't be able even to talk to Dante if the need arose?

Emilia seemed to realize that, too, for she said, 'Mario and I will do it together.'

'No,' I said. 'He's my child. When the ransom has to be handed over, that'll be my job and mine alone. I'll never allow you to put your lives in danger because of me.'

Emilia said, calmly, 'We are old, you are young. Your child should grow up in your care.'

I burst into tears. All of a sudden, I wished Jonas was there. Had I not brought a terrible guilt upon myself by denying my child his father? The kidnappers would never have found their way to his farm if Béla had been growing up there.

Then Cora asked, 'Shouldn't we maybe ask around in the café to see if we can find out what this alleged "uncle" looked like? Has anyone any idea whether the police in Sicily are corrupt and incompetent, or whether, in the end, we should consider putting them in the picture?'

Emilia gave Mario a questioning look, then both of them shook their heads slowly. 'There are good ones and bad ones,' she said mysteriously, 'we can't be too careful. Maybe the criminals aren't keeping a watch on us, maybe they're a bunch of amateurs – but how are we to know for sure?'

Mario was writing again: *I'm going to have a look around. They don't know me.* He left the room with Pippo.

The waiting was unbearable. Cora called room service and ordered something to eat, telling them I was running a fever. When a tray was brought, loaded with antipasti and accompanied with all good wishes, none of us could touch a thing. We were missing Mario; he had such a reassuring effect on us.

When Dante phoned again, he demanded right away to talk to the grandmother, not to Cora. Emilia was very pleasant, but she pursued her own plan. 'We're poor people,' she said. 'My husband worked as a gardener, and I'm just a charwoman. You gangsters live the high life and can have no idea what amounts of money like that mean to us.'

Dante gave himself away. 'Surely you don't think we're rich, do you? My brother and I have nothing but debts, we're much worse off than you. We're unemployed . . .'

Emilia said she was sorry to hear that. 'I'm sure we can come to some agreement,' she suggested, 'but you mustn't be unrealistic. What you don't have – I mean, what the Signora Kornmeier doesn't have – you can't very well give away, isn't that so, signore?'

Dante's next demand was that Cora should have a think about how much she reckoned the life of my child was worth. He would call again. I tore the receiver out of Emilia's hand. 'I'm the little boy's mother. Now listen – he needs his meal at seven, he'll be starving! And he doesn't like going to sleep in the dark, leave a light on or else he'll get scared and start crying.'

'Signora, we are men of honour, we wouldn't do anything to frighten a little fellow. He has already had his meal and is lying happily in bed.'

'Please, Signor Dante,' I pleaded humbly, 'that child is all I have in the world, you can't take him from me. Signor Dante, I know now what they mean by "the Inferno", do you understand it too? I'm going crazy at the thought that my son and I have been separated for the very first time and this could damage him for life!'

'No, no, you mustn't talk like that,' said Dante. 'Nothing is going to happen to the little one, you can rest assured. As soon as your friend pays up, you'll have him back – upon my word of honour. So now, have a talk with her, and I'll call back in an hour.'

In a way, I was relieved. Dante was no monster, far less a professional kidnapper or killer; he sounded like a young, perhaps even very young, man who, because of the picture in the papers, had thought up some stupid scheme. Couldn't the police be of some help after all? But supposing the sensitive Dante cracked at the very sight of the police and blew himself to bits along with my child, or did something equally terrible?

Cora was doing some arithmetic. She had laid all her traveller's cheques out on her bed – an excessive pile of them; how thoughtless can you get! – and was counting them. 'We'll offer them what's here, or, let's say, just a little less. If they bite, then everything's fine. If not, I'll have to fly back to Florence and try to drum up some ready cash from somewhere.'

'Cora,' I said, 'I promise you I'll work as long as I live to pay back what I owe you. But please, just pay, do it for me, do it for Béla, please!'

'Yes, right, that's what I'm going to do! But we don't have to shell out any more to Dante than is absolutely necessary. And besides, we'll soon be making more money again – that's going to be no problem for us.'

Suddenly, I couldn't help thinking of my mother. When I was five, I had got lost in a crowded department store at the time of the sales. I wasn't crying, and I wasn't afraid, because a boy had led me into the pets department, where I stood, holding his hand and gazing at puppies and parrots and baby rabbits. As I remembered it, even then I experienced that uplifting feeling of having thrown off my chains. When at last, as a result of various messages over the public-address system (which I was never able to make out), I was found, taken in tow and led back to my mother, she was absolutely beside herself. I'll never forget the tremendous relief on her face when she saw me. Later, of course, all hell was let loose.

Mario came in with Pippo on his lead, looking pretty excited. Unfortunately, in that state, he couldn't even stutter. Emilia held out his slate to him. *Car park, man in car with binoculars*, he wrote.

'That must be Dante's brother,' Cora thought. 'Is he young and well built? Does he look dangerous?'

Mario stammered, 'Quite young!' Then he went back to writing, since that took less time: *If I had another man to help me, we could grab him.*

Emilia was suddenly all enthusiasm. 'I'm better than any man! And then, when Dante calls, we can just say, very friendly, "Guess who we've got here!"'

Cora began to laugh, but immediately had second thoughts. 'And what if he's packing a gun? Besides, what are people in the street going to think if we drag a stranger from his car and overpower him? They'd call the police! And anyway, who can say whether he is Dante's brother? He could be some harmless peeping Tom, or even a private detective keeping a watch on something else altogether.'

Mario wrote, *No!*

Emilia gave him a questioning look. 'How do you know it's us he's watching?'

Mario pointed to our window.

I leapt to my feet to go and look out, but Emilia grabbed me by the sleeve. 'Are you crazy? If we're to have a chance, he mustn't suspect that Mario has spotted him.'

At that moment, the phone rang again. Wouldn't the hotel staff get suspicious and start eavesdropping if a Signor Dante kept on phoning and asking for us? He must be pretty careless or inexperienced to take a risk like that. Cora now made her offer, and Dante again asked for time to consider it. Apparently, he wasn't in a position to decide everything by himself.

Emilia took off her slippers and put on her shoes. 'I'm going down to the lobby, because after all, Mario and I still haven't got the keys for our room. We came rushing straight up to you, because we knew your room number.'

I could tell by looking at her that she had other plans in mind and probably wanted to go and have a look at the figure in the car, but I trusted her implicitly.

Dante called before Emilia got back. 'Signora,' he said to Cora, 'we've checked up on you. While you were telling the truth when you said the child wasn't yours, you do own a house in Florence, and its value is very different from the pathetic amount you have the cheek to offer us. Stick another couple of zeros on the end of your offer and then we can talk terms.'

Cora protested, 'My house in Florence is a dump. I hope you've found that out as well.'

'Signora, just stop lying! Even the bill for your studio windows amounts to a great deal more than the pittance you're trying to fob us off with.'

'How am I to know the child's even still alive? And anyway, it must be obvious to you that I can't raise so much in cash just overnight, especially since your banks here are closed practically all the time.'

'Well now, you'll just have to get yourself to Florence tomorrow. The sooner you're back here with the money, the sooner we hand over the little fellow.'

'And how is the handover to be done?'

'I'll decide that later. First, I want to see that you're on that plane tomorrow morning. It takes off from Catania at eight.' He hung up.

Cora cursed. 'There's something very fishy about all this. Where has he got all his information about my studio windows? I'm going to phone my glazier right now; I've got a sneaking suspicion.' Cora called information, phoned around for a while and finally, sure enough, she had the glazier on the line. She asked him whether Ruggero, her one-time lover, was a Sicilian. No, she heard, Ruggero was born in Florence, but his father was originally from Taormina. Had the lad got himself into some kind of bother?

'No, no, not at all. We just had a bet that I could recognize any Italian dialect.'

'Signora, you speak excellent Italian, but I'm afraid you've lost this bet. Ruggero speaks purest Tuscan.'

Cora thanked him, hung up and started racking her brains. 'What's his surname? Damn! I've forgotten it, and it's too late now to ask his boss.'

Emilia came in. 'Sherlock Holmes has come up with something,' she said proudly. 'Dante has been phoning from here in the hotel! You see, there's a woman sitting down at the reception desk, and it was a man that connected you with Dante. I've had a bit of a chat with the woman; I spun her a story about you having an admirer you couldn't shake off, who kept ringing you up all the time and she shouldn't take too much notice of it all. She said she had been on duty for six hours, and nobody had phoned for you. It is of course possible she's lying, but then, why should she?'

'So Dante is either one of the staff or he's a guest in the hotel,' said Cora. 'He has a phone in his room, so he can get straight through to our number. That probably means Béla is somewhere here in the hotel, too, who knows?'

'We have our suspicions,' I told Emilia, 'that Ruggero, the glazier's apprentice in Florence, might be mixed up in this, or at least he has supplied them with information. Can you remember what his surname was?'

'Mandorlo,' she said. 'I couldn't forget such a lovely name. If Ruggero is a cousin of Dante's, then they could have the same family name. I'll have a look in the hotel register to see if there's any Signor Mandorlo booked in.'

Mario wrote: *And I'll have a look to see if the man in the car is still there.*

Cora and I were left alone; every now and then, I would be overcome by a bout of tears. Then I started praying. Cora said, 'I know how you feel, but instead of just hanging around waiting, don't you think you'd do better to apply your sharp wits to this whole thing?'

I gave it a try. 'I reckon these kidnappers are anything but pros. On the one hand, that's a bit of luck for us, because it's unlikely they could bring themselves to do anything to hurt Béla. On the other hand, though, they're not likely to be cool customers – they could easily lose their nerve.'

Cora phoned the airport and made a booking on the flight to Florence the next morning. 'Mario will have to drive me to Catania first thing,' she said. 'I'll try to arrange a mortgage on the house. I'll phone you as soon as I get to the bank.'

'Oh, Cora, I'd dearly love to come with you and help, but I've just got to stay here in case Dante phones.'

'You must all stay here. I'm just wondering whether I shouldn't track down that little shit Ruggero in Florence and give him a piece of my mind. It may well be that he has nothing at all to do with the kidnapping and has just been bragging to his cousins about his love affair with me. I mean, he would have seen my picture in the paper, and then he could boast to them. "I've slept with that woman – have a look at that!"'

'That's probably what happened. But maybe he's taking his revenge for you having given him the elbow.'

Emilia came in. 'There's nobody among the hotel guests by the name of Mandorlo,' she said, out of breath. 'I didn't want to ask too many questions about the staff.'

Then Mario, too, came back. *Man in car has walkie-talkie and he's talking into it*, he scribbled.

Emilia brought him up to date on what we had found out. He took the dog on his lead and stumped out. In contrast to Emilia, he was no use at all for sounding people out, but he would do everything he could to help after his own fashion.

Cora packed her toilet bag. 'Dante won't be phoning again today, I'm sure of that,' she said, 'so I'm going to have a lie-down for a few hours, although I won't get any real sleep. If anything special happens, wake me.'

Cora rolled herself up in her clothes on the bed in the next room. I had a quiet cry to myself and let Emilia stroke my head. She was crying too.

An hour later, Mario reappeared. Excitedly, he took out his slate. *Pippo has a scent*, he wrote.

'Where?' I yelled. *Attic. Staff quarters. Maybe Pippo smells Béla.* We went to waken Cora.

'I remember a film with Doris Day,' said Emilia. 'A little

boy is held prisoner in an embassy. Doris sits down at the piano and sings a song her son knows well and has always whistled the chorus along with her. He hears her from his room and starts whistling loudly . . .'

'I remember it too,' said Cora. 'What was it? – *The Man Who Knew Too Much*. Only Béla can't whistle, and you can't play the piano.'

But Emilia was sticking to her film idea. 'I can sing, though, and he can clap his hands.' She demonstrated by crooning, *'Ma come balli bene bella bimba,'* clapping when she came to the word *'bella'*, as she had taught my son to do.

'Stay here, I'm off to do some singing,' she said. 'If I hear clapping coming from that room, then Béla's there.'

'There's no point,' I said. 'Béla's generally sleeping by this time, you know that yourself.'

'I'll give it a try, all the same.'

Emilia and Mario slipped out, and we waited expectantly.

Ten minutes later, they were back. Mario shook his head dejectedly; no clapping could be heard. But Emilia insisted she had caught the sound of Béla's breathing through the keyhole, which seemed rather far-fetched.

Cora snuggled down again on her bed. Pippo whined and scratched at the door. 'Has he got to go again, or does he really have Béla's scent in his nose?' asked Emilia. 'Mario did the rounds of all the rooms with the dog, but he reacted at only one.'

Cora called from the next room, 'There could be a cat or a dog in that room, or maybe nothing more than a lump of meat.'

'You two get off to bed, you're bound to be dead tired,' I said to Emilia and Mario. 'I'll come for you the moment it's necessary.'

Emilia and Mario shook their heads. 'Old people need less sleep,' said Emilia. Mario took my hand and kissed it, a gesture of friendship and sympathy that set me off crying again. He took up his slate and wrote something, but only for Emilia. She read it, smiled, and gave him a kiss. All at once, I realized – crystal clear – what real love was.

Once, deep in the night, the phone rang. Emilia beat me to it in the dash to pick up the receiver, but it was a wrong number. Naturally, I didn't sleep a wink, but at least I was lying down, while Emilia and Mario sat on chairs next to me, with their feet propped up on my bed.

Suddenly, I could stand it no longer. 'You can think I'm mad if you like,' I said, 'but all the time, I can hear my baby crying and calling to me in the night. I'm going to that room you talked about now, and I'm going to see whether Béla is there. It could take two days for Cora to get back with the money, and I'll have gone off my head before then.'

'Me too,' said Emilia. 'I'm coming with you. The worst they can do is kill us both.'

We pulled on our shoes. Mario was not in favour, but was lacing up Don's shoes all the same. Cora came staggering out of the other room. 'What's up? Has he phoned again? Why didn't you wake me?' she demanded, half dazed.

'We're going up into that suspicious room in the attic,' I said. 'I've just got to do it.'

Cora reckoned it was a mistake, and much too dangerous, to confront Dante face to face. 'Then he'll have no option but to kill us,' she said.

Mario wrote: *We'll take him by surprise, overpower him.*

Taking Pippo with us, we sneaked along the darkened hotel corridor till we reached the back stairs leading up to the attics. I was in a panic, but even that was more bearable than simply hanging around doing nothing. None of us spoke, and we tried to prevent the old steps from creaking, but with little success. Emilia had brought along her pocket torch – which had already served her well during the expedition to Don's last-but-one resting place. As we stopped at the door, Pippo snuffled loudly at the gap at the foot, snorting his breath into the mysterious room so as to get clues about its occupants from the air that streamed back. He gave a brief wag of his tail, which was a sure sign for Emilia that Pippo's best friend and playmate was behind that door.

'It's bound to be locked and bolted,' whispered Cora, 'and

we don't have a pass-key or any kind of tool with us.'

With a shake of the head, Mario held up a small screw-driver.

Emilia put her hand on the door handle, and it gave immediately. It wasn't locked at all. 'Tina?' asked a voice from within. In a high-pitched girlish voice, Emilia responded with great presence of mind, '*Sì!*', threw the door open and switched on the light.

In a narrow bed lay Béla and a stranger, who shot bolt upright and made a grab for a revolver. Everything happened with incredible speed: I threw myself on my child, Mario dived on the man, the bed collapsed with a crash under the four of us, and a shot went off. Béla slept through it all. Holding him tightly in my arms, I leapt to my feet and immediately tripped over Pippo, who wanted his share of the action. Just for a moment, I was stunned.

Emilia was holding the gun in her hand; Mario must have wrestled it out of the man's grasp. He was still lying on top of Dante, pressing him down on the wrecked bed with all his weight.

Cora got on the phone to the night porter. 'Lock the main door at once and don't let anybody in but the police. Call the security guards and tell them to surround a battered blue Fiat in the car park and arrest a man with binoculars. And we need a couple of policemen and a doctor up here in the attic as well.'

I slunk out of the danger area, and as I did so, I noticed Mario was bleeding. Cora helped him to subdue the strug-gling Dante by pressing a pillow over his face.

'If you don't keep still, you're dead,' she said.

Emilia stood stock still, pointing the gun at our captive.

Cora said, in German, 'If it was up to me, we could have settled this without the police, after all; I do have a weakness for desperados, I admit. But snatching kids is going too far.'

I stood out in the passage with my soaking-wet Béla and Pippo, since I had no desire to stay a moment longer in that room; on the other hand, I didn't want to desert my helpers either. The police arrived, not exactly in a tearing hurry, and snapped the handcuffs on. Then an interminable, jabbering palaver cut loose.

Mario had been wounded. We learned later that his slate had saved his life, or, you could say, Emilia had in a round-about way. She had given him a useful Christmas present – a new slate with, on the front, his standard introductory message about his speech handicap, done out in oil paints. To accommodate this slate, she had sewn large pockets into both his jackets.

Dante's bullet had ricocheted off the slate and changed its course, finishing up embedded in Mario's arm. The doctor bandaged it up, but said that, although the wound was not dangerous, it would require hospital treatment. Poor Mario was carted off in an ambulance. His eyes were shining – he was the hero of the night. Emilia kissed him and Béla in turn, praised her clever doggie, and went off to the hospital with him.

Half the hotel staff were up and about, standing around in pyjamas and dressing-gowns, talking excitedly. Dante – of course, that was not his real name – was friendly with the room maid. But Tina was just as innocent as cousin Ruggero from Florence; both had acted unwittingly as informants. That day had been Tina's day off, and she had gone to see her parents. Dante, whom Cora nicknamed Diledante, had prepared the kidnapping extremely sloppily, and had planned to move to a suitable hideaway for himself and Béla the very next day. But these were all things we found out only gradually.

That night, we managed to get a few hours' sleep after all, Béla to my right and Pippo to my left. In the early morning, Emilia came back from the hospital in a taxi to report that Mario had been successfully operated on and just needed rest.

Around midday, as we sat at the breakfast our sympathetic waitress had brought up to our room, Cora said, 'You know, I can't help feeling sorry for him, poor old Diledante. No money, out of work, and totally unsuited to being a gangster. He should take up a course of study! I'll have to see what I can do to help him . . . Besides, he's not a bad-looking lad.'

209

'I've no sympathy for his sort,' said Emilia. 'He stole our Béla and gave him a strong sedative – and he shot at Mario.'

'We can't say that for sure. The gun went off by itself,' I said. 'It can happen quite easily – I know that for a fact.'

'Well, now we've saved a lot of money,' said Cora. 'We ought to treat ourselves to something special. Emilia, what would you like?'

'I'd like a pair of sunglasses. The sun's so dazzling today.'

'Your wish is my command, O faithful member of our happy band,' said Cora, and we went to a chemist's and bought three snazzy pairs of sunglasses shaped like slanting cats' eyes.

'Maya, what about you?'

'An enormous ice-cream.'

The sun was shining and it was warm enough to sit outside. A huge pyramid of Christmas stars mounted on a wrought-iron frame transformed the summer terrace into a winter garden. The Italian women were parading their furs. Street kids were playing with balloons, while one especially privileged boy had got an electric Vespa for Christmas.

We went off for our ice-cream, spooning it into the still drowsy Béla and the faithful Pippo until they were almost at bursting point. All of a sudden, my son yelled, '*Basta!*' and thumped his fist on the table with such force that the chocolate sauce splashed up around all our ears.

CHAPTER 16

White Heat

Some days, I wake up in the best of moods. I feel light and free, happy and thankful, and life seems to be a wonderful present. Unfortunately, there are other days, when I believe in all seriousness that I have inherited Mother's fundamental depressive outlook. The idea of suicide has accompanied me since I was very small, and has even been something of a comfort. Against that, I am convinced that Béla will never leave me in the lurch, not as long as he needs me.

Such swings of mood are alien to Cora. She is almost perpetually in good spirits, but she does show understanding for my black days; more than that, she is the only one capable of dragging me out of my black depths.

All little girls play at 'Mummies and Daddies and Children'. I sometimes feel I'm still playing at these Happy Families. The one I was born into no longer exists, so instead I have created a new one for myself: Cora is the father, I'm the mother, Béla the child. Our parents and Béla's grandparents are Emilia and Mario. As her role demands, it falls to Cora to provide for our daily bread. Of course, I earn a bit from the tourists and can afford to buy my own clothes; but things like insurance, taxes, heating, the car, food and Emilia's wages are taken care of by Cora.

If an outside observer were to describe Cora, what would emerge would be a very feminine figure. But she does have definite masculine facets: her dominance and her cold sexuality. She enjoys her superiority to the full, and whenever I have one of my attacks of depression, she rescues me from it. In fact, it's precisely this saviour aspect that establishes her as the father in our little game, but I doubt whether she will ever be able to iron out the kinks in me that my natural father left.

However, even Cora has hurt me a few times, but then perhaps that, too, is all part and parcel of the games little girls play.

After Béla's kidnapping and rescue, we were desperate to set off back to Florence right away, but we wanted to wait until Mario was discharged from hospital. In the hotel, we were spoiled right, left and centre; the people of the land of the Mafia proved themselves to be warm-hearted folk, very compassionate, and they did everything they could to help us get over the terrors we had been through. We often sat out in the sun, drove to the *ospedale* in the Cadillac and pushed Béla in his buggy down to the Teatro Greco. Like so many other tourists, we scratched our names into the leaves of the aloes, even though there was a notice stating VIETATO SCRIVERE SULLE PLANTE. In the middle of the corso, a Russian played his accordion, and an elderly woman sang 'Black Eyes' and 'Kalinka' to his accompaniment; we were among their greatest admirers, and Béla was allowed to toss money into his Cossack hat.

Whenever we lounged around in our hotel room, we switched on the television; Emilia loved a programme called *Club della lirica* on the RAI TRE channel, in which corpulent tenors sang Donizetti arias.

Driving around Taormina's narrow streets was an art in itself, in which even Cora found no enjoyment. The parking places were set out so haphazardly that, often enough, we couldn't use our broad car, because it was boxed in.

Mario came out of hospital after four days' treatment, although he still had to go easy on his injured arm for the time being; driving the car was out of the question.

Cora had caught a cold. 'I want to get home,' she said. 'I've just got to get back to my painting. This lazing about doesn't agree with me.'

'Well, so what's the new sequence to be about?' I asked, half joking, half in apprehension.

'What about variations on the theme of the Naked Maya?' she said in all earnestness. 'I've always been attracted by quotations from the classics as modern paintings, as you know. And the Judith series is now closed.'

We decided that Mario should fly home on my ticket, along with the feverish Cora. I was to bring the car home with Emilia. What else could I do? The motorail service didn't operate in winter. 'Let our little treasure fly home with Cora, the drive is very tiring,' Emilia advised me.

Yet, although I was really dreading the prospect of the long car journey, on no account did I want to be parted from my child for so much as a single day. I drove Cora and Mario to the airport. To my utter astonishment, she behaved like a mother hen. 'Now, drive carefully! You're still on edge since your encounter with Dante! On no account pick up any hitchhikers! Here's some money – no, it isn't too much. I'd much rather you stopped for an extra overnight than . . .'

We threw our arms around each other. Emilia and Mario had already said their affectionate farewells back at the hotel, even though we would be seeing each other again in a few days.

The next day, we set off to catch the ferry to Reggio di Calabria. I drove, while Emilia sat in the back with Béla and Pippo. While she did in fact have her driving licence now and was no bumbling beginner, she tired quickly and could never stay at the wheel for more than half an hour at a time. By five o'clock, it was getting dark, and we didn't feel like driving any farther. We stopped at a far from high-class hotel, booked a double room and went for a meal. In the evening, we went to bed early, since we had no intention of going out and leaving Béla in Pippo's care.

'Oh, Emilia, I'm sure I'm turning into a real twitchy old fusspot of a mother . . . That can't be right, can it?'

'It's perfectly normal after the shock you've had,' Emilia consoled me. 'None of us has got over the scare yet.'

During that night, someone smashed in one of the side windows of the Cadillac. Nothing much was stolen, since we had taken our cases up to our room with us. A woollen rug was missing, as well as my small camera and Emilia's woven shopping bag full of provisions for the trip. At the garage, they told me that, for an American car like ours, they would have to order the right kind of side window from Rome. 'And how long will that take?' I asked.

'Hard to say – three days at the outside.'

I phoned Cora. 'What are we to do? Wait here for three days, or leave the car and come home by train? Then I'd have to come back again to collect the car.'

'If it's not too awful and dreary in your hotel, just stay the three days there,' she said. 'In this weather, you can't drive with a window missing. Oh, by the way, Jonas phoned – stupid of me, but I told him about Béla being kidnapped. I'm afraid he got into a terrible state. I'm just mentioning it so that you're forewarned.'

'Oh, Cora, you shouldn't have done that . . .'

'Yes, I know, but what's done can't be undone. Right then, you stay in your hotel and have a boring time; I'm very busy, I've just started a new picture. And by the way, Mario has made a marvellous job of the patio; no one can say Don is lying under a cheerless stone! I'm absolutely delighted with it, and when spring comes, we're really going to make the most of that corner.'

Emilia snatched the receiver from me. 'Is Mario there with you?'

'No, I took a taxi back from the airport and dropped him off at his own place. He's not allowed to do any work for the time being, he has to take things easy. Do you need any cash for the car repairs?'

The next day – we really were finding it tedious in our ugly room, and it was raining outside – the foreman at the garage delivered the bad tidings that the window they had ordered wasn't expected for at least a week, since it wasn't in stock in Rome either. I was furious. They could do a provisional job and close up the window, he said, we were lucky after all that it was only a side one. I agreed to that, and we got a sheet of plastic stuck over the window that would keep out the wind and the rain. I cancelled the repair job and decided to leave it until we were back in Florence.

Again I phoned Cora, but there was no reply.

I didn't fancy another overnight stop. After that night when Béla was snatched, I was thoroughly sick of hotel rooms. While we still had a long stretch before we got home, I wanted to sleep in my own bed and not run the risk of another broken window, far less a stolen child.

We arrived in Florence at dead of night. I was overtired, and overwrought as well. Emilia's conscience was bothering her because she had hardly relieved me at all. 'You go off and get some sleep,' she offered. 'I'll put Béla to bed and bring in the luggage. You don't need to bother about another thing.'

I accepted her offer.

The house was in darkness, Cora was sure to be asleep. I undressed, cleaned my teeth and opened my bedroom window. All of a sudden, I had an irresistible urge to look in briefly to tell Cora we had got back safe and sound. She would be relieved and would get straight back to sleep.

Quietly, I tiptoed into her room and switched the light on. She was fast asleep, her red hair curling over her pillow; I was touched by the sight and decided not to disturb her after all.

I was just about to switch the light out again when I discovered, next to her, a shock of black hair. Don! I rubbed my eyes to dispel this illusion, then looked more closely – Ruggero?

The light woke Cora. She sat up, smiled sleepily, yet at the same time there was almost something deceitful in it. As she drew herself up, the bedcovers slipped off her bedmate, and I recognized the soundly sleeping Jonas.

Cora rubbed her eyes. 'Back already, are you?' she asked, half dazed. I stood like a marble statue. 'Ah, yes,' she said with a grin, 'well, there you are, the things one does in the cause of education . . .'

I slammed the door behind me, rushed into the kitchen, threw myself on to a chair and started to howl my heart out. Despite the lateness of the hour, Emilia was busy filling up the washing machine – she never liked to let too much dirty laundry accumulate. 'My dear child, what's the matter? It's all been a bit too much for you, hasn't it?' she said, stroking my hair.

'Jonas is lying there, in bed with Cora,' I sobbed.

Emilia dropped Béla's jeans. 'What did you say?'

'You heard me!'

She sat down beside me. 'Cora's a very bad girl,' she said. I went on crying. 'Have you two poison pills left?' I asked.

'Well, of course, more than two,' she said gently.

I opened the fridge and discovered some of the freshly made blood sausage and liver sausage that Jonas, with his lack of originality, brought along as a present on all his visits; and this time, because it was the Christmas season, there was also a large jar of goose dripping.

'Go straight upstairs,' I shouted at Emilia, 'and bring me two of those capsules! I'm going to serve up liverwurst sandwiches for breakfast for the happy couple, but with a kick in them!'

'Yes, sure, of course, my darling. In fact, I'll bring four, and you can take care of Mario and me while you're at it.'

I looked at her, enraged. 'I'm not joking. Mario and you I love. I don't need any poison for you.'

'You love Cora and Jonas, too,' she said, 'otherwise you wouldn't be getting in such a state. You can't just go around killing off everyone you love.'

I let out a howl.

Emilia stroked my back, which did me good. 'Come on now, off to bed with you. You're dead tired. It'll all be different in the morning. Why has Jonas come here anyway?'

'I've no idea, but I can imagine. Cora told him on the phone about Dante. No doubt he wants to drag Béla and me back home.'

Emilia took herself off to bed, and, ignoring her advice, I sat on in the kitchen. In a rage, I spread liverwurst on a slice of the Black Forest farm bread that Emilia despised. At the sight of the kitchen knife, sinister thoughts came into my head. False friends and unfaithful husbands deserved to be hacked down. I had taught her how to steal, and she had stolen my husband from me! I rammed the knife into the wooden tabletop.

Then I was struck by the dreadful suspicion that, early the next morning, Jonas would simply disappear with my son. Knife in hand, I went out into the street. How on earth had I failed to see Jonas's car as we returned home, when it was parked directly in front of the next-door house? I thrust the knife into the right rear tyre. That made me feel a lot better. I repeated this bloody deed over and over. I let the other three tyres live. Now Jonas would have to change a wheel first and not simply make the quick getaway he intended.

After this orgy of stabbing, I went to bed, although sleep was out of the question. I tried to reason with myself that I had deceived Jonas, too, that I no longer wanted him for a husband, that I could now, after this incident, accuse him of self-righteous hypocrisy and tell him we were quits. He could have slept with every girl in his village and it would have left me cold, but, with my best friend – that was unforgivable. Against Cora, too, I felt a fiendish rage. She, who could have any man she wanted, why did she have to do it with Jonas of all people, when she didn't love him? Why did she want to humiliate him in this way? It was obvious that he was bound to feel utterly ashamed of himself for having betrayed his principles. Or was Cora afraid that, after the shock of the kidnapping, I would go back to Jonas in Germany? In my state of terror, I had expressed such thoughts several times. It was just possible that she wanted to thwart any such plans before I got round to considering them again.

Increasingly bloodthirsty images rose in my mind: of Cora and Jonas lying next to Don under the exquisite patio, discreetly buried there by Mario. I felt demeaned, cheated, betrayed. I had to have my revenge. Would it be worth the death penalty, or life imprisonment?

Suddenly I hit upon a new version: early in the morning, I could slip into bed beside the two of them, either in a transparent nightie, or – better still – as a Naked Maya. 'My dear Cora, you wanted to paint me à la Goya! My dear Jonas, here I am, your eager wife . . .'

My pious husband would die of shame, and Cora would laugh.

I had an urge to throw a bucket of ice-cold water over the

sleeping pair, to destroy Cora's pictures with acid, to dig up Don and lay him in the bed between them. Instead of icy water, petrol was also a possibility – one spark, and that witch, along with that hypocrite and the pink villa, would be dispatched to hell! Or should I drive off now, tonight, flee back to Germany with my child, and leave the adulterous pair to their fate? Should I leave a farewell note that would pitch them both into a state of depression? In my young days, I had been called the she-elephant, because I had a tendency to trample my foes underfoot. Most of my sufferings had been at the hands of my blood relations, but only Cora had managed to rouse me to such a white heat as I was in that night.

Had she been painting while I was away, or had she been rolling around between the sheets with Jonas for two whole days? I wondered. I left my own crumpled bed and slipped into the studio. To my amazement, there stood a little Christmas tree, a Black Forest pine, decorated with stars made out of straw, red apples and beeswax candles. Everything the genuine article, no cheap tinsel, no electric-lit plastic stars, like in Sicily; Jonas was all for simplicity and reverence. Clearly, he had brought this bonsai for Béla. I slipped off my wedding ring and hung it on the green tree.

There were sketches lying scattered about the floor. Cora had been painting Jonas, with the full atmospheric background: next to him, the little Christmas tree and a German liver sausage. On all three sheets, his facial expression had been cruelly caricatured: handsome, yet simple-minded; diligent, yet plodding; pious, yet lecherous. Cora was certainly highly talented.

The liverwurst in the picture stirred my appetite again, even though the real thing always had too much marjoram in it for my liking. I ghosted through the house and, back in the kitchen, stuffed another sandwich in my mouth. Fatty stuff like this brings you out in pimples, I thought dejectedly, because, for once, as a result of the stress with Dante, my skin looked very much the worse for wear. I checked in the bathroom and found, sure enough, that I had red blotches on my face, my eyes were puffed up and my hair was all straggly. I reached out for Cora's night skin cream, 'for sensitive skin', the most expensive Japanese luxury. Angrily, I slapped the stuff on my cheeks, then I poured half the bottle of her favourite perfume over my sweat-soaked nightdress and emptied the whole pot of cream on to the Art Nouveau floor tiles. Then I had an even more diabolical idea: from the kitchen, I fetched the jar of goose-fat and filled the tubs of skin cream – both the day and night varieties – with onion-reeking grease. The smell was a giveaway, so I sprayed her perfume all round the bathroom till I had emptied the bottle. Once I had the bathroom – a dream, Cora had once called it – looking like a pigsty, I felt a whole lot better.

I swore that in future, I would never again allow myself to be financially dependent on Cora. I resolved to earn my keep with the efforts of my own fair hands – and the idea of stealing didn't even enter my mind. As a tourist guide, I wouldn't exactly get rich, but it would pay for my own skin cream.

Only towards morning did I manage to fall asleep, to be plagued by a series of horrendous dreams that revolved in turn around fat liver sausages, heavy perfumes and traumatic experiences. Fitting neatly into these dreams, it seemed, a piercing scream rang out, which tore me out of bed and had me rushing off, still half asleep. Béla! my mother's instinct told me.

The shriek had come from the bathroom. I covered the distance in record time, much faster than any hundred metres I did at school. My momentum sent me crashing down next to Cora on the cream-smeared tiles, which were like a skating rink, and now I, too, was screaming in pain and horror.

Emilia, with Béla in her arms, and Jonas, in his underpants, had gathered round and were trying to make sense of the whole thing. We were whisked off to hospital after being given painkilling injections by a paramedic, right there in the bathroom. The x-rays showed that Cora had broken a leg, and I an arm.

In our room at the hospital, we lay in neighbouring beds, moaning at each other. Emilia came to visit us every day.

Jonas took Béla back home with him, so that his mother could at last get to know her grandchild. He promised tearfully that he would bring him back in a fortnight. I took the opportunity to demand to have my celadon-green dish back, and he assured me he would bring it.

'I've got something I must tell you both,' Emilia informed us on one of her visits. 'As soon as you're both well again, I'm going to leave you.'

'What do you mean?' we asked as one.

'I'm going to move in with Mario.'

We were staggered. 'Emilia, you're going to get married! Congratulations!'

'Children, you are old-fashioned, aren't you! You don't have to rush off and get married in order to live together!'

She's right there, I thought.

Cora asked, 'Wouldn't Mario like to move in with us, in our pink villa?'

Emilia doubted it. 'I don't think he would want to live under one roof with three women . . .'

'You're forgetting Béla and Pippo,' I said. Emilia asked for time to think it over.

When she had left, I drew a heart on Cora's plaster and wrote clumsily with my left hand, MARIO + EMILIA in the middle of it.

Next to it, Cora drew a dainty little Cupid.

The next day, we were presented with Emilia's conditions. 'The attic has to be renovated and extended. And as well as that, you must promise me that you will never again . . . you know, with one and the same man . . .' And she blushed.

Laughing, we promised. And we meant it sincerely.

CHAPTER 17

Mother-of-Pearl

Cora and I have asked lots of people what their favourite colour was. As a result, we have found out that men generally prefer to evade such conversations, treating us as silly little girls; Jonas is a good example of that. Friedrich is another who is unwilling to settle for a particular colour, insisting he has more important things to think about. As for Cora's mother, I've known for ages that she favours Persian pink, while the professor said, to my great alarm, 'Celadon green, h'm, yes.' Mario just points to his brown trousers, an earthy, unimaginative colour. Cora wavers between kingfisher blue and emerald green. Emilia, for her part, loves a warm red, which she finds is a 'motherly' shade. My own favourite is mother-of-pearl. Emilia balks at this, protesting that, 'That doesn't count. It's not a real colour.'

Oh, but it is, I assure her, all colours are amalgamated in mother-of-pearl, the whole spectrum of the rainbow. I keep oyster shells and sea-snails' shells, the inside of which is coated with a mysterious glaze, iridescent with all sorts of colours, silvery pink like moths' wings or thunder clouds. My favourite shell is one I discovered, not on the beach, but in a little souvenir shop. It doesn't come from the Mediterranean, but from the South Seas. Sometimes I sit meditating with this shell in front of me, for it seems to me to be the embodiment of all life's mysteries. The goddess of love, Venus, is shown by many painters adorned with pearls, because she rose from a seashell. Even the human ear is shaped like a shell, and it would be much more beautiful if Nature had lined it, too, with a mother-of-pearl glaze. The

Muslims decorate the columns at their men's graves with turbans, their women's with shells.

Cora always gives a sneering laugh whenever she stands looking at my collection.

Mario built me a display cabinet. From some dark canals or other, he brought me twelve miniature pillars, which, almost certainly, originally formed part of the balustrade of some noble villa. Ruggero, who, lately, keeps popping up from time to time to show off his newest girlfriend to Cora, cut some glass shelves for me, which rest fair and square on the little flat-topped marble columns. This showcase is big enough to house all my treasures, stolen ones and found ones, collected ones and purchased ones.

Whenever I gaze at my favourite shell, I am happy I haven't decided in favour of one particular colour, but instead have chosen the whole palette. This variegation seems to me like a symbol for the whole rich variety of life itself. How on earth can a painter possibly pass up such wealth and limit himself to black, white and red?

There are times when I am filled with pity for my father's restricted life, for his inability to let his own talent unfold. I have now taken my favourite shell to Henning's grave, in a tiny corner of which the urn with my father's ashes lies buried. There, the shell lies next to some white plastic lilies that Emilia placed there for decency's sake. Béla sometimes wants to take the shell away with him, and then I catch myself saying, 'No, that belongs to Grandad!'

'Grandad?' my child asks.

Then I give him a kiss, and we start back on the walk home. We always pass a garden with an old willow tree in it. Its pale-green fronds overhang the garden wall, and I always try to pick my steps in such a way that a tender young shoot trails caressingly across the top of my head. If I miss the right spot between the wall and the edge of the pavement, I turn back and try a second time (provided, of course, nobody is watching me). I imagine Father, Mother or Carlo stroking my hair, which is, sadly, something they never did.

The way home is not very far, yet I nevertheless have a

very long march ahead of me. My goal is difficult to achieve, although it is not an unfamiliar one: I would like to be able to forgive my dead parents.